THE THRONE

Published in Canada by Red Deer Press
195 Allstate Parkway, Markham, ON, L3R 4T8

www.reddeerpress.com

Published in the United States by Red Deer Press
311 Washington Street, Brighton, Massachusetts, 02135

Edited for the Press by Peter Carver
Cover and text design by Daniel Choi
Cover photo courtesy of Elizabeth Ballantyne. Photographed with thanks at the Thornhill
School of Music, www.thornhillmusic.com.

We acknowledge with thanks the Canada Council for the Arts, and the Ontario Arts Council
for their support of our publishing program. We acknowledge the financial support of the
Government of Canada through the Canada Book Fund (CBF) for our publishing activities.

ONTARIO ARTS COUNCIL
CONSEIL DES ARTS DE L'ONTARIO
50 YEARS OF ONTARIO GOVERNMENT SUPPORT OF THE ARTS
50 ANS DE SOUTIEN DU GOUVERNEMENT DE L'ONTARIO AUX ARTS

Canada Council
for the Arts
Conseil des Arts
du Canada

Library and Archives Canada Cataloguing in Publication
Goobie, Beth, 1959-
    The throne / Beth Goobie.
ISBN 978-0-88995-496-0
    I. Title.
PS8563.O8326T47 2013   jC813ʾ.54   C2013-901673-2

Publisher Cataloging-in-Publication Data (U.S.)
Goobie, Beth.
    The throne / Beth Goobie.
[288] p. : cm.
Summary: A girl who decides to make her mark in school attracts
unwanted attention from the school's "kingpin of the underworld"—a
smart, determined enemy capable of holding a long-term grudge. But
with the help of her friends, she will have to find a way to stand up for
herself and survive high school with her dignity intact.
ISBN-13: 9780889954960 (pbk.)
1. Bullying in schools – Juvenile fiction. 3. Friendship in adolescence
– Juvenile fiction. I. Title
[Fic] dc23   PZ7.G66354Th 2013

MIX
Paper from
responsible sources
FSC
www.fsc.org   FSC® C103113

Printed and bound in Canada

THE THRONE

Beth Goobie

Red Deer Press

This book is dedicated to Kevin Hogg.

chapter 1

On most days, Polkton Collegiate was a snake pit, and the first day of the year was no exception. As Meredith came through the east tech-wing entrance, the halls closed in with their familiar mayhem, catcalls and laughter ricocheting off the walls. Short for her age and slight of build, she instinctively braced herself against the oncoming flow of students, many of whom towered a full head above her. One of these months, she thought resignedly, she was going to hit a genetic-defying growth surge and her eye level would finally pop up above other kids' nipples; for now, she was condemned to fending off the occasional Slurpee cup that had been placed on her head by some out-and-out moron.

Ducking to the right, Meredith sidestepped advancing traffic and headed past an overhead security camera and on down the corridor. Ten meters in from the outer entrance was the door to her home form—the school's only music classroom—and, as she approached, she quickened her step. Anticipation surged through her, tingling her palms; glancing to either side, she swallowed once and slipped through the open doorway. Ahead, the room sat empty, not even Mr. Woolger, her home form teacher, to be seen, and for a moment Meredith stood motionless, surveying what lay before her. Then, striding past shelves of numbered instrument cases and tubas positioned upside down on their stands, she began to climb the risers that contained the students' chairs. At the third and highest riser, she paused and scanned various nearby percussion instruments before turning her attention to the drum set. A smile hesitated in one corner of her mouth, and, almost disbelievingly, she touched a fingertip to one of the cymbals. Here it was—the moment she had been pondering for weeks—and now, with one last glance around, she stepped behind the drums and parked her butt.

For a second, she felt disoriented. Having spent the previous year seated in a floor-level, front-row chair, the view from the third riser felt surreal—three descending rows of chairs and music stands, and a full seven meters away, Mr. Woolger's front-of-the-room conducting podium and desk. There was so much space, Meredith wanted to stretch out her arms and holler. The drum set was, simply put, *the* place to be in Home Form 75, and the fact that she had snagged it for her Grade 10 year was sweet.

Last year, the drums had been claimed by Eddie van Holst, a Grade 12 muscle-building fanatic, and many of Meredith's Grade 9 memories were haunted by the secret mind codes Eddie had tapped onto the largest horizontal drum's surface whenever he had gotten bored with the PA announcements. From her position in the front row, those codes had sounded restless, seductive—a quiet but tangible undercurrent calling her toward the unknown. In addition, a year's experience had taught her the utter inadvisability of allowing herself to get stuck anywhere near Mr. Woolger's desk again. Close to retirement, the teacher teetered constantly on the edge of a nervous breakdown and kept the world adamantly at bay with a conducting baton that he seemed to have glued permanently to his right palm. Whether standing in front of a music class or not, Mr. Woolger conducted nonstop, keeping time even when seated alone at his desk and muttering only to himself.

One morning last spring, he had grown so upset while lecturing the home form class about the gum wads he kept finding stuck to various objects around the room, that he had shattered his trusty baton by pounding it hysterically on his desk. While Meredith had been sympathetic—particularly about the still fresh, *OOZING!* (as Mr. Woolger had put it) Double Bubble wad that he had recently discovered affixed to the inside of a tuba bell—still, without having to be told, she had shown up the following morning along with the rest of the home form class, methodically chewing a stick of Wrigley's Spearmint gum.

Recalling the incident now, Meredith gave the drum set a cautious once-over, checking for anything damp, squishy, or *OOZING!*, then straightened just as several guys entered the room and started toward her. Engrossed in loud guffaws, they didn't notice her until, glancing up out of a shared joke, one of them fixed on her sitting bolt upright behind the drums and came to a dead halt.

"Who's that?" he asked, as if he had never seen her before. Last year, his seat had been one row below and slightly to the right of Eddie van Holst. If he had noticed Meredith at all, it would have been only as the rear view on a decidedly diminutive head of short black hair. Warily, she assessed him, then his buddies. Of the three, two were now in Grade 11 and the third in Grade 12, and all of them had spent last year's home form periods clustered around Eddie and his secret drum codes. So they probably figured they had put in their apprenticeship, and one of them was now due to inherit Eddie's position—presumably Seymour Molyneux, the oldest, and the one most likely to have left a trail of moist, illicit gum wads all over Mr. Woolger's *joie de vivre*. Like the other two—Morey Jampolsky and Gene Bussidor—Seymour had grown a lot over the summer. These were guys, Meredith thought, observing them carefully, who *ruled*.

Well, she decided, so did she! And if she didn't let them know that right off, they would be crowding her all year. So, picking up a drumstick that was lying on one of the smaller drums, she pointed it at Morey, the guy who had asked the question, and said, "My name, for your information, just so happens to be Meredith Polk. As in Gus Polk, great and illustrious founder of the pukey, poky megalopolis of Polkton."

For a moment, the guys just stared at her. Then Gene broke into an easy grin. "You know how to play the drums?" he asked.

"No," she said. "But I know how to sit on one."

His grin widened. One of a handful of Cree students attending Polkton Collegiate, he had shoulder-length black hair and deeply tanned skin. "You get a good rhythm going," he said, "and you won't need sticks."

Then, without seeming to think twice about it, he climbed the second and third risers and sat down next to her, behind the xylophone. "Come on, you guys," he said to Seymour and Morey. "What're you waiting for?"

Narrow-eyed, Seymour's gaze flitted between the two of them. His answer was obvious—*for her to get her ass out of there*—but he didn't say it. Gene played double and electric bass in the school's Concert, Jazz, and Greaser bands; he was popular, respected, and from a distance appeared to be utterly lacking in a mean streak. While he might have taken to chewing gum daily during home form period for several weeks after Mr. Woolger's Double-Bubble outburst, Meredith couldn't imagine him depositing a gum wad anywhere on school property except in a wastepaper basket.

"Charlie Watts would be turning in his grave," Morey said disgustedly.

"I doubt it. And anyway, he's not dead yet," said Gene. "You ever read anything about the guy? A Stone, and he's never cheated on his wife. Not even once."

"What's that got to do with it?" demanded Seymour.

Gene shrugged. "Never stereotype anyone," he said. "Not even a Stone."

"A philosopher," muttered Morey as Seymour stood, his gaze neutral, almost blank, eyeing Gene. *Assessing*, thought Meredith. *He's assessing Gene for something.* But before she could nail down what that something was, Seymour's gaze had shifted and was sweeping the rear-riser row of empty chairs positioned behind the various percussion instruments. From the looks of it, he was considering taking up home form residence in one of them—probably the chair dead center, one over from Gene. The moment passed, however, and with a grimace he dropped into the second-riser seat directly in front of the drums.

Following his cue, Morey ducked past Seymour's knees and parked his butt in front of Gene. Chubby, with gold wire-rim glasses, he had a habit of patting his thick blond frizz of hair, and he did so now, nervously—as if trying to keep it from flying off his head. "Hey!" he said, turning to Seymour. "You heard anything about the new football coach?"

To Meredith's right, Gene leaned forward, instantly absorbed into a discussion about this year's football roster—a discussion, she realized with a sinking feeling, to which she was obviously not expected to contribute. She had been dismissed, and while this more or less solved the question of who was to occupy the drum set, at least for the present, it left her feeling as if she didn't exist. This wasn't something she had considered when she had made her beeline for the most cherished seat in home form—that she would be surrounded by great hulking male seniors, none of whom saw themselves as engaging in regular chit-chat with an undersized, nondescript Grade 10 twerp.

At that moment, Mr. Woolger entered the room, gave it a quick scan, and fixed on her with a look of surprise. Behind him, Meredith could see several students coming in—Sina Sun and Kirstin Rawls, two girls she had sat with last year, as well as a few terrified-looking minor-niners. For a second, she considered admitting defeat, handing over the drums to Seymour, and descending to the comfort of relative obscurity in a front row seat. But then she ditched the idea. Maybe she hadn't been welcomed to the back row riser with open arms, but time would tell. And for now, she had it—the epicenter, Nerve Central of Home Form 75.

Placing her hands tentatively on the largest horizontal drum, she tried tapping out a few secret thoughts.

Later that day, as Meredith headed along a crowded hall en route to her afternoon history class, she saw Seymour again, leaning in an open doorway and talking to a girl. Instinctively, she homed in on him, sizing him up the way she would a tennis or debating opponent—not that there was any reason to see Seymour as an enemy combatant, she told herself reassuringly, but something about the set of his back that morning as he had sat down in the seat one riser below her, and the way he had kept his head turned carefully away, refusing to acknowledge her presence, had communicated loud and clear that he hadn't accepted the situation as it currently presented and would be seriously mulling things over.

So, as Meredith approached, she mulled him over—the conspicuous height that placed him two to three heads taller, the broad, almost rough-looking face and dark collar-length hair, and the energy that ran constantly through him like a current, drawing in everyone in his vicinity. Although Seymour wasn't what most girls would consider good-looking, and was more likely to be found in a heated cafeteria game of laptop poker than shooting baskets with the jock crowd, still, he was popular; both girls and guys liked him. In fact, he was the sort of person Meredith would have chosen as a friend, given the chance—quick, verbal, and at the center of things. Consequently, when Seymour happened to glance up out of his conversation and meet her eye, she didn't look away, but met his gaze head-on and continued walking.

Briefly his eyes narrowed, and then he said something to the girl he had been talking to and started toward Meredith. Startled, she glanced around, looking for someone nearby from the senior cool crowd, but found herself surrounded by a flood of short, bewildered-looking minor-niners, who had probably all just been let out of the same class.

"Well," said Seymour, coming to a halt in front of her. Raising a hand, he placed it against the wall and leaned in, effectively cutting her off from hallway traffic. "If it isn't Charlie Watts."

His dark eyes studied her—so casually, it felt as if he was sitting well back inside himself and observing a situation that might or might not have something to do with him. Inexplicably, a soft warning sensation crept up Meredith's back, lifting the hair on her neck. "My name," she said carefully, trying to suss out what he was after, why on earth he would have crossed a busy hall to talk to her, "is Meredith."

To her dismay, she felt a flush heating her face. Backed into a wall, with Seymour looming vampire-like over her, Meredith found it difficult to hold his gaze ... something of which he was well aware, she realized, reading it in the slight curve of his lips.

"Meredith," he said slowly, as if tasting her name on his tongue. "Meredith Polk. *The* Polk."

Meredith was starting to get it—Seymour's reason for backing her into the wall was becoming more obvious by the second. "Seymour," she said, imitating his tone syllable by syllable. "*The* Molyneux."

One of his eyebrows lifted. "Come on now," he said, his voice taking on a coaxing tone. "Charlie Watts isn't really your style, is it? I mean, the progeny of a *founding* father and all. Don't you think, all things considered, tomorrow you would rather be sitting in the front row with your buddies from last year?"

Nothing changed in his gaze as he spoke; he didn't bare fangs or start breathing ominously, but still Meredith felt it—something unspoken, vaguely threatening, leaning in.

"No!" she shot back, her voice cracking nervously. "I don't think that. I don't think that at all." Stepping backward, she tried to move around him, but unexpectedly he reached out and took hold of her arm.

"Come on," he repeated, his voice still coaxing, but with a harder edge. "When you think about it, Meredith—can't you see yourself walking into home form tomorrow morning, catching sight of your old buds smiling at you in the front row, and going over to your old familiar seat and sitting down where you belong?"

Where you belong? Full-out dumbfounded, Meredith could only echo the phrase in her mind as she stared, open-mouthed, at Seymour. Still nothing changed in his gaze; it remained cool and remote, as if he had yet to decide whether or not the conversation included him. By contrast, there she stood—heart thudding, palms sweaty, her voice stuck halfway down her throat. It was the size of him that did it, she thought, gazing upward. The guy seemed to grow taller by the second. Without warning, it made her angry—the way Seymour assumed he could just stand there towering over her ... as if that was where *he* belonged. Surging onto her toes, she shoved her face up at him.

"I like where I'm sitting in home form," she said, heated but slow. "And I got there first, so it's my seat for the rest of the year. What's it to you, anyway?"

With an audible intake of breath, Seymour took a step back, and his gaze lost some of its remote quality. Finally the conversation had grabbed his full attention. "I ... *want* to sit there," he said. "That's where the oldest guy always sits. It's a tradition."

"Too bad," Meredith said flatly. "That tradition just got broken."

Seymour's eyes narrowed, and something flickered in their depths—surprised, maybe even a little mean. "What're you after, Polk?" he asked, his mouth twisting. "Power?"

Taken aback, Meredith stared at him. Power had been the last thing on her mind when she had headed for the drum set that morning. Or had it? *Epicenter*, she thought. *Nerve Central.*

"I thought ... it would be a fun place to sit," she said, feeling oddly guilty. "That's all, just fun. No big deal—"

Her voice trailed off and they stood, faces centimeters apart, observing each other. Knowingly, as if he had read her mind, a smile crept across Seymour's mouth. "Tomorrow," he said quietly, not so much coaxing this time as giving a matter-of-fact command, "you are going to walk into home form, go over to your old front row seat, and sit down with your buddies, where you will have a rip-roaring good ole time for the rest of the year. Right, Polk?"

Without waiting for a response, he pushed out from the

wall and set off down the corridor. As Meredith watched him go, an unexpected wave of fatigue passed over her and she felt sucked dry, as if something giant and invisible had been vamping her. Confused, she glanced around, but saw only a nearby security camera implacably filming and other students streaming past, oblivious to what had taken place. So, with an inner shrug, she filed the conversation for later consideration and headed off in search of History 201.

chapter 2

The first day of Grade 10 officially over, Meredith was lying around with her best friends, Dean Matsumoto and Rebecca Looby, in the Matsumoto family's back yard. More specifically, the three girls were lying under the willow tree near the rear fence, the crowns of their heads resting against the base of the trunk. That was their rule—the tips of their heads all had to touch the trunk, and then they had to lie in complete silence, cell phone ringers off and contemplating the way the light invited itself through the willow leaves for at least five minutes before they began to talk. "Invited itself" was Dean's phrase, but it had become part of the texture of Meredith's thinking the first time she had heard her friend say it. *Light always invites itself,* she now thought lazily as she observed the sun spark here and there through the willow branches. *Invites itself like a smile, the scent of a flower, or the beginning of a new year. Yeah—the* very *beginning.*

As if in response to her thoughts, Dean sighed, the sound wafting from her in pure pleasure. An instinctive echo, Reb sighed too, and then Meredith threw one in for good measure.

"A long summer it has been," murmured Reb. "Nothing, *nothing* in Kapuskasing or anywhere in the whole wide world, smells as good as it does under this tree."

"Uh-huh," the others murmured in reply, and then they lay simply watching the shift of a thousand leaves against sky. Two full months had passed since the three of them had been together like this, Reb having deserted Polkton at the beginning of July to spend the summer with her father at their lakeside cabin. Several weeks later, Dean and her family had taken off on a month-long camping trip to Florida.

"Disney World!" Dean spat abruptly, her tone filled with contempt. "I am telling you—*never* go there. Brouhaha and whiplash—I'd have more fun if someone threw me into a washing machine."

"Fun fascists," agreed Reb. "We had them up at the lake, too. Every second of the entire summer, they had to be out water-boarding and kicking up waves. If there wasn't a lot of noise, they weren't interested. Unless, of course, they could put in time staring at my boobs."

Reb was well-endowed. It was a Looby family trait and got her a fair amount of attention. Last year, several guys had asked her out, but she had turned them all down. "They weren't asking me out, they were asking my boobs," she had explained flatly. "Date me, date my face."

Of the three of them, Meredith had decided years ago that Reb was the prettiest, though Reb would have scoffed loudly if anyone had suggested it. Most of the time, she acted as if femininity was a disease, keeping her hair so short it clung in auburn curls to her head, and habitually dressing in jeans and a loose shirt. Anything she carried—laptop, books, etc.—she pressed flat to her chest like a shield.

"More ogle-eyes?" Meredith asked sympathetically.

"Ooga-booga eyes," replied Reb. "Booby Looby—nothing's changed. One night before we left the lake, it got so bad I told Dad that I wanted a boob-reduction. Y'know what he said?" An exasperated whoosh of air followed, and then Reb moaned, "To wear them with *pride*." Pitching her voice lower, she imitated her father. "'The size of your breasts comes from my side of the family, Rebecca,'" she intoned philosophically. "'From my mother, and her mother, and her mother. The Looby women are strong women, and strong women take up a lot of space.'"

The girls lay silent, contemplating this snippet of parental wisdom. The pain in Reb's voice had been obvious, a long, slow-cooking kind of pain—not the type that cut, healed, and was over and done with. "Take up a lot of space," she repeated musingly, and Meredith knew without looking that Reb was lying with her chin dug into her collarbone, surveying her temporarily flattened chest.

"He could be right, you know," ventured Dean. "That's actually a pretty good way of looking at it."

Reb groaned softly, then muttered, "Dads are boobless."

In the pause that followed, Meredith lay cautiously feeling her way through the moment. While she wasn't a father, she was, technically speaking, almost boobless, which left her decidedly lacking with regard to the kind of experiences Reb was talking about. "Boobless, yeah," she said finally, "but not brainless. Your dad is incredibly proud of you, Reb—anyone who's ever been around the two of you knows that."

"I know," sighed Reb. "I just think he doesn't quite *get* it."

"It's those guys staring at you who don't get it," Meredith said heatedly. "Someone must've ... I dunno ... oh, given them a brain reduction at birth. Like Seymour Molyneux. Remember what I told you at lunch about the drums in home form? Well, I ran into him again this afternoon." Voice quickening, she told the other two about the hallway encounter.

"Seymour Molyneux!" exclaimed Dean when she had finished. "Wasn't he the black Santa at last year's Christmas assembly?"

"Oh yeah," mumbled Meredith as the memory came back to her. It had been mid-December, and the entire school had been gathered in the auditorium. The Concert Band had just finished playing "I'm Dreaming of a White

Christmas," when a black-garbed Santa and his entourage of black-leotarded elves had abruptly strode onto the stage, apparently sabotaging the proceedings. In a sly singsong voice, Santa had called up various teachers to receive gag gifts such as a Tweety Bird whistle or a Frankenstein mask. Even the school principal, Mr. Sabom, had been summoned into the footlights to be presented with a large rubber "spanking hand." That Seymour had managed to pull this off while still in Grade 11 was ample testament to his ... well, *presence*, thought Meredith, unable to come up with a better word.

"So he's Big Man Jock," Dean continued dismissively, but was cut off mid-sentence.

"No," said Reb, who had a number of big-man-jock cousins, several of whom had played on last year's senior teams. "But he hangs around with them. He's sort of like a mafia kingpin. Not drugs, exactly—he's not into actual crime. Just Ruler of the Underworld, y'know? He runs things. You don't mess with him."

"Great," said Meredith, a sinkhole opening in her gut. "First day of Grade 10 and I've already messed with him twice."

"Don't worry about it, Mere," advised Dean. "He's a crustacean brain. You can't let someone like that tell you what to do."

"No," agreed Meredith. "But it's just *weird*, don't you think? Why would sitting behind the drums be such a big deal to him? It's a fun place to sit, sure, but ..."

"That's the way Lords of the Underworld think," said Reb. "I want it, so it's mine. Period."

The sinkhole in Meredith's stomach expanded. "Does he really run things?" she asked uneasily. "*Every*thing?"

"Not *every*thing," said Reb. "I don't know much about him, really. It's just things I've heard my cousins say ... and the way they laughed after they said them. You know, like, 'Don't mess with the Mol.' Or 'Check that one out with the Mol.' Things like that."

"Great," Meredith said again, her unease growing. "No wonder he talked to me like that—as if I was some *thing* in his path that had gotten out of line and had to be straightened out."

"So don't listen to him!" cried Dean. "The *Mol*! So what? He's just ego-flexing. You want to sit behind the drums and you got there first—go ahead!"

Meredith wanted to agree, to believe it was that cut and dried, but the silence coming from Reb was speaking volumes. Besides, she thought, there were so many unanswered questions. For instance, how was she, realistically speaking, supposed to handle tomorrow morning? What if she walked into home form to find Seymour had gotten there ahead of her and was seated behind the drums? Would it be worth kicking up a fuss? Why, in the end, was it so important to *her* to sit in that particular seat?

"I'm not telling you *not* to sit there, Mere," Reb said carefully, breaking into her thoughts. "But you know how it is. If you've got something and someone else wants it ... someone bigger than you ... well, things can get complicated. My guess is the Mol can hold a grudge—a complicated one. Is that something you want to deal with every home form period for the rest of the year?"

"Yeah, but ..." Dean protested. "I mean ... well, this is the 21st century! She's got her rights!"

"I know what century it is, Mount Matsumoto," snapped Reb, using a nickname the Matsumotos had bestowed upon their fiery daughter. For several breaths, an uncomfortable silence leaned in on the three beneath the tree.

"Huh," hedged Meredith, looking for a way to change the mood. "I'll have to think about it some more. I mean— Kingpin of the Underworld, and all that."

"Not actual *crime*," repeated Reb, her tone defensive.

"Hey," said Meredith, not sure how to connect, but wanting to. Reaching over, she patted Reb's arm and added, "Actual *friend*." Then, not wanting Dean to feel left out, she patted her arm, too. "Actual friend," she repeated.

Smiles were breaking out on both sides, chasing away the awkwardness. Suddenly, Meredith was filled with the urge to let loose—yell, holler, *boom*. "Beware, Polkton High!" she proclaimed, feeling her voice resonate in her almost-boobless chest. "This year, we three are going to take up *a lot of space*! Thus sayeth *The* Polk!"

Beside her, Reb erupted into giggles. "Thus sayeth the Looby!" she shouted. "Beware, Polkton High! Beware the Looby boobs!"

Dean let loose with a howl. "Thus sayeth Mount Matsumoto!" she bellowed fiercely. "This is the 21st century! We demand our rights!"

Above them, the willow sighed agreeably, lulling them into complacency about the possibilities of the coming year. "Pocky is what we need," murmured Dean. "Mom just bought a box. Anyone hungry?"

"Pocky for me," agreed Reb. "Pocky for you. If your brothers haven't devoured them all already, that is."

Getting to their feet, they trooped inside to indulge.

The apartment that Meredith shared with her Aunt Sancy sat above a small bakery at one end of a row of adjoined red-brick stores close to Polkton's downtown core. Located in an older area of town, the entire block had been constructed in the 1920s, and the apartment's external rear-entrance staircase, with the small closed-in porch at its peak, certainly looked like it—badly in need of demolition, or at least a new coat of paint. Inside, however, the place felt like home, with a small kitchen directly inside the door, and the rest of the rooms opening off the left side of a hall that extended to the building's front end. Meredith had lived there since she was five, soon after her aunt had adopted her and upgraded to a two-bedroom apartment.

"I loved you and all," Aunt Sancy had told her several years ago, "but your quick puffy breathing drove me crazy at night. You had your own bed in that room we shared, but you somehow managed to puff right into my ear all night from way the heck across the room."

Aunt Sancy worked full-time as a mechanic for a trucking company. As a result, she and Meredith shared the cooking chores, and on the days Aunt Sancy made supper, it was Meredith's responsibility to get home in time to put her aunt's prefab casserole into the oven so it would be piping hot for 5:30 PM. At the moment, the two of them were seated at the kitchen table waiting for the oven timer to go off, Aunt Sancy snorting her way through the day's edition of the *Polkton Post* while Meredith perused her Grade 9 yearbook.

With yet another pronounced snort, Aunt Sancy set down the newspaper. Politics in any form always seemed to go straight up her nose. "So," she said, taking a swig of iced tea. "How are the Philosophical Feet?"

"The Philosophical Feet" was the nickname Ms. Matsumoto had given Dean, Reb, and Meredith last year after taking a snapshot of them communing under the willow tree with only their feet in view. Copies had, of course, been made, then distributed to Aunt Sancy and Reb's parents, who were divorced.

"Okay," Meredith said vaguely. "The willow's okay, too."

Her aunt nodded. A short, wiry woman, most people found it difficult to imagine her crawling around a semi's insides. Meredith, however, had spent much of her childhood on the back of her aunt's Harley, traveling to various racetracks. The sound of a revving engine was music to Aunt Sancy's ears; she even had the Montreal Grand Prix's logo tattooed onto her right bicep.

"And your first day of Grade 10?" asked Aunt Sancy.

Meredith shrugged. "So far, so good," she said carelessly. "Don't worry, Ms. Goonhilly—I attended every minute of every class."

Aunt Sancy's last name was, unbelievably, Goonhilly. Next to Looby, it was the surname Meredith would have voted Most-Awful-To-Inherit. Several years ago, her aunt had explained that the lifetime of trials and tribulations the surname Goonhilly had caused her was the only reason she hadn't had Meredith's last name legally changed to her own during the adoption proceedings; ten years later, Meredith remained devoutly grateful.

Aunt Sancy nodded again. "What's with the yearbook?" she asked.

"Just seeing how people changed over the summer," said Meredith. In fact, she was busily scanning every page for mug shots of Seymour Molyneux, wanting to study him at length, get some kind of fix on him. So far, she had located several beaming images—one dead center in the Science Club's annual photo, another off to the side of a slightly out-of-focus Student Council picture (Seymour had been Home Form 75's class rep three years running), and a third, in which he was seated with a group of students who called themselves the Serene Knitter's Fellowship. A quirky school club, they devoted themselves to the production of various handicrafts, and in this snapshot, Seymour appeared to be completely absorbed in crocheting an afghan. Most likely he was faking it, though, Meredith decided. It was hardly likely the Mol spent much time knitting cardigans and mitts. Probably he had been in the vicinity when the picture was being posed, and had been invited to join in as a joke. To his credit, it only added to his *presence*, which seemed to be everywhere.

"Here," she said, sliding the yearbook across the table and pointing to a fourth photo she had discovered—a candid in which Seymour was goofing off in a school hall with two other guys. "Give me your psychological assessment of the guys in this picture."

Pursing her lips, Aunt Sancy focused on the snapshot. "That guy," she said sternly, tapping her finger on one of the grinning faces, "is psychotic. Stay away from him."

"What makes you say that?" asked Meredith, hiding a grin. Knowingly or unknowingly, Aunt Sancy had just nailed Neil Sabom, the only son of Polkton High's principal.

"Bulging cranium," said her aunt, delicately patting her own forehead. "Obvious deformity of the brain. Not a good sign. Watch out for the guy."

"Okay," promised Meredith, knowing her aunt was fooling around. "We won't let him join the Feet." Pointing to Seymour, she forced an offhanded note into her voice. "How does this guy strike you?" she asked.

Aunt Sancy snorted. "Boggs blood," she said tersely. "Stay away from him, too."

"But he's a Molyneux," protested Meredith, intent on keeping her aunt going for as long as possible.

"There's Boggs in him somewhere," muttered Aunt Sancy,

glaring at the picture, and Meredith realized that she was serious. "You can see it in the bones and the eyes. Same shaggy black hair, too. He's a Boggs, all right."

"As in Boggs Street downtown?" asked Meredith, her interest quickening.

"As in," nodded Aunt Sancy, settling back in her chair. "That family goes back a long way in Polkton."

"So he's from a founding father, too," murmured Meredith, recalling the sarcasm in Seymour's voice as he had said, "*Progeny* of a founding father and all."

"Not quite," said Aunt Sancy. "The Boggs weren't part of *that* group of scallywags. From what I recall, they moved here two or three decades after the city was founded. One of Polkton's early mayors was a Boggs. On his retirement, he had one of the downtown street names changed to deify himself. The family's always been big in the legal profession."

Her tone was scathing; Aunt Sancy never bothered to hide her contempt for what she usually called the "lethal profession," even though Meredith's father, James Polk, had just graduated from law school when he and her mother were killed in a car crash. Nor did Sancy Goonhilly attempt to conceal her dislike for James and his extended family. After Meredith's parents' deaths, there had been sporadic visits with her Polk grandparents, but in the face of Aunt Sancy's obvious antagonism, these had been awkward. When, five years later, her Polk grandparents died in a yachting accident, Aunt Sancy's relief had been palpable.

"Huh," said Meredith, studying the photograph. So, she mused, Seymour Molyneux was an undercover Boggs ... *the* Boggs bloodline that intersected directly with Polkton's main downtown thoroughfare—named, of course, Polk Avenue, in honor of her own illustrious ancestor. Superstition would call that destiny—as in, destiny whether you liked it or not.

Glancing up, she found her aunt observing her. "What's with the guy?" asked Aunt Sancy. "Why the interest?"

For a moment, Meredith teetered on the edge of telling or not telling—not because she didn't want her aunt to know, but because she sometimes needed mental space to work out things on her own. But then, deciding Aunt Sancy's perspective might prove helpful, Meredith launched into a detailed description of both run-ins with Seymour. When she had finished, she sat watching her aunt gaze thoughtfully out the kitchen window. Meredith knew from experience that any response she received wouldn't come quickly; her aunt tended to go at everything as if it were a mechanical device, poking and prodding each aspect of a situation until she had all the parts fitted together and running smoothly.

To Meredith's surprise, however, even after several minutes her aunt remained quiet, with only the odd thought flickering across her forty-year-old face. Abruptly, the oven timer kicked in, and Aunt Sancy got up to shut it off.

"So, what do you think?" asked Meredith, after the meal had been served and they had begun eating. "About

Seymour and the drums, I mean."

"I'm still thinking," her aunt said slowly. "What do *you* think?"

Still thinking herself, Meredith poked at her steaming shepherd's pie. "I don't know exactly," she admitted. "I know how I feel. I want to sit there and I don't want to back down. But the fact is that sitting there might not be that much fun. The guys who sit around the drums are all older than me, and I won't be high on their social chit-chat list. And Sina and Kirstin—the kids I hung around with last year—are still sitting at the front of the room." Briefly she hesitated, then added, "Besides, taking Seymour on ... he *will* be pissed, no question. It might not be worth the effort. In the end, it's just a place to sit—not a big-deal issue like racism, y'know?"

Eyes lowered, Aunt Sancy nodded. Silently, the two chewed, swallowed, and contemplated the Polk-Boggs connection.

"Try this one on for size," suggested Aunt Sancy, pouring herself another glass of iced tea. "Say you decide not to sit behind the drums. Now I want you to fast-forward ten years and pretend you're looking back on that decision. How are you feeling about it now? How do you think it's affected you—the way you think about yourself, the kinds of things you've chosen to take on since?"

From across the table, her dark eyes pinned Meredith's, direct and challenging. And in that moment Meredith saw it loud and clear, what her aunt was getting at—this decision wasn't just about a seat in home form, it was about how she thought about things in general, how she thought about *herself.*

"Yeah," she said, breathing deeply, startled at the sensation of internal vastness that had opened up. "I *want* to sit there, I really do. It's kind of scary, maybe even a little dumb, but ..."

Aunt Sancy sat silently, waiting her niece out, watching her resolve swing back and forth. "But, yeah," Meredith said again, more firmly this time. "It's what I *want* to do." A quick grin cut across her face and she added, "Well, what my *butt* wants to do."

Aunt Sancy grinned back. "Now you're talking like a Goonhilly," she quipped. "A Goonhilly always knows what her butt wants to do."

And she got up to get some ice cream.

chapter 3

It was the following morning. As Meredith strode through Polkton Collegiate's corridors, shouts and whistle shrieks could be heard resounding from the gym. Other than that, the building was unnaturally quiet, the open doorways of classrooms revealing only the odd teacher or maintenance staff. Several minutes earlier, she had arrived at her usual entrance to discover it still locked, and had been forced to reroute through the school's front door. Now, glancing at a nearby wall clock, she quickened her pace. "8:10 AM," she whispered under her breath. "Please God, *please* don't let him already be there."

Heart in a steady thud, she descended the stairwell to the tech wing's first floor and turned the corner. *Empty*! she thought, her relief so tangible she had to stop momentarily to absorb it. Ahead stretched the corridor that led to Home Form 75, its walls a dull yellow and a single row of closed olive-green lockers to her left. To her right, the door to her home form also stood closed; for an instant, Meredith wondered what she was going to do if she found it locked. When she tried the doorknob, however, it turned easily in her hand and, swallowing hard, she edged open the door.

There it was, directly across from her—the drum set, perched on the back riser in a completely vacant room. Either Mr. Woolger was in one of the adjoining practice rooms, or he had temporarily stepped out. Feeling a trifle shaky, Meredith crossed to the three risers and climbed them, then paused beside the drum set, studying its gleaming, steel-ribbed outline. What on earth was she doing here? she wondered. What, after all, did she know about the drums, Nerve Central, or the kind of popularity that went with such a position? Bitter and stinging, doubt swamped her, but she pushed back and it gave way. With a deep breath, she stepped forward, intending to finally, *gloriously* park her butt, when she heard a sound behind her. Startled, she glanced around to see Seymour walk into the room. As he caught sight of her, he let loose with a loud hiss and stopped dead in his tracks. Their gazes locked; their breathing froze. Quickly, in an explosion of determination, Meredith sat down.

Seymour's eyes narrowed and he took a step forward, but then another sound from the doorway caused him to whirl around just as Mr. Woolger entered, carrying a stack of music folders and his ever-present conducting baton. Eyebrows lifting, the teacher glanced from Seymour to Meredith, and a knowing expression flashed across his face.

"My, my—aren't you the early birds," he said, his tone slightly mocking. "Looking for the worm?"

Seymour flinched visibly. Then, without speaking, he ducked past Mr. Woolger and out into the hall. Alone by the door, Mr. Woolger stood gazing through the classroom windows, a smug expression on his face.

The gum wads! thought Meredith. *He's always suspected it was the Mol.*

"So, Meredith," said Mr. Woolger, walking to his desk and setting down the music folders. "You have ascended the throne."

His words brought Meredith a moment of intense headiness, followed by a flicker of satisfaction like a ripple across the surface of a lake. *Power*, she thought, almost overwhelmed—it was a smooth, cool, snake-slither kind of feeling, there and gone, but once you experienced it, you wanted more, you *knew* you wanted more.

"Yes sir, I have," she said, trying to sound offhand.

"Well," he replied, waving his baton vaguely as he spoke. "Rule wisely and well."

Then, crossing to one of the practice rooms, he went in, leaving her alone with her decision and the memory of Seymour's expression just before he had turned and left the room—angry at an assumption that had been overturned;

betrayed, as if he had felt Meredith owed him obedience to that assumption; and *ashamed* ... the latter an emotion he probably rarely felt, and even more rarely displayed. The Ruler of the Underworld, Meredith realized with dismay, would not be happy about the fact that she had seen him in such a humiliating moment; he would not be happy at all. And, as Reb had said, he could carry a grudge—a complicated one. So while she still had it—the drum set, the throne, and her self-respect—she had just made an enemy, and a complicated one at that.

With a sigh, she eased her knapsack to the floor. *Tell me your secrets*, she thought, splaying both hands lightly across the largest horizontal drum's surface. *Every single one of them. But tell me especially how I'm supposed to ride this damn thing out.*

It was going to be a long year, sitting high above the world behind the Mol's rigid back, but she wasn't ready to give up yet—not by a long shot.

Tap tap, went her fingers, wandering across the drum. *Tappety tappety tap tap tap.*

Determined to consolidate her claim to the throne, Meredith decided to put off going to her locker until after home form period. With approximately forty minutes to kill, the situation looked bleak, but she passed the time imagining the school's far-from-noteworthy Concert Band playing songs by AC/DC and Nickelback. Around 8:45, students began to wander into the classroom, and both

Kirstin and Sina left their front-row seats and climbed the risers to talk to her. Immediately, Mr. Woolger shooed them off the third riser, claiming too many students crowded in together would damage the percussion instruments. Relegated to floor level, the two girls stood at the riser's outer edge, gazing up admiringly at Meredith as they chatted.

About this time, Gene and Morey came through the doorway, engrossed in an argument over whether or not David Beckham was worth his salary. Not a big soccer fan, Meredith kept one ear tuned to their conversation and the other to her floor-level friends. Looking down at Sina and Kirstin from her perch behind the drums, Meredith felt an undeniable flush of importance that faded only with Seymour's entrance, seconds before the last warning bell. Without a glance in her direction, he strode to the second riser and sat down, then launched himself into Gene's and Morey's debate, which had since morphed into a discussion concerning the relative merits of Oh Henry! and Mr. Big chocolate bars. Siding with Gene, he pronounced Mr. Big a "patently obvious second-rate imitation" before falling into the obligatory, if resigned, silence required during the playing of the national anthem.

After the morning announcements, the three again took up the Oh Henry!–Mr. Big debate, Gene scooting his chair out from behind the xylophone in order to get closer to the action. "Mr. Big's peanuts are a bust," he declared, interrupting Morey's enraptured description of the Mr.

Big taste explosion. "Soggy. Inferior. Like chewing wet cardboard."

"Rubbish!" cried Morey, waving a dismissive hand. "Mr. Big's peanuts snap, crackle, and pop between the teeth. They are veritable dining *ecstasy*. Face it, Bussidor—Oh Henry!'s an Oh Goner. Mr. Big came along, and after that the competition became very smaaaaaaall."

"Smaaaaaaall is the size of your brain," grunted Seymour. "*And* your taste buds. Anyone who's taken a nibble of an Oh Henry!, caught a whiff of its delicate scent—"

It was at this point that Meredith, heart pounding, reached for her knapsack and began rooting around the contents, pulling out her binder, math supplies, and gym shoes. A chocolate-bar addict, she usually had a mound of empty wrappers collecting at the bottom, but try as she might, she couldn't remember if she had bought an Oh Henry! or Mr. Big recently. Ears glued to the ongoing dispute, she pawed impatiently through the candy wrappers currently inhabiting her knapsack. An Oh Henry!, that was what she was looking for, she decided—an Oh Henry! to bring another smile to Gene's face, and hopefully appease Seymour. But to her dismay, she couldn't locate either an Oh Henry! or a Mr. Big wrapper and, finally, in one swift movement, she upended her knapsack onto the surface of the largest horizontal drum, spilling out an entire summer's worth of chocolate-bar wrappers.

"Whoa!" said Gene, staring at the mound of Mars Bars, Caramilk, and Big Turk wrappers. Then, with a glance toward the front of the room, he added, "Lucky Woolger just went into a practice room. He'd freak if he saw that."

"It's just chocolate-bar wrappers," Meredith assured him. "I took everything else out first."

"Aha!" cried Morey. Leaning forward, he snatched the edge of a bright yellow wrapper and extracted it from the pile. "A Mr. Big!" he proclaimed triumphantly. "A Mr. Big that was eaten by a Grade 10 student—the wave of the *future*! I rest my case."

"Your case needs resting," grinned Gene. "It needs burying alive."

"May I keep this wrapper?" Morey asked Meredith, pointedly ignoring Gene's last comment. "It will be a ... a ..." Morey's face screwed itself up tightly as he went into deep thought, chasing the words he was seeking, and then he announced, "a symbol of our mutual pact against the evil Oh Henry! eaters!"

An ear-to-ear grin split Meredith's face. She had done it, she realized jubilantly—had broken through the unspoken but constantly assumed barrier that existed between junior and senior students ... and it had been so easy. "Sure!" she shrugged. "I just keep them in my knapsack to make my binder smell like chocolate."

"Ah, yes," said Morey, taking a voluminous sniff of the Mr. Big wrapper. "Exquisite, the scent of the gods—"

The end-of-home-form bell erupted, cutting him off mid-sentence, and Meredith began frantically scooping the candy wrappers back into her knapsack. Amiably, as if it were the most natural thing in the world, Gene and Morey leaned down, picked up several that had dropped to the floor, and handed them to her. "A Mr. Big," said Gene as he got to his feet. "You're a bit short to be eating one of those, aren't you?"

"Not if I keep eating them," Meredith shot back and he grinned, acknowledging her scored point before starting down the risers after Morey. Alone behind the drums, Meredith sat for a moment, watching the two of them head out the door. That had been fun, she thought—certainly more interesting than any of last year's home form periods. In the end, all her concern and advance scheming had been for naught, and the three male seniors had welcomed her easily into their camaraderie.

No, not *three*, she realized, doing a quick review of the conversation. From the point at which she had joined in, Seymour had said nothing, retreating into a silence so icy, he had actually turned himself physically out of the discussion and sat facing the front of the room. The debate had been at its most animated, and neither Morey nor Gene appeared to have noticed; nor had they taken note when the end-of-period bell had gone off and Seymour had leapt to his feet, leading the rush for the door.

Would things have gone differently, wondered Meredith, if it had been an Oh Henry! wrapper that Morey had spotted in her knapsack pile? That would have put her on Seymour's side, square in his camp for once. *But no*, she thought, considering, *probably not*. It wasn't as if the Mol cared what brand of chocolate bar she favored; it was her butt he was interested in—as in the absence of her butt with regard to its current home form placement.

Well, she decided, picking up her knapsack and starting down the risers, *whatever*—if that was the way Seymour wanted to be, she wasn't going to make it her problem. Ruler of the Underworld he might be, but as far as she could see, that didn't mean much; she was the one with the throne, after all, and Gene and Morey hadn't even *noticed* Seymour's silent temper tantrum.

Heading out the door, she booted it to the nearest girls washroom.

The rest of the day passed without incident, and it was only as Meredith was leaving the school building with Reb and Dean that the events from home form period came back to her. Animatedly, a wide grin on her face, she recounted the entire episode, giving a sentence-by-sentence replay of the Oh Henry!–Mr. Big debate. With the laughter and remarks interjected by her friends, it took several blocks to complete the tale—just enough time to reach the nearest 7-Eleven. "Seymour was sitting there like an ice pick!" declared Meredith as they turned into the parking lot. "I mean, that *frozen*, like he really wanted to chop me into little pieces."

"Psychologically disturbed," muttered Dean, gearing herself up for another Mount Matsumoto eruption, but was cut off by Reb, who had reached out to touch Meredith's arm.

"Don't look now," Reb said quietly, "but there he is—the Mol. In that yellow Jeep opposite the store door."

Instantly Meredith's eyes zeroed in on the Jeep, scanning the male driver and female front-seat passenger before settling on Seymour in the back. Sprawled beside a second girl, he was regaling his audience with an apparently captivating tale, and they were all turned in their seats, sucking down Slurpees and throwing in the occasional comment. Rooted to the spot, Meredith stood observing the scene before her so intently, she was practically absorbing it through her skin. Gradually, only gradually, did she become aware of the pounding of her heart and her white-knuckled grip on her knapsack shoulder straps.

"Big Man Jock," sniffed Dean to her left. "More like Big Man *Jerk*."

"I told you," Reb corrected her, "he's not a major jock. More like a jock sidekick."

"Yeah, okay," agreed Dean. "Big Man Side-Jerk." Glancing at Meredith, she added quickly, "What's the matter, Mere? You look like you've seen a ghost."

"A ghost?" echoed Meredith. Letting go of her shoulder straps, she flexed her fingers. "I ... didn't expect to see him here, I guess," she mumbled. "Especially when we were just talking about him."

"Come on," said Dean, glaring at the Jeep. "We'll go in and buy three Mr. Bigs, then come back out eating them and walk right past him. Show *him* who's going to take up space!"

Giggling nervously, Meredith started across the parking lot in Dean's purposeful wake. By the time she reached the store entrance, her heartbeat had slowed, but still she was jittery—her voice overly loud, her laughter too high-pitched. Once inside the store, she followed Dean to the chocolate bar display and they each selected a Mr. Big. To their surprise, however, Reb bypassed the candy bars and walked to the rear of the store, where she pulled a bottle of fruit punch from the drinks cooler.

"I like Oh Henry! better—evil me," she shrugged at them. "But I won't betray you by buying one."

"I like Oh Henry! better, too!" protested Dean, waving her Mr. Big like an accusing finger. "It's the point of the thing, isn't it?"

"The point is that it'd probably make my boobs bigger," responded Reb, and the three crowed with laughter as they turned toward the till.

And saw him—Seymour, a half-empty Slurpee in one hand, coming through the doorway with his friends. Immediately Meredith felt a kind of cloud settle over her— dense, wary, apprehensive. Her reaction was irrational, she knew that. There was no reason for Seymour's presence to alarm her; this store was regularly frequented by Polkton Collegiate students, and he most certainly was not here today to irritate her.

On the other hand, he and his friends had already purchased their Slurpees, so why would they all feel the urge to re-enter the store *now*, just after she had come in?

Eyes narrowed, Meredith stood beside the drinks cooler, watching Seymour and his entourage approach the till. The effect of their presence was tangible—all over the store heads turned, conversations faltered, and, when a male student second in line waved Seymour into position ahead of him, grimaces and sighs broke out, but no one further back protested. With a smug grin, Seymour placed an order for several lottery tickets; while the clerk processed his purchase, his friends lounged nearby, their laughter breaking out sporadically as they ignored everyone in the vicinity.

No, not everyone, Meredith corrected herself. Though no one in the group looked directly at her, she realized that she was being observed as closely as she was studying them. Rapidly flitting glances took in her crumpled T-shirt and shorts; suave peripheral vision assessed the Mr. Big clutched in her sweaty right hand and the two friends standing beside her. By the time Seymour had bought his tickets, pointedly keeping his back to her the entire time, his buddies had not only established that Meredith was right-handed, they knew the brand of her running shoes and knapsack, and exactly how many days it had been since she had last shaved her legs. Their expressions said it all: *Minor-niner, graduated by default. Tempest in a teaspoon.*

Then, turning, the group meandered out the door, the swagger obvious both in their voices and hips. Just outside the store, Seymour made a comment, and all four broke into uproarious laughter. Though Meredith hadn't heard what had been said, and had no concrete reason to believe it concerned her, still, a flush swarmed her face. *So what if they're talking about me?* she thought, chagrined at her response. *I was just talking about him, wasn't I?* Striding to the back of the line, she took up position, ninth from the till. Behind her, she felt Dean and Reb step into place, and knew without looking that they were staring through the store window, eyes fixed on the yellow Jeep as it pulled out of its parking spot and exited the lot.

Not me! Meredith decided. Not the butt that owned the throne—*she* wasn't going to be caught standing with her gaze fixed on Seymour and his loser lottery tickets as he roared off into the sound of contemptuous laughter. A silent, rigid backside might be all he intended to give her for the rest of the year, but if so, that was his loss, not hers— she was fifteen, this was her Grade 10 year, and she fully intended to take up every millimeter of available space.

When Meredith got outside the store, she unwrapped her Mr. Big to find she had been clutching it so tightly, some of the chocolate had melted, leaving the indent of her grip clearly outlined on the bar.

chapter 4

The following morning, Meredith waited until
8:50 to walk into home form, figuring that having
gotten to the drums first three days running had
consolidated her butt-rights to the throne. As expected,
she entered the room to find the drum set uninhabited;
Seymour's, Gene's, and Morey's seats were also empty. To
celebrate what she considered her now uncontested status,
Meredith spent several minutes talking to Sina in the first
row before climbing the risers and taking her place at the
peak of the room. A minute before nine, Seymour, Morey,
and Gene breezed in, caught up in another of their endless-
yet-amicable disagreements, and took their seats. Meredith
felt it immediately—a hum in the air, a tangible field of

energy the three created between themselves. Just being close to it made her feel buzzed, as if she had been plugged into an invisible circuit.

She had left yesterday's Mr. Big wrapper stashed inside her knapsack at the bottom of her locker, having decided that to show up with it today would be an embarrassingly blatant plea for attention. But as the 9 AM bell sounded without Gene or Morey having acknowledged her, she began to wonder if blatant was the way to go. Silent and uncomfortable, Meredith endured the national anthem and PA announcements, trying out various possible conversation starters inside her head, then ditching them all as not only blatant but pathetic. As it turned out, however, there was to be no time that morning for home form chitchat, pathetic or otherwise. The instant the announcements ended, Mr. Woolger got to his feet and rapped his baton on his desk. In a monotone, his face devoid of interest, he said, "Yesterday, you were asked to think about whom you would like to be your class rep to Student Council. Are there any nominations?"

Mute and brooding, Meredith continued to slouch at the back of the room. She had heard yesterday's PA announcement regarding the nomination of home form reps, but hadn't given the matter any thought. As far as she was concerned, Student Council was something that went on in the stratosphere, sort of like NASA satellite launches or God—unarguably out there, but nothing that required her direct attention. Besides, Seymour had been the rep for several years running; with his established fondness for the institution, she had assumed he would want to carry the tradition through to graduation.

To her surprise, however, when Mr. Woolger glanced questioningly at Seymour, he shook his head. "Not this year, sir," he said easily. "Too much homework."

With a nod, Mr. Woolger scanned the rest of the class. "Any nominations?" he asked.

The response he received was one of categorical disinterest, the entire class simultaneously dropping its gaze to the floor and taking up an intense study of the linoleum. "Come, come," said Mr. Woolger, irritably rapping his baton. "We must have a representative. Any volunteers?"

Again, the response was deadpan. Then, casually, Seymour raised a hand. "I have a nomination, sir," he said, his voice smooth, almost purring. "I'd like to nominate Meredith Polk."

Astonished, Meredith gaped at the back of his shaggy head. Mr. Woolger, on the other hand, looked distinctly relieved, and once again rapped his baton. "Do we have anyone to second the motion?" he asked.

All across the room, eyes rose from the floor and hands shot up, seconding, thirding, and fourthing Meredith's nomination. "Anyone opposed?" asked Mr. Woolger, and then, without waiting for a response, he glanced for the first time in Meredith's direction. "Well, Meredith," he said, his expression returning to one of complete boredom. "The position appears to be yours by acclamation."

Stunned, Meredith stared at him. *Me, a class rep?* she thought. *A class rep to Stupid Council? What do they do, except vote on new team uniforms and ... and ... Well, what else?*

At that moment, the end-of-period bell went off, and the class began clambering to its feet. Suddenly indignant, Meredith stood up, leaned around the drums, and poked a rising Seymour in the back. As he turned, startled, to face her, she hissed, "What did you do that for?"

To her dismay, he loomed annoyingly taller, even when standing one riser lower. For a moment, he stood gazing down at her, his expression remote and at the same time calculating. Then, with a twitch, his lips curved into something he probably considered a smile. "I thought you were *big* enough to handle it," he said carelessly. "Eater of Mr. Bigs, and the progeny of a *founding* father and all."

With that, he stepped off the second riser's outer edge and headed for the door, leaving her open-mouthed and staring after him.

Mid-morning, Meredith sat on a wad of gum. At first she didn't notice; she was in math class, Reb seated one desk ahead, and they were practicing their paper-airplane pilot's skills, launching 777s and Airbuses at friends on the opposite side of the room. Then the class got underway, the teacher, Mr. Jiminez, scrawling a series of indecipherable algebraic equations across the chalkboard that, as usual, left Meredith drawing a complete blank. Scowling down at her notes, she doodled tentatively, trying to get this x to communicate with that y, and let her in on their unknown quantities. Unfortunately, today was a day when x's and y's appeared to be incommunicado; surrendering to the inevitable, Meredith leaned forward, intending to consult with the algebraically-inclined Reb, just as Mr. Jiminez raised his stick of chalk and pointed it at her.

"Meredith, would you come up to the board and work out equation number three?" he asked.

Stifling a groan, Meredith fought the urge to crawl under her desk and got to her feet. Ahead stretched the empty aisle, and beyond it the unsolved, probably unsolvable, mystery of equation number three. Reluctantly, she started toward it. Within several steps, a gasp sounded behind her but she ignored it, her attention focused on the looming chalkboard and the incomprehensible equation number three. Seconds later, however, a scattering of cackles erupted, followed by a roar of mirth that swept the room; whirling, Meredith caught sight of the entire class, faces incredulous as they surged collectively to their feet. At first she thought she was about to be swarmed, then realized her classmates were staring at something approximately hip-high that ran the length of the aisle in which she was standing. Dropping her gaze, she saw it—a moist, elongated tendril of orange gum that stretched from somewhere directly behind her all the way to the seat she had just vacated.

For a moment, she stood gaping at the gum, not connecting its long, stretched journey along the aisle to her own butt. Then, abruptly getting it, she glanced over her shoulder, trying to get a look at the seat of her shorts and inspiring another wave of laughter. Quickly, Mr. Jiminez stepped in, shushing the hysterical students and ordering them back to their seats. Sheepish, Meredith stood at the front of the room, cautiously patting her butt, then wishing she hadn't as her hand came away sticky with soggy gum threads.

"Well, Meredith, I guess you'd better get yourself cleaned up," said Mr. Jiminez, his face simultaneously sympathetic and fighting off the chuckles. "Then come back to class."

"Yes, sir," said Meredith. Sidestepping the elongated gum tendril that had by now sagged to the floor, she made her way back down the aisle. The urge to cup both hands protectively over her posterior was enormous, but she fought it off, focusing instead on Reb, who was on her knees and leaning over the front of Meredith's desk. "It's a monster!" Reb hissed indignantly, pointing to the massive orange gum wad flattened across the metal seat. "It must be two or three gumballs."

Which meant two or three mouths to chew it, thought Meredith, observing the wad—a conspiracy of mouths, conspiring that morning from the looks of it. Breaking off the tendril still stuck to her butt, she reattached it to the monster wad and headed out the door. Luckily the halls were empty, and she was able to make it to her locker unobserved. There, she pulled out a pair of gym shorts, then scurried to the nearest girls washroom, where she entered a stall and slid off the shorts she was wearing. Holding them up, she inspected the large orange splat mashed across the rear central seam.

Still sticky, the gum clung to the fabric—a mean, insolent presence. Heat flooding her face, Meredith stared at it. *Who would do something like this?* she thought. *And why?* That it had been an act of deliberate social sabotage, there was no question; monster gum wads didn't materialize out of thin air, especially onto metal desk seats. *But why my desk seat?* she wondered. *Who's after my butt?* As far as she knew, she had no enemies in math class; it was only the third day of the school year, and there hadn't been enough time to create that much resentment. *Ah, whatever*, she decided finally, working the wad off her shorts. *It's just a random attack—could've happened to anyone.*

Well, she could live with that—leaving a gum wad on a desk seat hardly qualified as a terrorist attack, and her shorts, being dark blue, wouldn't show the stain. Still, it was unnerving, knowing there could be something moist, squishy, and massively full of germs, lurking on desk seats all over the school. *From now on*, Meredith thought grimly, *I am checking* and *double-checking every desk seat, chair, and bench before parking my butt. No one will catch me napping like that again.*

Stashing her blue shorts in her locker, she headed back to class.

School had let out, the day was yet young, and the Philosophical Feet were wandering Polkton's downtown core, T-shirt sleeves rolled up and enjoying the late-season warmth. Tucked under Dean's arm was a set of pastel pencils she had just bought for her art class; errand accomplished, the girls figured they had ten, maybe twenty minutes to kill before they had to head home for various pre-supper chores.

"What d'you think?" asked Reb, as they meandered over to a large fountain at the center of the downtown intersection. "A soda at Murphy's or a milkshake at McDonald's?"

"Soda," said Meredith.

"Milkshake," said Dean, her answer overlapping Meredith's.

"Glad that one's solved," muttered Reb, sitting down on the fountain's curb and stretching out her legs. "A soda-milkshake would exactly hit the spot about now."

They sat quietly, sun-dazed and watching the late-afternoon light spark the fountain's falling water. "I wonder," Meredith said idly, "what good ole Gus would think of this place if he could see it now."

"As in Gus Polk, ancestor emeritus?" asked Dean.

"Ancestor Great Hand," Meredith replied solemnly, and, following her example, the other two girls each raised a hand and shifted it back and forth until they had aligned their fingers with the five-cornered intersection in front of them. "Left," said Meredith, staring through her fingers at the busy scene. "I'm sure it was the left."

"Nah, Mere," said Dean. "It was the right. The guy wouldn't have founded a city with his left hand. It's too ... nefarious."

"Creepy," agreed Reb. "Gothic. And Polkton is ... well, it's McDonald's and the Gap. Definitely right-hand stuff."

They had rehashed this argument frequently over the years, and still hadn't come to a collective agreement. Admittedly, Meredith had more invested in the subject than the others; it was her bloodline, after all—her poky-Polk surname, not theirs. The matter at hand, so to speak, was historical, a basic Polkton fact learned by every Grade 8 city resident—that in 1827, founding father Gus Polk placed a hand on the ground near Lazy Man's River and drew a line around that hand with a stick, then used this outline as the center-point for the map of the town he planned to build. When Meredith had first heard this story, she had marched downtown to Polkton's core intersection, a busy five-cornered junction that included Polk Avenue, Boggs Street, and a short two-block roadway called Dieffendorfer Boulevard, and had tested out the theory, taking up various positions around the central fountain and holding up first one hand, then the other. As far as she had been able to tell, her illustrious ancestor Gus Polk had fudged a little on what must have been his original map—Polk Avenue, which ran north-south, intersected the east-west Boggs Street at right angles, and a person would have to be double-jointed to accurately align every digit. But what had bothered her most about the story had been its egomaniacal aspect. Even now, almost two centuries after Gus had originally planted his hand in that long-ago dirt, she could feel the arrogance of that decision—five dark, gothic fingers rising out of the earth and reaching for the sunlight and life going on above it.

It is like the left hand of darkness, she thought. *Creepy. Not as in the supernatural—a ghoul or a ghost, anything like that. More just human darkness, complete self-centeredness, as if everything Gus Polk saw had to have his name plastered across it—not just while he was alive, but even after he died. This entire city is sitting on top of his arrogant reaching hand. That definitely belongs to the left side of things, not the right.*

"It had to be the left," she argued, still observing her upraised hand. "Most people are right-handed, right? And if you're right-handed, you'd put your left hand on the ground if you wanted to outline it. Gus Polk was probably right-handed like most people, which means Polkton was founded using a map drawn around his left hand."

Triumphant, certain of her point, she turned to watch her friends' faces twist into skeptical grimaces. "Maybe," Dean allowed slowly, "*if* he was right-handed. You don't know that. Anyway, so what if he was? That left hand-right hand stuff doesn't mean anything. It's just fairy tales, superstition."

"*The Exorcist*," agreed Reb. "Or Stephen King."

Not quite sure how the conversation had arrived at Stephen King, Meredith was, nevertheless, unwilling to bypass the opportunity for a joke. Faking spasms in her left hand, she pretended to attack the other girls' right ones. "Evil," she intoned in a guttural voice. "My great-great-great-great-great-*great*-grandpappy Polk was evil, and consorting with Lords of the Underworld. That's why Polk Avenue crosses with Boggs Street, y'know. Seymour Molyneux has Boggs blood, and *he* is of the nether regions."

"Seymour is a Boggs?" asked Reb, hastily sitting on her right hand to protect it from further assault. "How d'you know that?"

"Aunt Sancy said so," said Meredith, settling her left hand onto her knee and patting it gently to calm it down. "I showed her his yearbook pictures."

"So the Mol is a creature that crawled out of a bog," mused Dean. "Figures. Crustacean brain, like I—" Interrupted by her cell phone, she pulled it out of her back pocket and held it to her ear. "Yeah, Mom," she said quickly. "I'm downtown with Mere and Reb. I got my pastels. Yup. Okay. Bye." Getting to her feet, she sighed, "I gotta go. I'm supposed to rake the lawn before supper. See you." Long black hair floating out behind her, she took off along Boggs Street.

"I gotta go, too," said Reb, standing up. "I promised Mom I'd get in a half-hour of piano practice before supper every day this week. She wants me to make up for missing out on it all summer. Not my fault there was no piano up at Kapuskasing."

"Kapuskasing was probably relieved," observed Meredith.

"Hey!" said Reb, bouncing a textbook lightly off the top of Meredith's head. "Bach happens to *flow* off these fingers like water."

"But actual music?" teased Meredith.

Feigning rage, Reb glared. "My mother likes it," she pouted.

"I rest my case," smirked Meredith. "You go home and play Bach for your mother, and I'll go listen to my aunt rev her Harley."

Reb looked wistful. "Your aunt is so cool," she said. "D'you think, if she was my mother, she'd let me get a boob reduction?"

"If my aunt was your mother, you wouldn't have boobs," said Meredith. "Booblessness runs in the Goonhilly family."

"Lucky you," sighed Reb. "Well, Bach calls. I really gotta go."

Without a backward glance, she headed south down Polk Avenue, shoulders hunched and books glued, as usual, to her chest. Watching her go, Meredith wished she could reach out an invisible hand and gently straighten her friend's shoulders, somehow make her entire body *relax*. Reb was always so ... clutched up, bracing herself against the next glance or comment. Why did life have to be like that—overloading one girl with womanhood and leaving another practically prepubescent? Why not just make every female on the planet the same bra size? It would make things so much easier.

Meredith for God, she thought wryly. Yeah, if Meredith Polk was put in charge, she would have a few ideas to throw around the universe.

chapter 5

Later that evening, Meredith was lying on her bed, studying a picture in a book on local history that she had propped open on her chest. The image in question was a line drawing of a man from the early 1800s— her illustrious ancestor, Gus Polk, to be exact. Forehead creased into a frown, Meredith repeatedly ran her gaze over every millimeter of the sketch. Several years ago, she had bought the book at a library discard sale; she had long since read it, and this particular page was the only one that continued to draw her interest.

Nothing in the man's face—not a single feature— resembled her in the slightest. Tall and apparently fair-haired, broad-shouldered Gus stood in centuries-old dress, a rifle in one hand as he gazed off contemplatively into the horizon—a horizon that at that point was crowded with maples and poplars, but now was probably occupied by several blocks of Polk Avenue. Eyes narrowed, Meredith zeroed in on the man's face. *Is this really what you looked like?* she wondered, observing the aquiline nose and high forehead. *Or is this maybe Zeus, showing up a thousand years later in some kind of time warp?* Because, truth be told, in the line-drawing Gus looked suspiciously Walt-Disneyish— as in too good to be true. *A wart, a zit, some vampire fangs,* thought Meredith, irritation curling her upper lip. *Come on, Gussie—you don't even look like a Polk.*

Reaching out lazily, she picked up one of three framed photographs standing on her night table. Two faces gazed back at her—the beaming, laughing expressions of her parents, Ally and James Polk, caught on their wedding day. In their mid-twenties, they looked as if they were living at the center of the universe—as if the world, and everything life held in store for them, was just spare change in their pockets. Ally's dress was frilly and white, her thick black hair piled up under the veil cascading from the back of her head. *Prettier,* sighed Meredith, as she usually did when studying this photo. Her mother had been prettier than her—Ally had had a smile that would light up any room, and she looked as if she knew it. James, beaming away beside her, was almost as good-looking, but other than the blond tint to his hair, he didn't resemble the line drawing of ole Gus in the slightest. *Well, maybe the shoulders,* conceded Meredith, her gaze flicking between the two pictures. *But Dad's hair is curly where Gus's is straight, and Dad's nose looks like it lost an Olympic boxing match.*

Mom. Dad, she thought, touching their glassed-in faces. *If only* ... A gulping sigh took her, and Meredith blinked back a rush of tears. If only she could have five minutes with them now, she reflected—to hear what their voices had sounded like, the kinds of things they had liked to say. *The true things*, she thought fervently. *The real things.* Not the endless stories she made up inside her head—scenes of being welcomed home from school by her mother, or playing catch in a big back yard with Dad. It wasn't that Meredith didn't like Aunt Sancy—love her, in fact, but ... *Well*, she thought, touching the two faces again. *Parents are where you come from. They used to have bits of you inside their bodies. They* are *you, sort of. Aunts can never be that.*

Possibly the saddest thing in her life was that she could remember next to nothing about her parents. Try as she might to dredge up something tangible, all Meredith could recall were blurred fleeting moments—a memory of her father's laugh, or of standing in warm window-light and holding her mother's hand. At least, she *thought* that what she was remembering was her father's laughter and her mother's hand, but if she was really honest, she didn't know. Life before her fifth year was pretty much a blank space, like an erased chalkboard; Meredith was only able to recall specific experiences after her parents' deaths, when Aunt Sancy had taken over. And these memories tended to involve the Goonhilly side of the family, due to the ever-present tension that had existed between her aunt and her Polk grandparents before their deaths.

Letting Gus Polk's picture drop onto her stomach, Meredith picked up a second framed photograph and set it next to that of her parents. Taken a year after Ally's and James's deaths, it showed her Polk grandparents, Johanna and Dave Polk, leaning against their BMW in their front drive. Tanned and golf-course trim, they looked like the ideal retired couples portrayed in investment ads. *And,* thought Meredith, homing in on her grandfather's face, *they look like Dad—Granddad Polk even had that same mushed-up looking nose.*

Even with her grandfather's boxer's nose, however, she had to admit that, like ole Gus, her grandparents looked too good to be true. In their late fifties, both were laughing blonds without the slightest sign of gray hair, and not a wrinkle lined either forehead. *Face jobs?* pondered Meredith, studying them. *Botox? Even Granddad?*

Aunt Sancy's open hostility had restricted both the number and length of Meredith's visits with her Polk grandparents, and, as a result, her memories of them were sparse—a big house that echoed as she ran through it, a vast manicured lawn, the scent of the BMW's leather-covered seats. Overriding all of this had been the weight of her grandparents' sadness over their only child's death—invisible but constant, even behind their photogenic smiles. "A brilliant law student," Meredith could recall her

Grandfather Polk sighing. "He graduated at the top of his class. Prominent firms were lining up to interview him. Such a tragedy. Such a *waste*."

And then there was the way that sadness had mutated into a flash of disappointment at every visit, the moment her grandparents had initially laid eyes on her. As if, somehow, her physical appearance *took* something from them— something they had been anticipating, had somehow assumed belonged to them. At the time, Meredith had felt it but hadn't understood it. Now she did. *It's the way I look*, she thought, observing her grandparents' carefully arranged smiles. *Not like him. Your son. No, your only grandchild turned out looking like the daughter-in-law—a Goonhilly. And the Goonhillys look like aliens from outer space next to the Polks. If ole Gus somehow managed to come back from the dead and we met up on Polk Avenue, he wouldn't look at me twice.*

Instinctively, Meredith glanced right and found herself smiling fondly at the elderly couple displayed in the last photograph standing on her night table. Dressed in matching velour track suits, her Goonhilly grandparents were snuggled together on a psychedelic, flower-power couch. Both were wearing the fuzzy rabbit-head slippers Meredith had given them the Christmas before they had died, within a month of each other, at a nearby seniors' home. While Meredith didn't currently resemble either of them, she knew she would someday. *Right down to the rabbit-head slippers*, she thought, smiling affectionately at their chubby faces. In contrast to her limited recall of her Polk grandparents, Meredith's memories of her Goonhilly grandmother and grandfather were endless. And not in one of them, not even for the most fleeting of moments, could she remember seeing hesitation in their eyes when they caught sight of her. She lit up every room for them, and they let her know it. There had been no BMWs parked in front of the Goonhilly bungalow, no velvety, manicured lawn. The back yard had been dominated by her grandfather's rabbit pens; his hair had resembled Einstein's; and Grandma Goonhilly had thought dieting was for the birds. "Grandma Goonie" was what she called herself, and when Meredith had enthusiastically taken up the habit, the elderly woman had chuckled with delight.

Picking up the book on local history, Meredith again pondered the line drawing of her acclaimed ancestor. *I don't think this is really you,* she decided, scowling at it. *It's just a guy—the way some artist imagined the great Gus Polk would look. You're an illusion, Gussie. A fake. Complete and utter.*

Briefly, her gaze flicked down to the rifle in the man's hand. *See!* she triumphantly told herself. *Even the hand is wrong. It's in the right, but it should be in the left. I'm sure it was the left.*

Decisively, she snapped the book closed.

Friday morning, Meredith arrived at home form to find the music classroom door closed and half the class milling around the already busy hall. *What's up?* she thought. *Concert Band practices are Tuesday and Thursday mornings.* Weaving her way through the crowd, she joined Kirstin, who was peering in through the window in the classroom door.

"What's going on?" Meredith asked, edging onto tiptoe to see in.

"Some kind of meeting," said Kirstin. "The Concert Band, Woolger, and the Phoenix."

Meredith snorted. "The Phoenix" was Mr. Sabom, Polkton Collegiate's principal. A man with a large balding spot, he had taken to combing a long length of hair across the top of his head. Several years ago, this had led to unforeseen repercussions when an enterprising yearbook photographer had snapped a picture of the principal running across the teachers' parking lot on a particularly blustery day, the long length of hair lifting vertically from his scalp. The ensuing yearbook candid had been labeled "The Phoenix," and, years later, the nickname continued to rise from students' lips on fiery, if giggly, wings.

"They don't have their instruments," said Meredith, scanning the scene before her. There, on the other side of the window glass, sat four rows of students, listening intently as Mr. Sabom spoke. Conspicuous on the rear riser was Gene, leaning against the back wall beside the double bass. Two meters to his left sat the drums, presided over by a set of blond dreadlocks, which, in turn, presided over a decidedly bored face.

Larry Navasky, thought Meredith, observing the drummer

carefully. In his grad year, Larry was the sort of person one would expect to find inhabiting a drum set; his was a butt predestined to rule rock 'n' roll thrones. Eyes narrowed, she scrutinized the tip of the cigarette pack peeking from his shirt pocket, the ragged tear in one jeans knee, and the casual way the drumsticks hung from his hands even when he wasn't playing—so loosely, they appeared almost fluid. *Bach, flowing from these fingers like water,* she remembered Reb saying, and suddenly Meredith wondered if the same could be said about all musical instruments—if, for instance, notes from the tuba, the trombone, or Gene's double bass also felt like flowing liquid to the musician. Personally, she didn't have a clue—as far as she knew, no one in her family, Polk or Goonhilly, had ever displayed an aptitude for music—and it had never occurred to her to wonder about playing an instrument, what it might feel like, what the gift of that experience might be.

Turning to Mr. Woolger, Mr. Sabom nodded; with a wave of his baton, Mr. Woolger dismissed the band, and four rows of attentive faces dissolved into individual students rising to their feet. Then the door swung open and Meredith stepped back to avoid the surge of exiting bodies. For a second, she saw him so close she could have reached out and touched him—Larry Navasky, boredom flushed from his face as he tossed a comment at the band's lead trumpeter. Then he was gone, his cool rock 'n' roll butt passing through the doorway at the end of the corridor and out of sight.

Pressed to the wall, Meredith waited out the stream of

departing students, then followed her classmates into the music room. Several band members were still lingering in their seats; over by Mr. Woolger's desk, the teacher and the principal continued to talk; at the back of the room, Gene was running his hands carefully over the double bass. Stepping up onto the third riser, Meredith checked the drum-set seat for gum wads, Double Bubble or otherwise, and parked her butt. A moment later, the xylophone shifted slightly as Gene slid in behind it and sat down.

"Hey, Ms. Big," he said congenially.

Meredith radiated light. "Hey, evil Oh Henry! eater!" she replied. "That was pretty quiet for a band practice."

Gene grinned wryly. "We start practicing next week," he said. "Sabom and Woolger called today's meeting to discuss a possible band trip."

"Cool!" said Meredith. "Where to?"

"Miami," said Gene. "Some kind of high school band festival."

"In February, I hope," said Meredith. "Ditch the parka for a swimsuit."

"I wish," said Gene. "It's early May. And it'll mean fundraising all year—car washes galore, selling calendars and chocolates."

"Your soul?" Meredith added helpfully.

"Not my soul!" gasped Gene, cringing in mock horror.

Meredith snorted. "Hey," she said again. "I have a question—about playing music. I don't know anything about it."

"Nothing?" asked Gene, looking surprised.

"Well," admitted Meredith, "there *was* playing the recorder in music class in junior high. But other than that, riding the back of my aunt's Harley is the closest I've ever gotten."

Gene's eyebrows rose. "You've got the bass section down, then," he said neutrally.

Meredith giggled. "Well, what I was wondering," she said, then paused as Morey stepped onto the second riser ahead of them and sat down. Unexpectedly, a flush rose in Meredith's cheeks. There was no denying it—the question she was about to ask felt, well ... *dumb*. Next to debates about David Beckham and the Stones, it was decidedly uncool. Unfortunately, she hadn't realized this until she had opened her big mouth, and now, with both Gene and Morey watching her, it was too late to back out.

"Well," she said again. "The notes you play—and the tuba guy, and the drummer, and all the other players ... do they feel like water flowing off your fingers? I mean ..." Overwhelmed by the enormity of her looming dumbness, Meredith faltered. No two ways about it—she sounded *so* Grade 10. "Well, is it like something you can actually touch?"

Her flush deepened; there was definite heat eating up her face. On the second riser, Morey was observing her with an openly quizzical expression. Gene, however, didn't appear to have noticed anything amiss.

"Notes," he said thoughtfully, staring off into the middle distance. "Something you can touch? Yeah—that's a good way of putting it. But only when you get good at what you're playing. *After* you've been practicing it for a while." Turning to look directly at Meredith, he smiled, his eyes quiet but intent—as if noticing her, really taking her in, for the first time.

"What's that like?" asked Meredith, trying to work out what he was telling her. "Touching music?"

"Touching music?" repeated Gene, small surprise flickering across his face. "Like touching the wind, I guess. Except, just like it is with the wind, music is mostly touching you, rather than you touching it."

"Yeah, but with music, *you're* playing *it*," Meredith reminded him.

"True," agreed Gene. "But the music you're playing was around *before* you played it, just like the wind comes from somewhere else before it touches you."

"Okay," said Morey, breaking into their conversation. "But *you're* still the one playing the music. So you're the one in charge—you're directing it."

Gene smiled, his eyes going vague. "What's your instrument, Morey?" he asked mildly. "What d'you play?"

Pulling himself upright, Morey emitted a distinct huffiness. "The accordion," he said with pronounced dignity. "I had three years of lessons—from Grades 3 to 6."

"What happened to kill your illustrious career?" asked Gene.

"A broken arm," said Morey. "I lost interest while it was

healing ... okay, *before* I broke my arm. But I can still play a damn good polka."

"'Roll Out the Barrel?'" interjected Seymour as he slipped into place beside him.

"I can roll out the barrel anytime," affirmed Morey. "What about you, Seymour? What can you play?"

"On the accordion?" asked Seymour.

"On anything," said Gene.

An expansive expression on his face, Seymour leaned back in his chair. "Other than the recorder in junior high, not much," he admitted.

A slight grin caught Gene's face, and he glanced sideways at Meredith. "That just so happens to put you in the exact same category as Meredith," he said. "Still stuck in junior high. She never got past the recorder, either."

Seymour stiffened noticeably, and Meredith thought she saw Gene's grin widen. "I guess I'll have to take up the accordion," Seymour said evenly. "Catch up to Morey, here."

"Eat my dust," said Morey. "'Barrel House Boogie,' here I come."

The final bell rang and the national anthem kicked in, ending further conversation. As Morey turned to face the front of the room, his hands took up position on an invisible accordion, cranking out a raucous "O Canada" boogie. An unmitigated grin split Gene's face, and he raised an eyebrow at Meredith. Instinctively, she grinned back.

Pulling a sheet of foolscap from his binder, Gene scribbled something across it and passed the page to Meredith. She scanned it quickly. *Music*, the note said, *touches you. Outside and in, where you didn't know you could be touched. Places you didn't know you had inside you—music finds them for you. Like riding a Harley that can fly.*

The smile that found Meredith then was pure and full of light. Glancing at Gene, she beamed and he nodded, his gaze warm but careful. For a second, she wondered if she had done something wrong—smiled too brightly, perhaps—but then, rereading the note she realized, *No, it's what he wrote. It's so ... open. Anyone would be careful after that.*

Gently, almost reverently, she folded the sheet of foolscap, opened her own binder, and slid the page into the front pocket under a Big Turk wrapper.

Later that afternoon, she discovered gum on her bum again. This time she was in a corridor, headed to her last period history class, when someone abruptly stumbled against her from behind. A muffled *oomph!* sounded, followed by an even more muffled apology, but by the time Meredith turned around, the stumbler had vanished, leaving no one in the vicinity—at least, no one looking guilty or off-balance. With a shrug, she continued down the hall until someone tapped her shoulder. Turning around, Meredith saw a Grade 11 student she knew from afar as Ronnie Olesin.

"Hey!" said Ronnie, a mocking grin on her face. "I've got news for you, dozo."

What Meredith knew about Ronnie was that she was

someone best avoided. Burly and obese, Ronnie had a habit of throwing her weight around and had been suspended twice last year for fighting.

"Oh, yeah," Meredith said carefully. Unease walked softly up her back. It wasn't just Ronnie's reputation that was putting her on edge—there was something in the girl's pale blue eyes, their strangeness ... the way they grabbed onto whatever they were looking at and hung on. Frankly, she gave Meredith the creeps. Trying to be subtle, Meredith took a step back.

Ronnie stepped forward. There, in those blue eyes, Meredith could see it—triumph at having made Meredith cede space.

"On your bum, moron!" said Ronnie, her grin widening. "You sat on some gum."

"Gum!" repeated Meredith. For a second, she gaped at Ronnie, then pivoted, positioning herself with her back to the wall.

"That's what it looks like," singsonged Ronnie, obviously enjoying Meredith's discomfort. "Unless you got some kind of weird disease growing on your butt."

With a dismissive snort, she turned and moved off down the corridor, leaving Meredith with her back to the wall and cautiously feeling her own butt. To her dismay, she felt it almost immediately—a gooey lump plastered across one of her rear pockets, freshly chewed like yesterday's, but much smaller. Which made sense, she reasoned to herself, if it had been planted by the fake stumbler a moment ago—a hit-and-run act like that would have been harder to pull off with a giant wad.

But why, she wondered, her thoughts churning, would someone choose *her* butt out of a crowded hall? And why had gum wads materialized on her person twice in one week? The chance of either being a random attack was pretty much annihilated by there being two of them. Well, she decided miserably, the next step was to get to the closest washroom unnoticed and check out the damage. Yesterday she had been wearing navy; today her shorts were pale blue.

Please please *don't let it be grape-flavored*, she thought, and headed down the hall.

chapter 6

The weekend passed quickly, a golden blur that Meredith absorbed from the back of her aunt's Harley as they traveled to and from a Hamilton car rally. The following Monday dawned with her feeling sunburned, content, and a long way from Friday's hallway gum-wad attack, but still cautious enough to don a pair of black shorts. The second wad appeared to have been Wrigley's Spearmint, and her pale blue shorts would thus live to see another day, but just barely; the stain was discernible, even after washing, if you knew to look for it, and someone did seem to be looking for it—her butt, that was, rather intently.

As she wove her way through the hallway crowds en route

to her locker before home form period, Meredith found herself suddenly struck with inspiration. Instead of pulling off her sweatshirt and hanging it in her locker as she had intended, she removed it and tied the sleeves around her waist, allowing the bulk of it to hang down behind her body. The effect was immediate—a sweet, protected feeling that spread out, body-wide, from her butt. *Take that, Mr. Bum-Wad Creep!* she thought cheerfully. Her sweatshirt was black to match her shorts, and no gum flavor in the world could stain it. With an exuberant swagger, she closed her locker and headed off to home form.

Upon arrival, she discovered Gene, Morey, and Seymour already in their seats and engaged in animated debate. Climbing into position behind the drums, she leaned forward slightly, trying inconspicuously to tune in.

"No way!" exclaimed Morey. "Your main competition is yourself. It's always that way. You start thinking someone else is better than you—you psyche yourself out and take yourself out of the running."

"I've seen him play," said Gene. "I swear he has extra knuckles on each finger. His hands are waltzing spiders."

Morey shrugged. "Spiders," he said carelessly. "Octopi. Who even notices?"

Seymour waved a dismissive hand. "It all depends on how you run your audition, Gene. You've got to do this like reality TV. You're a survivor; everything you do has to be on the edge."

"The edge of what?" Gene asked mildly.

"That's the point," said Seymour. "You *create* the edge. You make the conductor think it exists and you've got it, and that's why he wants you. Otherwise, what are you—just another bass player."

Gene frowned. "Thanks," he muttered. Then, turning his head, he smiled at Meredith. "Hi there, Ms. Big," he said.

Meredith lit up. "Hi!" she beamed. "What do you need waltzing-spider fingers for?"

"I've got an audition coming up," said Gene. "Bass player for the Toronto Youth Orchestra. At least one of the other guys trying out—David Chang—is really good. And these two geniuses here are telling me I have to handle it like a survivor show. What'm I supposed to do—kill my opponents, then dine on their raw, frozen flesh in the Arctic to prove I can play the double bass?"

Seymour's chin jutted, and he swiveled in his seat so he sat facing the front of the room. "It's your audition," he said huffily. "You don't want advice, just say so."

"Come on!" said Gene, leaning forward to swat his shoulder. "We're just kibitzing here. Don't get all wounded on me."

Still staring straight ahead, Seymour harrumphed under his breath. Tentatively, Morey raised an eyebrow at Gene. "The Mol," he said significantly, "is moling."

"Moling?" asked Meredith, without giving it a second thought. Instantly, Seymour's back rigidified, emitting unmistakable disapproval, and in spite of herself Meredith flushed. *What?* she thought, stung. *Now I'm not allowed to speak? I have to turn off my ears and hear nothing if it's about you?*

If Gene noticed Meredith's flush, he didn't let on; neither did he give any sign of having noted the abruptly vertical line of Seymour's spine. "Moling," he explained amiably to her, "means like a mole burrowing around the underground. Which is where the Mol lives and breathes—down under, in the dark, where everything germinates."

For a moment, the three guys sat silently, as if mulling over Gene's words, and Meredith tried to absorb what she had been told. *Don't say it*, she told herself sternly. *Not a damn thing about Lords of the Underworld or mafia kingpins—crime or no actual crime.*

"Keeps me ahead of the pack," Seymour muttered finally, his spine relaxing.

"Granted," said Gene. "But sometimes ... things get too much like Dungeons and Dragons around you. I'm auditioning for bass player in a youth orchestra, not viceroy of the dark realms."

"Yeah, yeah," Seymour said impatiently. "The question still is: How do you get what you want? You've got to be prepared to make compromises. I say you need an edge. It doesn't have to be Satan, although you've got to admit—the supernatural would be a nice touch."

"I don't think the conductor would go for it," said Gene as the bell went, signifying the start of home form and the inexorable blare of the national anthem. Tuning it out, Meredith sank into a studied contemplation of the back of

Seymour's head. A cymbal was blocking the right side and she had to lean to the left to get a clear view, but once she had it, she let herself go into a flat-out stare. *What is it with this guy?* she wondered, analyzing the shaggy black mop of hair, the casual slouch, and the blue-and-white rugger shirt. Resting on one knee, Seymour's left hand continually flipped a pen end over end. If it was an indication of the speed at which his mind worked, his thoughts burned rubber, all right.

With an impatient sigh, Seymour glanced at the clock, bringing the left side of his face into view. Immediately Meredith homed in on it—the jaw motion, its slow, regular chew. Wordless, she watched, her mind working so quickly there was no time to form actual thought. But by the time the national anthem had drawn to a ponderous close, she had put two plus two together to form the inevitable four, and had her mystery equation; x and y had surrendered their unknown quantities and presented her with *drum + bum = gum*. Whether or not Seymour had been the actual offender in either attack, the message was now clear: *Get your bum off my drum.*

And, thought Meredith, it was a message designed to be abundantly clear only to her. There was no way to prove his involvement; no one in their right mind would demand a DNA test on gum-wad saliva to pin down someone else's guilt on something like this. No, Seymour had simply known in advance that she would eventually figure it out through osmosis.

And then what? she pondered, glaring at his oblivious left ear. How many more gum-wad attacks did he have planned? And how long did he intend to keep it up—until she was finally overwhelmed in sticky, gum-wad butt-stains, and retreated to a front-row seat in defeat?

Screw that! she thought. *So what if you're a poet. I'm not living out your King-of-the-Underworld fantasies. You're not controlling me.*

At the same time, she couldn't just up and accuse him without proof. She was going to have to think her way through this carefully—*very* carefully. Giving her own impatient sigh, she slouched down in her seat and waited out the end of home form.

"You think it's Seymour?" Dean said disbelievingly. "Really?"

"A complicated grudge," murmured Reb. "I told you, Mere."

"I know," sighed Meredith. "But how was I supposed to know it would be something like this? I mean, Seymour Molyneux—a bum-gum pervert?"

Dean let out a sharp laugh. "I doubt he'd think of it like that," she said.

"I don't know how he's thinking about it," replied Meredith. "But I've got him now. He'll never get through this sweatshirt." Smugly, she patted the sleeves tied around her waist.

It was Monday lunch and they were lying on the school's

east lawn, munching sandwiches. The sky was an effortless blue, the weather warm enough for shorts, and the air, thought Meredith, breathing deeply, smelled of that clear September, going-on-forever happiness. "What d'you think—" she started to ask, but was interrupted by a voice calling from a nearby basketball court.

"Hey!" shouted a boy she recognized from her math class. "You three want to join us for a game of pick-up?"

"Sure!" Dean called back, and the girls were on their feet and moving toward the court.

"Great!" grinned the boy—Barry was his name, realized Meredith. "One of you come onto our team and two of you are on that team."

Quickly Dean crossed to join his team, and Meredith moved to the sidelines to discard her sweatshirt. Then, giving Reb a high-five, she shifted into position on the court. Their teammates were all from Grade 10—guys she knew well enough to nod at vaguely on the street—but still the invitation to play surprised her. *It's Reb*, she thought, sizing them up. *One of these guys has the hots for her*. Nevertheless, as the play began, the first pass came not to Reb but to her, and when she managed a respectable bounce-pass back, she was passed the ball again. This time she fobbed it off to Reb, who lost it to a guy on the opposing team. Runners squeaked, eyes squinted against the noon sun, and Meredith was soon pulling out the front of her T-shirt and flapping it to cool off.

"Hey!" grinned Reb, slapping her butt as she passed.

"Hey!" cried Meredith, pivoting to return the favor, but Reb was already halfway across the court, chasing a guy who had the ball. In spite of their best efforts, however, the score gained rapidly in favor of the other team and, to Meredith's relief, the warning bell rang before the end of the game.

"We'll call it a win for us!" one of her teammates proclaimed grandly—a tall nerdy-looking guy with a mop of curly brown hair.

"Yeah, a win like rocks swim," retorted a guy from the other team.

"Hey, who you calling a rock?" demanded the curly-haired guy, and they moved off, arguing amicably.

"See you two—I've got to get to my art class," called Dean as she took off for her locker, leaving Meredith and Reb standing on the sidelines.

"That was fun," sighed Reb. "No one fouled me—I mean my boobs. They kept their hands off. It was a boobs-free game."

"And we took up space!" grinned Meredith. Leaning down, she scooped up her sweatshirt and draped it over one arm, then thought better of it and began to tie it around her waist. "It's too hot for this," she grumbled. "I'll be a sauna by 2:00, but if I don't—"

Behind her a gasp sounded, followed by a tugging sensation at her back. "Don't tie it," Reb said tersely. "Let go of it. Just let me take it."

Mystified, Meredith let go of the sweatshirt's sleeves, and Reb pulled it away from her body. "Like I thought," she said as Meredith turned to face her. "Look." Holding up the front of the sweatshirt, she showed Meredith what she had been about to place next to her butt.

The sweatshirt displayed an image of a large horseshoe waterfall and the words I LOVE NIAGARA FALLS. But the logo wasn't what had attracted Reb's attention—it was the sticky, stringy network of purple gum tendrils that had been worked all over the picture, the end of each tendril ground deeply into the fabric. There was no possible way the action hadn't been deliberate. Open-mouthed, Meredith stared at the mess. She was speechless—not at the fact that it had happened again, but at the sheer meanness of the act.

"Whoever it was, he sure was thorough," said Reb.

"It wasn't Seymour," said Meredith. "I would've spotted him."

"I wasn't paying attention," said Reb. "I didn't think of it."

"Me neither," Meredith said glumly. "That was stupid. I'm going to have to be more careful."

"Oh, Mere," said Reb. "Don't blame yourself. You can't be on guard *all* the time."

"Seymour is," sighed Meredith. "Right now, it's like his whole life is this grudge. Did I get any gum on my shorts?"

"No," said Reb, checking. "Your shorts are fine."

"Do you think," asked Meredith, gingerly taking the sweatshirt, "the guys in the game were in on it? Could Seymour have gotten them to ask us to play so I'd take off my sweatshirt, then be too distracted to notice anything else?"

She reviewed the game in her mind—the surprising number of passes she had received, the guys' unusual friendliness. Before today, she had barely known their names.

"No," stammered Reb, her mouth falling open. "I mean, it's just the Mol and some of his mangy friends, not *everyone*. Don't let this make you paranoid, Mere."

A tremor ran through Meredith's mouth, and she sucked in her lower lip. "I guess not," she muttered. "This is real life, not Dungeons and Dragons, right?"

Shoulders slumped, they walked toward the school.

Setting her knapsack on the kitchen table, Meredith opened it and pulled out her Niagara Falls sweatshirt. Balled-up, with the gummy area on the inside, the sweatshirt was stuck together so thoroughly that when she placed it on the table, it remained in tight, crumpled formation. With a hiss, she pulled it apart and surveyed the mess. An afternoon's fermentation in her locker had done nothing to improve the sight; if anything, the purple tendrils appeared to have taken permanent root in the fabric.

What kind of mind works like this? she wondered bleakly. *You'd have to get some kind of fun out of it to do it. What kind of fun would that be?* Brow furrowed, she studied the sticky mass of gum. Radiating outward, it thinned into tendrils, as if someone with massive Neanderthal jaws had removed a three-gumball wad from his mouth, pummeled it into the center of the waterfall image, then pulled out the tendrils to affix to the picture's outer edge.

Five tendrils, to be exact, realized Meredith, counting them up. Five stretched-out tentacles of glee, assuming the jerk had enjoyed the process. Also, she reminded herself, assuming it was a he; Seymour had plenty of female friends. But male or female, what could possibly have possessed one of those friends to do something like this? It wasn't, after all, something he or she would benefit from directly— only Seymour could eventually ascend to the throne ... *if*, Meredith reminded herself, he succeeded.

Furthermore, she thought grimly, gumming up her sweatshirt hadn't been a spur-of-the-moment prank. It had involved forethought, and enough brainwork to chew through several gumballs, then figure out how to get at the sweatshirt. Though the latter bit, she mused, could have been accomplished by Seymour in home form. He had seen then what she was wearing; a bit of "moling" and he had probably germinated a plan before morning announcements had finished. No matter what Reb said, no matter how much Meredith wanted to believe she and her friends had been the targets of random peer friendliness, the lunch-hour basketball game invitation had the Mol written all over it.

Glumly, she stared at the dried gum. *Dull*, she thought. Rather than angry, the whole thing made her feel dull and tired. This wasn't the way she had imagined Grade 10, but it looked as if things were going to continue like this for a while—Seymour had a wide network of friends from which to call in favors, and his intentions appeared to be well-germinated. Was sitting on the throne really worth the effort? So what if she gave up on this one? It didn't mean she was going to give up on everything that came along in life. Wasn't it important to pick and choose your battles, to know when you had bitten off something too big to chew?

Absent-mindedly, she traced out several gum tendrils. Then, without consciously thinking about it, she settled her palm onto the center of the gum-wad mass and aligned her fingers with the five stretched-out tendrils. It was awkward; she had to bend her thumb out of its natural position and skew her pinkie—so much so, it would have helped to be double-jointed. As she realized this, a shiver passed through Meredith, and blood began to beat quietly, insistently, in her throat. The thing was, she thought, staring at her hand, the gum-tendril network on her sweatshirt looked somewhat like downtown Polkton's main intersection. It wasn't exact—the north-south and east-west lines were hardly what you could call straight—but close enough to bring the five-cornered junction to mind.

Just a coincidence, obviously, she decided. No matter how much moling Seymour did, he couldn't possibly get into her mind and read her from the inside out. There was simply no way he could know how much time she had spent thinking about Gus Polk's arrogant hand-map, or how that minor historical detail bugged her. Still, creepily enough, it was the *left* hand that she had just placed on the five-tendriled gum wad, and she was right-handed. So, here it was again—the left hand of darkness reaching up out of the nether realms to mole around her personal life.

With a grimace, Meredith reclaimed her left hand from the Underworld and washed it thoroughly at the kitchen sink. *Germs!* she thought briskly. *H1N1! Herpes! That thing is OOZING!* Pulling out a pair of latex gloves from under the sink, she got to work picking dried gum bits off her sweatshirt.

chapter 7

The next morning, Meredith stood in a school washroom stall before home form, once again pondering the situation before her. A possible solution had presented itself the previous night as she was drifting off to sleep, but it was weird, and following through on it wasn't going to be easy. A sweatshirt tied around her waist was one thing; this, on the other hand, would target her for immediate attention, gossip, and who knew what else.

Reluctantly, she pulled a folded bit of plastic from her back pocket. Thin but sturdy, the rain hat unfolded into a pattern of cheery daffodils splayed across a transparent background. *Great*, she thought. *Spring growing out of my butt.* Already she could hear the comments. Ignoring their imaginary acid, she stretched the rain hat across her posterior and tied the chin-strings over her abdomen. Fortunately, the rain hat wasn't the thick, brightly colored type portrayed in children's picture books, but one more likely to be pulled out of a senior citizen's purse. Aunt Sancy had given it to her one year in a Christmas stocking; Christmas stockings from her aunt were like that—practicality mixed in with cheap, and a whole lot of warm woolen love.

Every time Meredith moved, she rustled. Wincing, she sashayed her hips and listened to the crinkling. *This*, she thought heavily, *is going to be a drag*. With a sigh, she unlocked the stall door and walked through the empty washroom. Beyond its outer door, the school halls resounded with voices, footsteps, and the clamor of closing lockers. If she changed her mind and took off the rain hat now, she could sidle into that mayhem as one more unnoticed body floating within its slipstream; the next few seconds of her life were about to determine the rest of her Grade 10 year.

The door handle slipped under her sweaty grip, but after fumbling, she had it and was pulling open the door and stepping directly into her decision. Head down, she swallowed, swallowed again. Then, sliding into the flow of the crowd, she headed for home form. Surrounded as she was by hallway cacophony, she could no longer hear the rain hat rustle, but she could feel it—minor earthquake tremors resonating across her butt. To her surprise, no one else appeared to notice; at least, she didn't hear anyone comment. Abruptly, the open doorway to Home Form 75 loomed, and she was stepping through it into the sound of familiar voices, a glimpse of Mr. Woolger in profile, conducting absent-mindedly at his desk, and the flash of Seymour's dark eyes flicking across hers, then away, as she walked, heart pounding, toward the third riser and the throne.

From where he was seated, Seymour couldn't see her butt and had no way of knowing what the plastic strings tied around her waist portended. Keeping the daffodils carefully out of his line of sight, Meredith stepped onto the third riser. Today, for some reason, Seymour had arrived ahead of Gene and Morey and was sitting alone, but he didn't acknowledge her arrival and she didn't greet him. Quickly, Meredith scanned the drum seat for gum wads, and was about to sit down when a voice behind her demanded, "What's that—some new kind of flower power?"

Flushing, Meredith turned to see Gene and Morey approaching.

"Don't tell me," grinned Gene, stepping onto the third riser and slipping past her. "It makes you smell like chocolate."

Meredith spurted laughter. The joke was what she needed, ejecting a hundred small pockets of fear from her body. "Whatever," she said. "I crinkle as I walk." With a flourish, she sat down into a small explosion of sound. "See?" she added, rocking back and forth. "It's like applause, sort of, for every move I make."

Gene's eyebrows rose. "Okay," he said. "You're a megalomaniac. But why be so obvious about it?"

Meredith glanced at Morey, who had turned around in his seat, then at Seymour, who hadn't. "Well," she said, hesitating, then rushed headlong onward, "someone has this thing for sticking gum on my bum. Here at school. It's happened three times this year already, so this is my defense."

Both Gene and Morey looked bemused. "D'you know who it is?" asked Morey.

Again, Meredith's eyes flicked toward Seymour and away. "No," she said. "Not for sure."

"Not for sure?" repeated Morey. "But you think you know?"

"Well, it doesn't matter if I *think* I do," stammered Meredith. Though she couldn't see the invisible ears growing out of the back of Seymour's head, she could feel them devouring her every word. "You have to have proof before you go around saying something like that, don't you?"

Gene and Morey sat mulling over what she had said. "Why would anyone want to go after you?" Morey muttered finally, just as the bell went and the PA kicked in with the national anthem. Settling back into her seat, Meredith didn't know whether to feel complimented by Morey's comment or not, but she had learned one thing from the guys' reaction—

there was no easy answer to this problem, or they would have come up with it. So she wasn't a dork for not knowing the solution; she hadn't missed anything obvious. Her only option, really, was to continue muddling onward in the hope things would eventually work themselves out in her favor.

Once again, no one in the halls noticed the daffodils dancing across her butt. Perhaps this was due to the number of students packed in and rushing along together, or maybe the majority of them had better things to do than scrutinize someone else's behind. Either way, it was fine with Meredith, and she slid, gratefully unnoticed, into her math class seat.

Crinkle, crinkle, she thought, bouncing slightly, and still no one noticed—not even Reb, who had arrived ahead of her. But that was because Reb's attention—her *smiling* attention, Meredith noted—was focused on Barry, the guy who had asked them to join yesterday's lunch-hour basketball game. Standing beside Reb's desk, he was leaned in and animatedly describing something, the words pouring from his mouth almost as quickly as he was chewing ... *a wad of gum*! Meredith realized. Horrified, she leapt to her feet and checked, but no—today's math class seat held no freshly chewed gum wad, monster or otherwise-sized. Knees shaky, she sat back down, scolding herself for her overreaction. *It's just a guy chewing gum*, she thought disgustedly. *Not an amber alert.*

Still, she mused, her gaze flicking back to Barry's chomping jaw, all things considered, his behavior could be deemed suspicious. Was it possible his pronounced gum-chewing was some kind of warning that Seymour had cooked up after spotting the rain hat this morning in home form? She hadn't been able to keep his eyes off it entirely— when the bell had rung signaling the end of the period, he had remained in his seat until she had been forced to leave first, and she had felt his stare glommed onto her butt all the way to the door. If Barry's prominent gum-chewing display was something Seymour had indeed arranged, Meredith pondered, he would have had to work fast, math being her first class. But say he had had a post-home-form meeting pre-planned with Barry ...

Thoughts in a crazed whirl, she sat staring at the chatting Barry and Reb. Then, like a train putting on its emergency brakes, she got a grip. *Stop this!* she shouted inside her head. *It's crazy! You're letting this drive you insane!* Immediately the inner whirl let go and she sank back, relieved, into her seat. Around her, students continued to chatter; Reb giggled at something Barry said; Mr. Jiminez got up to chalk some mystery equations onto the board. Other than the rain hat tied around Meredith's butt—which no one in her class appeared to have noticed—everything looked normal; it was only inside her that the world had gone skewed, distorted, crazy.

Don't let Seymour get to you, she counseled herself, taking a wobbly breath. *He's not God* or *Satan, and this is just about a few over-chewed gum wads. It can't go on forever.*

Shifting in her desk, she listened to the ensuing crinkling. *Yeah, baby!* she thought, reassured—the rain hat was still in place. And as long as it was, no gum could reach her bum. So for the present, she was safe—unless Mr. Jiminez got it into his head to call her up to the board to solve another of his murderous math equations ... in which case, all things considered, she might as well have an overdone gum wad for a brain.

One desk ahead, Barry chewed out a last comment to Reb and headed to his seat. As he passed Meredith, he didn't greet her—didn't, in fact, even glance at her. It was possible, of course, she thought, that, bedazzled by Reb, he simply hadn't noticed her. For now, she was willing to live with that option. It was better than any of the others.

Shifting in her seat, she listened to her butt rustle.

The first comment came as she was headed to English, her second morning class. Even Reb hadn't noticed the rain hat in Math, but as Meredith stopped to scan a Student Activities bulletin board mounted outside the front office, a voice behind her exclaimed, "Daffodils! Don't you think that's kind of perverted?"

Flushing, Meredith turned to see several Grade 11 students eyeing her. "It's a rain hat," she said lamely. Inexplicably, now that someone had finally noticed, every one of her preplanned explanations had fled her mind, leaving her with a dork's repertoire of responses. "That's why it's got daffodils on it."

The two girls in the group lifted their eyebrows. The guy grinned. "I was hoping you'd let me pick one," he said.

Again, Meredith flushed. "It's because of gum," she said desperately. "Someone keeps sticking gum there, and I got tired of pulling it off."

The girls' eyebrows rose higher. "Pampers," one said helpfully. "Put one on outside your jeans. I think they come in large sizes."

"You can get adult diapers for seniors," added the other girl.

"Yeah, but kids' diapers have cartoons on them," said the first. "That's better than *daffodils*."

"I dunno," said the guy. "I like flowers. How about some Venus fly-traps? That'd scare the bugger off."

"On my butt?" Meredith asked faintly, and the three laughed as they moved on. Watching them go, Meredith felt her flush begin to recede. That hadn't been so bad, she mused. Actually, it had been kind of fun.

Turning again to scan the bulletin board, she granted the passing crowd a full view of her flowery butt. *Try to relax*, she thought. *No one's going to go after it with a BB gun*. But in spite of the list of club activities before her, it was difficult to concentrate. Her butt felt neon, like a nuclear-powered pincushion waiting for someone to stick in a radioactive pin. As expected, the pin wasn't long in coming.

"My goodness," drawled a voice, breaking into her

thoughts. "Mary, Mary, quite contrary, how does your garden grow?"

Realizing her butt had once again been noticed, Meredith turned around. "Cockleshells and puppy-dog tails," the speaker continued as they came face to face, "and daffodils all in a row."

It was, she saw immediately, Neil Sabom, the principal's son ... and a personal buddy, she knew from last week's yearbook scrutiny, of Seymour Molyneux. "It's a rain hat," she explained quickly. "Someone keeps sticking gum on my bum, so I'm wearing it as protection."

Neil's expression grew pained. "Protection?" he repeated. "Daffodils?" Leaning toward her, he contorted his face as if it was a reflection in a house of mirrors, and singsonged, "Daffodils. Daffydils. Da-ffy-dil-dos."

Then, without saying anything further, he pulled back and walked off into the crowd. Mouth open, Meredith watched him go. *What in the world?* she wondered weakly. *Daffodils, daffydildos?* Had Neil Sabom's bulging cranium just released a flash of psychosis, or was the principal's son inhaling hallucinogenic chemicals between classes?

Braced for further weirdness, she headed off to English.

"Daffodil, daffydildo?" Dean repeated wonderingly. Cell phone ringers off, the Philosophical Feet were once again lying under the willow, gazing up into a gold-tinged afternoon and drinking in its warm, rich scents. Breaths of air glowed in Meredith's lungs, and the deep earth pressed solid against her back. Nobody could get at her here, she thought, contented. She was with friends; they would protect her against all comers.

"I mean, what *is* a daffydildo?" asked Dean. "Was he just talking nonsense?"

"Not nonsense, exactly," said Reb. "A dildo is a vibrator. You know—like they use in sex."

"Oh," said Dean, falling silent, and Meredith realized she hadn't known the meaning of dildo. Neither had Meredith, actually, and as she took it in now, a painful flush swept her face.

"Great!" she burst out. "Neil Sabom is going to send his crappy little joke all around school, and everywhere I go, I'm going to get comments about *that*. And I don't have a choice. I *have* to wear the rain hat or I'll get stuck with more gum wads."

Toxic despair blew through her and, for a moment, it was difficult to breathe. Daffodils on her butt was one thing, buggery quite another.

"Not everyone," Reb said swiftly. "Kids like you, Mere. I heard some of them talking today about your rain hat. They think it's funny that you're wearing it—that you're smart. Neil Sabom is the one who's perverted, not you."

"Yeah, but I still have to wear it," muttered Meredith.

For a moment, the three lay silently, watching the surrounding canopy of leaves shift and breathe. There didn't seem to be any reply to Meredith's comment; no matter how lovely or truthful something was, once someone smeared shit over it, shit was all it was.

"Maybe," Dean said cautiously. "But you don't have to wear his mind."

"What're you talking about?" muttered Meredith. What with gum on her bum and daffodil vibrators, today she didn't have time for philosophizing.

From beside her came the sound of Dean taking a careful breath. "I mean," her friend said tentatively, "it's all in how you *see* things, isn't it? I look at your rain hat with its yellow daffodils, and I see your sense of humor and it makes me laugh, and I like you all the better as my friend. It makes me *proud* of you for standing up for yourself and not letting someone else order you around."

Dean's voice trembled slightly, and Meredith realized she wasn't the only one blinking quickly. "And someone like Neil Sabom looks at your rain hat and sees *dildos*," Dean continued disgustedly. "I mean, what kind of mind is that? Most kids would never think of that, *never*. And I mean ... well, I mean ... I mean," she faltered. "Well, you can let one *jerk* come along and wreck everything that is you, and what you think, and who you are, or you can say, *Okay, that's the way* he *thinks, but it doesn't have anything to do with me!* Neil Sabom doesn't rule the world, he doesn't rule your mind—"

"And he doesn't rule my bum!" interrupted Meredith, finishing Dean's sentence for her.

"No, he doesn't!" Dean agreed emphatically.

Again, the three fell into a hard-thinking silence, loud with vivid beating hearts. "He didn't even get the rhyme right," Reb said finally, reaching over and squeezing Meredith's hand. "It's silver bells and cockleshells, not puppy-dog tails. And it ends with 'pretty maids all in a row.' There aren't daffodils in it anywhere."

"What a moron!" snapped Dean, her tone speaking for all of them.

"Your butt is going to take up space this year, Mere," Reb said softly, squeezing Meredith's hand again, and Meredith felt something inside herself—delicate and beautiful as a dandelion seed-head—swell and burst, then float off into the wild, perfectly blue yonder.

"Beware the poky-Polk butt," she murmured, fighting back tears.

"You bet," said Reb. "Butts *and* boobs."

"Beware *all* our butts and boobs," Dean added firmly. "Cuz we're right here with you, Mere. No one comes after your butt without having to deal with ours, too—right, Reb?"

"Of course, right," said Reb.

"Beware, Polkton High!" cried Dean. "Just beware. *Beware!*" Letting loose with a long howl, she pounded her fists and feet on the ground. Quickly Meredith and Reb joined in, howling and pounding until all thoughts of Neil Sabom and his depraved daffydildos faded into reverberating nothingness.

"That feels better," said Meredith, when their breathing had once again calmed.

"Does it ever," agreed Reb, letting out a sigh.

"You two are the best friends in the entire world," added Meredith. "The *very* best."

Dean and Reb lay quietly, but Meredith could feel them smiling.

"Well, and maybe the hungriest," said Reb.

"Pocky, anyone?" asked Dean.

"Pocky, everyone," replied Reb.

They dragged themselves out from under the willow and indoors to indulge.

chapter 8

I t was later that evening. Not yet ready to start in on the year's first homework, Meredith was sprawled on her bed, idly eyeing the three photographs on her night table. *Pictures of dead people*, she mused. Sometimes she wondered if it should creep her out that six dead ancestors watched every move she made in this room. If she thought about it, the situation was a little like living in a cemetery ... a friendly cemetery, of course, and a decidedly small one— but a place reserved for the dead, nonetheless.

She decided not to think about it. Instead, reaching over, she picked up her parents' wedding photograph. This particular copy had been with her since she had turned eight; previous to that, she had mauled a series of loose prints to fragments—carrying them everywhere she went, cuddling them as she watched TV, and kissing them goodnight and tucking them in beside her before she went to sleep. Aunt Sancy had never displayed any resentment over Meredith's attachment to this photograph; indeed, on her niece's eighth birthday, she had given Meredith the framed, glassed-over version that currently graced her night table. While this had interfered somewhat with the cuddling process, Meredith had continued to kiss the snapshot and tuck it in beside her at bedtime for several more years, before finally ditching the routine.

She still talked to the photograph, though. Not often, and rarely out loud—but there were times, even now, when she got the urge to take her parents' radiant faces, prop them up on her chest, and converse. *How,* she thought, smiling pensively at her father's image, *would you handle the Mol? Pampers? I bet it'd be something better than a daffodil rain hat. And I bet ... no, I know for* sure *you'd never give up the throne. Once James Polk parked his butt there, it'd be his until he graduated from poky-Polk Collegiate.*

Yeah! she thought decisively. That was the way the Polks were; they played for keeps. Not that they were warlords or anything—her father had been a lawyer, not a mafia kingpin. *Well ... almost a lawyer,* Meredith corrected herself. At the time of his death, James Polk had been scheduled to officially enter the lethal profession the following year, after he had completed articling.

Tentatively, she touched her father's face. It looked so

confident, ready to take on the world. Why *exactly*, she wondered, a frown crossing her own, did her aunt dislike James Polk so much? And, for that matter, Johanna and Dave Polk? For, truth be told, Meredith didn't know. While Sancy Goonhilly's antipathy had always been obvious, she had never given an explicit reason for it; the few times Meredith had tried to worm one out of her, her aunt had hemmed, hawed, and otherwise danced around the question. For hours afterward, the atmosphere in the apartment had been titchy, almost allergic, and, over the years, an unspoken commandment had come to rule the five small rooms Meredith and Aunt Sancy called home: *You are a Polk by name, a Goonhilly by blood.*

Getting to her feet, Meredith padded down the hall and into the living room, where she plopped down onto the couch beside her aunt. On the other side of the room, the TV screen flickered.

"Aunt Sancy?" said Meredith, propping her parents' wedding picture on her knees.

"Mmmm?" responded her aunt, her attention focused on a tea cozy she was crocheting. As far as Meredith could tell, the tea cozy was taking on the shape of a motorcycle. Aunt Sancy invented her own patterns.

"Tell me something about my mom," said Meredith. "What did she do as a kid for fun? What was her favorite candy?"

"Caramels," Aunt Sancy said without hesitation. "She liked the usual things—skipping and hopscotch, and, later on, video games. She was in gymnastics and aerobics. A cheerleader. You know all that, Meredith."

"Tell me something *new*," pestered Meredith. "So I have something more to remember her by."

"New," mused her aunt. "Let's see. She hated *Where Is Waldo?* puzzles. Her favorite breakfast cereal was Cream of Wheat."

"Yuck!" cringed Meredith.

"You aren't much like her," smiled her aunt.

Meredith hesitated. Asking Aunt Sancy questions about Ally Polk was easy, but James was a real tightrope act—a careful balance between questing for information and forestalling another rant about the evil Polks. So she took a cautious breath, then asked, "Am I much like him?"

"No," her aunt said shortly.

"Well ..." Meredith paused, then gave up on her quest for more info on her father. "Am I like you? What were you like as a kid?"

"Me?" said her aunt, surprised. "Kind of scrappy, I guess. I picked a lot of fights in elementary school. And *every* candy was my favorite kind. I used to pull gum off the street and chew it."

"Yu – uck!" gagged Meredith, now cringing in earnest.

"Black Cat was the best," her aunt said with satisfaction, ignoring Meredith's reaction. "I don't know if they make it anymore. It had a licorice flavor. Ten people could chew the same wad in a row, and it'd taste just as good. Had to watch out for small stones in those street wads, though."

Meredith gaped at her aunt in unmitigated horror. Aunt Sancy chuckled.

"I survived just fine, Meredith," she said. "Didn't pick up any rare diseases or grow an extra head. When you think about it, it's not much different than picking your nose and eating it."

"Picking someone *else*'s nose and eating it!" Meredith corrected her.

Aunt Sancy laughed outright. "Granted," she conceded.

"God!" Meredith said pensively. "I hope I never sit on a Black Cat wad. That's all I need." She had told her aunt about the math class and hallway wads, but nothing further. One peep about her suspicions regarding Seymour, and Meredith knew she would be spending the next hour listening to another tirade concerning Polkton's scallywag crowd—the Polks, the Boggs, and the degenerate genes they had no doubt passed on to their current progeny ... present company excepted, of course.

Aunt Sancy's eyebrows rose. "There haven't been any more, have there?" she demanded.

"No, no," Meredith assured her, and her aunt's relieved gaze refocused on her handiwork. "Tell me," she asked, scowling down at it. "D'you think this muffler looks right?"

"If I'm honest, will you give me this week's allowance?" hedged Meredith.

Mock fury crossed Aunt Sancy's face and she glared at her niece.

"It ... looks *wonderful*!" cried Meredith, raising both

hands protectively. "Really—I'd know it was a muffler for sure ... maybe ... if you told me first."

Grabbing a throw cushion, Aunt Sancy bopped her niece several times on the head. "Go do your homework!" she ordered.

Meredith went.

The locker room was cacophonous, girls coming and going from the showers, locker doors slamming. Standing at her locker, Meredith was halfway through changing, keeping pace with Dean, who had snagged the locker to her left. At the locker to her right, Reb was just getting started, having stayed behind the rest of the class to help the gym teacher put away field hockey equipment.

"Hey!" said Reb, opening her locker. "What classes d'you guys get next? Mine's a stinker. I've got Geo—"

A clamor of voices interrupted her. Turning to see what was going on, Meredith caught sight of several classmates playfully shoving each other as they came down the aisle. Not knowing them well, she turned again to her locker and reached for her rain hat, intending to tie it on over her butt. But as she did, Reb cried out sharply; a second later, something ... or someone ... fell hard against Meredith's back.

Pressed into her open locker, she struggled to regain her footing. Her head throbbed where she had bumped it, and one arm felt scraped. Abruptly, behind her Reb shouted, "Oh no, you don't!" and Meredith twisted around to find one of the girls from the carousing group sprawled against her, while Reb grabbed determinedly at the girl's right hand.

"She's got some chewed-up gum!" cried Reb, as the girl pulled free and ran down the aisle after her friends. "Penny Gugomos—she was reaching for you, and there was gum in her hand."

"The bitch!" Dean said indignantly. "She must've been trying to stick it on your bum! Come on, let's go get it."

"Get what?" asked Meredith, gingerly touching the sore spot on her head.

"The gum!" said Dean. "It's in Penny's hand, right, Reb? It'll be proof."

"Not anymore," said Reb. "She'll have ditched it by now."

"We'll get her anyway!" insisted Dean. "Confront her— make her admit it!"

Without waiting for a response, she started off down the aisle. Heart in mouth, Meredith hesitated, then followed, a dubious Reb at her heels. The fleeing girls had turned right at the end of the aisle but weren't difficult to find, clustered as they were around an open locker two aisles over. Storming toward them, Mount Matsumoto clamped a hand onto Penny's shoulder and pulled her around.

"You're the one who did it!" she declared to the astonished girl. "Come on, hand it over!"

"Lay off!" exclaimed one of the other girls, stepping forward and shoving Dean so she stumbled backward. "Keep your fucking hands to yourself!"

Instinctively, Meredith and Reb stepped forward,

buttressing Dean to either side. "Same to you!" Dean shot back, regaining her balance. "*And* your gum wads! You keep them off my friend's bum!"

"I'm not interested in your friend's bum!" yelped Penny. "You can have it, if that's what turns you on!"

In spite of herself, Meredith stiffened, and she heard Reb hiss angrily. A titter ran through some of the watching girls, but others looked uneasy. "Hey, cool it!" someone called. "Or we'll get Ms. Vickery."

"I'm cool!" Dean snapped back. "It's these girls who are the problem, not us."

"Oh, yeah?" demanded Penny. "We were just standing around talking. *You're* the one who came busting in here and grabbed me."

Dean's face jutted forward. "Because you were trying to stick gum on Meredith's bum," she insisted. "Admit it. Reb saw you."

"What gum?" demanded Penny. "I fell against Meredith when Rebecca pushed me. I don't have any gum."

Again Meredith heard Reb hiss, but before either of them could respond, another of Penny's friends stepped forward. "*I* have gum," she interrupted loudly. "Is this the wad you're looking for?" Opening her mouth, she stuck out her tongue and waggled it. On the tip sat a wad of purple-colored gum.

"Me, too," chimed in another girl, blowing a pink bubble. "D'you want my gum, Dean?"

"Hey, what about this?" asked the last of the group, reaching into her locker and pulling out a package of

Chiclets. "Want some of *this* gum for your bum, Meredith?"

Chiclets package outstretched, she observed Meredith, the taunt dancing in her gaze. *She knows*, thought Meredith, staring back at her. Maybe Penny was the only one who had tried to pull off the actual stick-it job, but all the girls in this group of friends knew; every one of them had been in on the intended prank. The smirks on their faces were a dead giveaway.

"Come on," she said, touching Dean's arm. "Let's go." Up and down the aisle, watching girls began to relax and turn back to their lockers, relieved the episode was over. But the current of anger pulsing through Dean was still strong and, for a long tense moment, she resisted, her body hunched forward, her eyes intent.

"We know!" she said heatedly, her words carrying clearly along the aisle. "It's Seymour Molyneux, isn't it? He put you up to this."

The surprise that blew across the group's faces was obvious. Eyebrows lifted and each girl looked down or away; suddenly, they had nothing to say. *Bingo!* thought Meredith, studying them, and then, *Shit*! Because the first thing this group of friends was going to do when it got out of the change room was, of course, track down Seymour and tell him what had happened. That could only escalate matters, and the last thing she needed was an escalation of gum wads.

"Come on, Dean!" she said urgently, pulling on her friend's arm, and this time Dean relented; turning, she scuffed along beside Meredith, with Reb bringing up the rear.

It was as they reached the end of the aisle, about to turn left, that the comment reached them. Spoken behind their backs, its source was anonymous—could have been anyone's voice, everyone's. "Nice rain hat, Meredith," it said coolly. Then, softly, it singsonged, "Daffydildos."

Instantly Dean stiffened, and Meredith grabbed one of her arms, Reb the other. "Just keep walking," Reb hissed and they turned left, leaving the silent aisle behind.

Ninety minutes later, they were under the willow tree and staring up into its gently wafting branches, trying to make sense of what had happened. In spite of the time that had elapsed since the change room confrontation, Meredith still felt bruised by the event, and not just on her sore head. Generally, she didn't spend much time contemplating her soul, but now she thought she could feel it—a confused, quivery presence inside her body that felt as if it had been shaken, rattled, and rolled.

"It happened so fast," she said wonderingly. "One second Reb was talking about Geography, and the next ... Well, those girls aren't wallflowers. For a bit there, I thought someone was about to get decked."

"I know," agreed Reb, quiet shock also lingering in her voice. "If it had gone on much longer, I would've fetched Ms. Vickery myself."

A passing breeze rippled the willow's green and gold

canopy, and instinctively Meredith found herself breathing in its rich, warm scent. "I doubt anything violent would've happened," she said, running the scene through her mind again. "Not with half the class watching. Most of them know about my rain hat and why I'm wearing it, so they probably figured out pretty quick what was going on. Two of them talked to me about it in my next class. What I don't get about the whole thing is—why Penny Gugomos? She's not really popular—just average, like us. How would she know Seymour?"

"She doesn't," said Reb. "At least, I don't think she does. But Sandra Clulee's older brother hangs around with him."

"She was the one with the Chiclets," said Dean, speaking for the first time.

"Okay," Meredith said slowly, studying the intricate sway of leaves above her. "So Seymour talks to Sandra, Sandra talks to a group of her friends, and Penny gets pressured into doing the actual bum-gumming while the rest distract whoever's around. But why would Penny agree to do it? She doesn't have anything against me. None of those girls do. They hardly even know me."

"*Because* they don't know you, Mere," Reb said matter-of-factly. "One wad of gum is no big deal to them. They don't know how many times it's been done to you already, how your clothes get ruined, or what it's doing to you—always having to watch out for it happening again."

"Maybe," hedged Meredith. "You're making it sound ... I dunno, *normal*—like sticking gum on someone else's bum is the kind of favor any friend would ask. But would *you* stick gum onto someone's butt because a friend asked you to? Someone you hardly knew, who had never done anything to you?"

"No!" Dean spat out immediately.

"No," Reb echoed after a thinking pause. "No, I wouldn't. And y'know what else is weird? We were the ones in the right, obviously. But when I go back over the whole thing in my head—to be honest, we looked stupid."

"I'll say *stupid*," muttered Dean.

"The ones who were in the wrong looked cool," continued Reb, ignoring her. "That's not the way it's supposed to be. When you're right, there should be some kind of ... I dunno ... a divine *light* that drops down onto you and proves you're telling the truth. Instead, those girls looked ice-queen cool and we just looked dumb."

"Dumber than dumb," mumbled Dean. "Daffydildos-dumb."

"Hey—did you notice?" asked Meredith, her heart quickening. "I mean *how* it was said?" Excitedly, she singsonged the word for them. "Da-ffy-dil-dos—that's exactly the way Neil Sabom said it to me in the hall. D'you think *he* was in on what happened today?"

Silence followed as Dean and Reb pondered her question, and then Reb said, "Nah. He's probably been telling his joke a lot, and it's getting around, and that's why kids are saying it the same way. Mind you," she added hastily, with a sideways glance at Meredith, "I don't think it's getting around *that* much. I haven't heard it yet, anyway."

"Wait a few days," sighed Meredith. "If only that was my biggest problem. What'm I supposed to do now Seymour knows that I know he's behind all the bum-gumming? What's he going to do next?'

"Oh, Mere!" burst out Dean. "I am *such* a moron. I thought if they knew you weren't alone, and you had friends who'd for sure back you, they'd lay off."

For a moment, all three blinked rapidly, swallowing hard, hard again. "Maybe they will," Meredith said hoarsely. "Because like you said, now they know for sure I'm not alone."

"No, you're not!" Dean said stoutly.

"We're with you all the way, Mere," added Reb.

"Thanks," said Meredith. "Now, if I only knew where this daffydildo stupidity was headed next."

chapter 9

Approaching home form the next morning, Meredith's footsteps slowed. Ahead loomed the open doorway, a stream of students pouring continually past. As she came abreast, laughter erupted through it—laughter let loose by three guys, caught up in yet another amiable debate concerning the merits of Mr. Big, the supernatural, or the CFL versus the NFL. Hit by a surge of anxiety, Meredith came to a halt outside the open door. *Seymour knows*, she thought, flustered. *He knows that I know it's him. So what's the best thing to do—act as if I know he knows? Or as if nothing happened yesterday in the change room; I haven't got a clue.*

At that moment, she felt her rain hat twitch, and whirled

around to see a senior male student grinning down at her. Eyebrows raised, he quipped, "Nice cheeks," then continued along the hall, warbling, "We all live in a yellow daffodil, yellow daffodil, yellow daffodil."

A grin cut across Meredith's face, dissolving her uncertainty. *Okay, Mr. Mol,* she thought as the revamped Beatles chorus receded down the hall. *You haven't won them all yet. Not by a long shot.*

Determinedly, she barged through the open doorway and fixed on him—Seymour Molyneux, Lord of the Underworld, leaning back in his chair and apparently pondering a point Morey was making. But only apparently, Meredith quickly realized, because the second she entered the room, Seymour's gaze homed in on her as if he had been awaiting ... no, *anticipating* ... the moment she would enter the room. Dark, direct, and speculative, there was surprise in that stare. As Meredith started toward him, it was obvious from Seymour's expression that he had not only heard about yesterday's change room confrontation, but something about what he had heard was piquing his interest—or rather, something about *her*, Meredith Polk, a Grade 10 nondescript whom he thought he could doom to an entire year of Stupid Council lunch hour boredom simply by putting up his hand and casually dropping her name.

For the second time that morning, Meredith came to a halt. Then, turning, she walked over to Mr. Woolger's desk. "Sir?" she said hesitantly.

Brow furrowed, Mr. Woolger was absent-mindedly conducting as he studied a musical score lying on his desk. "Eh?" he grunted, looking up. "Yes, Meredith. What is it?"

"Well, sir," faltered Meredith. "Um ... I'd like to resign as class rep. For Student Council, I mean."

For a moment, her comment didn't seem to register, and Mr. Woolger continued to observe her blankly. "Resign!" he finally exclaimed. "But you just accepted the nomination."

"No, sir, I didn't," said Meredith. In spite of herself, her voice wobbled but she forged onward. "I mean, I couldn't have accepted it, not really. It happened too quick. Y'see— Seymour volunteered me without asking me first, and then someone seconded it. No one asked what I wanted, and I don't want to."

Narrow-eyed, Mr. Woolger's gaze shot toward Seymour, then dropped to his desk. "Uh-huh," he grunted knowingly. "Still hunting the worm. Well, fine, Meredith. Your resignation has been duly noted. The class will just have to elect another rep."

"Thanks," breathed Meredith, relief coursing through her. Without glancing at Seymour, she crossed to the back of the room, stepped up onto the third riser, and sat down behind the drums. Seconds later, the final bell went, its strident tone blaring through halls and classrooms; in its wake came the first weary notes of the national anthem. Settling back into her seat, Meredith let herself relax into the ponderous flow of notes. A tiny smile crept across her mouth, and for the first time since she had claimed the drum-set throne, she felt as if it was hers, as if she actually belonged there.

My butt belongs to me, she thought. *I put it where I want it. And I don't want it sitting on Stupid Council. So there, Mr. Mol.*

The anthem was followed by several announcements, and then, before the class could begin chattering, Mr. Woolger rose to his feet. "I have just been informed," he said briskly, rapping his baton, "that our Student Council rep is resigning from her position. This means this class will have to elect a new rep. As you know, Friday is a Career Development day, which means no school. So I'll give you the weekend to think over whom you'd like as your next class rep, and we'll hold the nominations on Monday morning."

With that, he sat down and returned to studying the musical score on his desk. Perched high above most of the class, Meredith watched her perplexed peers swivel in their seats and glance back at her. For a second, she was tempted to raise one hand in a royal queenly wave.

"What gives?" demanded Morey, looking aggrieved. "It's been less than a week."

Meredith shrugged. "I never wanted to be class rep," she said. "No one *asked* me—you just all voted me in."

To her right, Gene frowned, reviewing the incident in his memory. "I guess," he conceded. "Too bad. That means we're going to have to strain our brains all weekend, trying to figure out how to convince Seymour to put in one more year as our esteemed representative."

One riser down, Seymour grimaced. "Nah," he said tersely. "I've put in my time—three years. Been there, done that."

"Morey?" probed Gene.

Morey shook his head. "My dad's on my back to bring up my marks," he said. "I can only join one club this year and that'll be badminton."

"Tell him it's not a club," persisted Gene. "It's your civic pride—training for your future career."

"More like my future going down the toilet," grumped Morey. "*If* my dad ever found out. Nah, this year it's one club and one club only—and badminton's better for letting off steam."

Defeated, Gene sighed, and Meredith was briefly tempted to withdraw her resignation. But another glance at Seymour kept her resolute. Leaned forward, his eyes glued to the door, the guy was practically poised to leap out of his seat—a position he had taken up only *after* Mr. Woolger had announced her resignation. Something about that announcement had made Seymour restless—as restless as it had left her feeling relieved. When the bell finally went, signaling the end of home form, he was a released cannonball, shooting to his feet and leading the rush for the door.

And then he was gone, leaving her with the throne and a gum-free butt ... for the present. Taking a deep breath, Meredith stood up. *Take nothing for granted*, she told herself. *Just keep checking—every seat, every chewing mouth, every da-ffy-dil-do jerk that's out there.*

It was late into the lunch hour. Chair tilted against a large filing cabinet at the back of the school library, Meredith was perusing "Leiningin Versus the Ants," a short story her English class had been assigned to read. Caught up in the details of Leiningin's desperate sprint through a horizon-wide invasion of soldier ants, Meredith had lost all track of her surroundings. Whatever was coming, she thought excitedly as she turned a page, with this kind of lead-in, it had to be good. Glancing at a wall clock, she noted she had fifteen minutes until her next class and was swiftly reabsorbed into the story. A paper ball sailed within centimeters of her nose and she ignored it. Someone sat down at a nearby study carrel and she barely noticed. A vaguely wet sensation came and went on the top of her head; frowning, she shifted in her seat and forgot about it.

The vaguely wet sensation came and went again, and again. Eyes still riveted to the page before her, Meredith raised a hand and patted the crown of her head. It was damp, but not as damp as the drop of unidentifiable fluid that had just dripped onto the back of her hand. Leaping to her feet, Meredith scanned in every direction. *Nothing!* she thought with relief. Just the filing cabinet—no bum gum, no laughing, shoving girls, but wait a sec ... There, out of the corner of her eye, came the flash of a single dark-colored drop of fluid splashing down onto the chair she had just vacated. Following the drop's trajectory upward, Meredith spotted a large 7-Eleven Slurpee cup that had been placed on top of the filing cabinet so a small section of its base protruded over the edge.

The drips were coming from the bottom of the cup. With a hiss, Meredith grabbed the cup and examined it. Almost at once, she located the small hole that had been poked into the bottom. Only a bit of the original slush still occupied the cup's base, most of the contents presumably having been slurped before the cup had been placed on the filing cabinet. *Was it there before I sat down?* wondered Meredith, staring at the cabinet. *Nah, there's still unmelted slush in it— it hasn't been there long.*

"Did you get a soaker?" asked the guy who had sat down earlier at the nearby carrel. Probably in Grade 11, he looked familiar—a hallway face. "Looks like you're wearing your rain hat in the wrong place."

"Thanks for the advice," snapped Meredith, giving him a hard glance. When he had first sat down, she hadn't spared him a thought, but now ... *Was it him?* she wondered, anger flaring in her gut. *Maybe.* But if it was, what was she supposed to do about it? Lace into him? Laugh? Treat it with the cool disdain it deserved?

"You could've let me know," she added curtly.

The guy's grin vanished. "I didn't notice," he protested. "Or I would've."

Maybe, thought Meredith, but let it pass. "You haven't seen Seymour Molyneux around, have you?" she asked, faking casual, and the guy shrugged an equally casual no. So, with a grimace, Meredith tucked "Leiningin Versus the Ants" under one arm, dropped the offending Slurpee cup into the nearest wastepaper basket, and headed toward the library exit. Sure, there were other kids around that she could have queried about the incident, but after yesterday's change room episode she knew better. Without proof, an allegation was a live grenade. Even with an eyewitness of unquestionable integrity like Reb, that kind of situation was likely to blow sky-high. All things considered, it wasn't worth the effort.

You never know, Meredith told herself half-heartedly. *It could've been just a random thing—like a bird flying by, or a meteorite.*

Yeah, right, came the answering thought. *A nuclear meteorite.*

Giving her rain hat strings a tug to ensure its daffodils were in place defending her honor, she headed out into the halls.

Later that afternoon, Meredith was making tracks along an empty tech-wing hall. Minutes into her history class, she had realized that she'd forgotten the homework she had completed the previous evening, and had asked permission to fetch it from her locker. Her history class and locker were halfway across the school from each other, but as everyone else seemed to be in class, she was making good time. Putting on a burst of speed, she passed the music classroom and veered around the last corner leading to her locker.

Well, not everyone, she realized. A third of the way down the corridor, approximately ten meters from her locker, lounged a clutch of male students. Leaning against a wall or sprawled on the floor, they were discussing something in low tones. The three standing had their backs to her, and the two seated were blocked from her view. None of them appeared to have noticed her and, after registering their presence, Meredith didn't pay them much mind. As she drew close, she noted casually that the three standing students were seniors. Either these guys all had a spare in the same time slot, she thought, or they had been allowed out of class to discuss a shared assignment.

She was wearing soft-soled shoes; it wasn't until she was almost on top of them that she was noticed. The nearest standing guy glanced over his shoulder and spotted her; one eyebrow shot upward and he turned back to the group. What he said then was too low for Meredith to make out, but the rising eyebrow put definite brakes on her pace. She didn't know the guy's name—even if her life had been on the line, she wouldn't have been able to cough it up—but he knew hers ... or at least he knew her face. In some way, she was significant to him—it had been written all over his expression.

The three standing guys turned to face her; as they did, they shifted, revealing the two who were seated—Seymour and Neil Sabom. As Meredith's gaze connected with Seymour's, she came to a dead halt. Furthest from her, the

Mol sat with his elbows propped on his knees, dark eyes fixed on her. Eyebrows raised, he looked slightly amused; otherwise, his gaze remained as remote as ever. Certainly *his* heart wasn't racing, she thought distractedly, nor were *his* hands clenched, palms sweating like hers.

All five, seated or standing, had now fallen silent, their collective gaze fixed on her. Swift as a heartbeat, Meredith scanned their expressionless faces; as she did, a weakness swept her—without form or meaning, but unarguable, absolute. The thought came to her to say, "Hi!" and continue onward as if nothing unusual was happening, but then the thought vanished as if snatched, leaving emptiness in its place. As Meredith stood staring at the five seniors, none of them spoke—the silence so dense, it was like a seventh presence. The instinct to turn and skedaddle back the way she had come was overwhelming and, for a moment, Meredith almost gave in to it—almost let her feet turn her body in the direction it wanted to flee.

But then she got a grip, set one foot in front of the other, and shifted into forward momentum. It was awkward— under that silent scrutiny, she felt oversized, a clunky machine composed of ill-fitting parts. This, of course, added to her growing sense that she could actually *feel* the guys' gazes on her ... especially on the daffodil rain hat. As Meredith began to pick her way carefully over various splayed legs, she thought she could hear the rain hat crinkle with every step she took. *Da-ffy-dil-dos*, she thought, cringing. The phrase was probably singsonging itself mockingly inside each of their minds.

Warily, she stepped over Neil's left foot, and his right. *Almost there*—the thought swept her, leaving her slightly giddy. Then, as she was rigidly bypassing Seymour's feet, the sound began—a repeated clicking that had to be coming from somebody's mouth. Loud and rapid, the clicks were startling after the intense quiet, and instinctively Meredith quickened her pace. As if on cue, the other guys also took up the jarring rhythm; while no one moved physically, it felt to Meredith as if something invisible had reared up from each one of them and was coming straight at her.

Arriving at her locker, she had to grip tightly onto her lock to regain focus; then she spun it shakily, but her nerves were so shot, she miscalculated and was forced to redo the combination. The clicking had now stopped, but this didn't help much. Without glancing back, Meredith grabbed her history notes, jammed her lock shut, and headed north along the corridor. North wasn't the route she needed to take—the only classrooms between her locker and the school's north exit were for shop, and her history class lay in the opposite direction. That she had headed this way in order to avoid further contact had to be as obvious to the five guys, currently lounging silently, as it was to her. But the only option was to turn and walk a second time through that dense, hostile scrutiny, and if she did, Meredith knew she would shit herself. She didn't have the guts—it was that simple.

Quickening her pace, she scurried on down the hall.

chapter 10

Friday morning, Polkton's main library branch was busy, its cavernous ground floor resonating with the many small sounds of patrons coming and going, dropping books into Returns slots, and clicking away at computer keyboards. Ensconced at a microfilm reader in a shadowy cubbyhole next to Information Services, Meredith was scrolling through back issues of the *Polkton Post*, specifically issues from the month of August, one decade previous. Last night, while she had been lying awake, studying her parents' wedding picture in the moonlight, it had come to her that in the ten years since their deaths, she had never seen an official account of the car crash that had killed them—including their obituaries. Even her personal recollections of their funeral drew mostly blanks. All she could remember of the event was sitting on Aunt Sancy's lap in a church pew, her aunt's arms wrapped protectively around her.

Those arms were still wrapped protectively around her, but, as Aunt Sancy had repeatedly made clear over the years—she wasn't talking. And so, rather than send Sancy Goonhilly into a pointless, three-day funk, Meredith had decided to check out back issues of the *Polkton Post* for the desired information. She had an hour and a half to complete her task, having made plans to celebrate the school-free day by meeting up with Dean and Reb at the Burger King for lunch. No one knew she was here—not her friends, and especially not her aunt. In response to Aunt Sancy's breakfast queries, Meredith had said merely that she would be meeting Dean and Reb for lunch, and had left it at that. It had been the truth, more or less, and her aunt had appeared satisfied with her reply. So why, wondered Meredith as she scanned the microfilm reader's screen, was she feeling guilty—guilty because, one decade and one month after her parents' fatal accident, she wanted to know the basic facts concerning their demise?

Because she did feel guilty, *obviously* guilty, her shoulders in a defensive jut and her head ducked as if to conceal her profile from possible passersby. That it was ridiculous to be feeling this way, she was well aware—reading past issues of the *Polkton Post* was hardly a crime. Still, she couldn't shake it, the sense of the betrayal she knew her aunt would feel if she found out—a betrayal Aunt Sancy would never voice aloud, but nevertheless make known in every weighted sigh and drawn-out silence. Hunching closer to the microfilm reader, Meredith pushed the image of her aunt's disapproving face from her mind and focused on the film advancing across the screen.

The problem was that she wasn't certain which day her parents' obituaries had appeared in the *Post*. They had died on August fourth, and the funeral had been held on the ninth, but an obit could have appeared any time between the two dates. *Or even after that*, she thought, studying the screen. So here she was, scanning every page of the *Post*, starting on August third, just to make sure. Front-page news on that day had been a provincial heat wave. Next came the Arts and Lifestyles section, followed by Sports, Business, and classified ads. As the latter section advanced onto the screen, fronted by the obituaries, a trembling passed over Meredith, surprising her with its intensity. Deliberately, she clenched both hands, digging in her fingernails to fight off tears. *Not yet*, she thought, her eyes skimming pictures of smiling, elderly faces. At this point, on August third, the accident hadn't taken place; the world was still innocent, without the slightest inkling of what was portended.

Carefully, she advanced the film to the August fourth edition, where she encountered headlines concerning a major drug bust in nearby Toronto, with possible local connections. Centimeter by centimeter, she scrutinized each page, her heart thumping uncomfortably as she passed through the Sports and Business sections, thinking, *This was when it happened. This was the day—people sitting around and maybe reading this very page ...*

Again her eyes skimmed Obits snapshots of unfamiliar elderly faces, and she quickened the pace through the classified ads that followed. And then, suddenly, there it was—the August fifth issue, with its front-page headline: *DEADLY CAR CRASH KILLS TWO.* In spite of the fact that she had been expecting it, Meredith felt broadsided by the words— as if they had collectively leapt off the page and tackled her. Shakily, she forwarded the film and spotted a color photograph of a small bridge that spanned the river just outside Polkton, its guardrail mangled, and the back end of a car just visible above the waterline. Breath stopped, her mind almost uncomprehending, Meredith stared at the photograph. She hadn't known the accident had happened at this bridge ... nor, for that matter, at any bridge. No one had ever told her where the event had occurred, and over the years, for some reason, she hadn't thought to ask. How many times, she wondered now as she gaped at the image on the screen, had she and Aunt Sancy driven across this bridge and her aunt had never commented on its significance, never flinched or given any sign of distress.

Blasted—from the inside out, Meredith felt blasted—torn open like the bridge's guardrail. It wasn't just the photograph of the mangled bridge—she had been betrayed, it was as simple as that. For Aunt Sancy not to tell her something like this, to act as if something of the utmost importance hadn't taken place where it so obviously had ... Well, Meredith thought bleakly, it was the same as telling a lie. How was it possible her aunt could have kept this information from her—this basic, mundane, *killer* aspect of the Polkton landscape?

The trembling was back, Meredith's head buzzing as if she had been wearing earbuds too long. When she had decided to look up her parents' obits, she hadn't realized the information would hit her like this; the incident had occurred so long ago, she had assumed she had adjusted to the loss, and it had become a fact like any other fact. Pressing fingertips to both temples, she breathed raggedly, trying to slow her thoughts. Gradually the buzz in her head diminished, and she found herself able to refocus on the screen. As she did, details she had always known about the accident came back to her—the day had been sunny, without rain or cloud, and the crash had taken place mid-afternoon and midweek, when traffic could be expected to be sparse. In the trees along that quiet, secondary road, birds would have been chirping lazily, cicadas keening in response. Nothing and no one could have foreseen how fate was about to intervene, take hold of the fundamental fabric of life and tear it irreparably asunder.

How, thought Meredith, reviewing her memories of the bridge, *did it happen*? How did a perfectly competent driver like her father—in his mid-twenties, a family man who had just graduated with a law degree—drive off a safe country bridge on a day with clear weather conditions? The bridge was small, sure, but the road leading up to it had no turns or blind angles. Anyone with a minimum of driving experience—heck, a student driver with a learner's permit could be expected to make it across easily. Advancing the film, Meredith scanned the article beneath the photograph, phrase after phrase leaping out at her: *James Polk and his wife Ally ... only child of Dave and Johanna Polk and direct descendant of Polkton's founding father ... promising law student articling at the law firm of Loye and Twemlow ... survived by a five-year-old daughter.*

And that was it, the sum total of what had been reported. *Wait a minute*, thought Meredith. *Check the obits*. Swiftly, she forwarded the film to August sixth, then the seventh, where she found what she was seeking. The picture displayed in the obituaries section was the familiar wedding photograph that graced her night table. All of the information listed was known to her—birth dates, school and work experience, surviving family members, and upcoming funeral details. Intently, Meredith read and reread the obit, her eyes sucking the words off the screen. When she had reread it a third time, she sank back into her chair, a feeling of defeat caving in around her.

There had to be more, she thought. Something to explain the way things were—the bridge, Aunt Sancy and the Polks, the decade-long ache of silence. Almost without thinking, she located the appropriate knob and began, once again, to advance the film. August ninth, the day of the funeral, came and went without mention of the event. Then she spotted the headlines for the tenth, blaring news of a possible federal election call, followed by page two and pictures of her parents' funeral—pallbearers carrying the two coffins into the church, and her Polk grandparents, their heads bowed, flanked by Polkton's current mayor and the local MLA. Neither Meredith, her Aunt Sancy, nor her Goonhilly grandparents seemed to have merited the *Polkton Post*'s attention, but knowing her aunt, Meredith thought wryly, they had probably all been kept well away from reporters' cameras.

Automatically, she began to read the article next to the photographs. To her surprise, several dignitaries had attended the funeral; the Polk family, at least ten years ago, had been well-connected. Details were given concerning the eulogy, hymns sung, even the flowers decorating the coffins. In passing, it was mentioned that the bodies were to be cremated. Then, in the last paragraph, almost as an afterthought, came the phrase: *Autopsies revealed both victims had above-legal levels of alcohol in their blood.*

Stunned, Meredith reread the sentence several times. A loud buzzing started up again in her head, and her right hand floated numbly toward the screen and touched the word "alcohol." *Drunk?* she thought, bewildered. *They were both drunk, mid-afternoon, in the middle of the week?*

No one had ever mentioned alcohol as being a factor in her parents' deaths ... *or their lives*, she thought, swallowing hard. *Is that what my parents were—two alcoholics? Drunks? Or was this a one-time thing—a fling to celebrate something?*

Well, whatever the reason for their alcoholic binge, she now had what she had been looking for—that one little fact to explain things. Unfortunately, that one little fact also now had her, whether she wanted it to or not. Without warning, Meredith felt sick in a dull, heavy way. Fighting back tears, she unloaded the film and slid it back into its box, then returned it to the Information Services desk.

"Thank you," she said, her eyes sliding across the librarian's face.

"You're welcome," smiled the librarian, handing back her library card.

Do you drive drunk? The question hovered on Meredith's lips; for a moment, she almost blurted, *Did you know it can kill people, important people—people you thought you knew?*

But then propriety dropped down onto her, and silence, and the realization: *Of course she knows. Everyone knows that, stupid.*

Listlessly, she left the library.

"Meredith!" called her aunt from the top of the staircase. "Come on up here. I talked to the Altgelds about repainting the inside of the porch and they said okay. I've got some color swatches and I need your advice. I was thinking a warm amber ..."

Without replying, Meredith laid her bike against the outside of the staircase's handrail. Then, slowly, she began to mount the stairs.

"I was thinking amber," continued Aunt Sancy, smiling at her from the doorway, "so it'd be September all year round when we stepped in here. I know how you love autumn—"

"Why didn't you tell me about the bridge?" blurted Meredith, cutting her off mid-sentence. Breath harsh in her throat, she stared fiercely at her aunt as she fought to keep a grip, hold herself back from shouting. All day, it had been building—the bewilderment, the anger ... through lunch at the Burger King with Dean and Reb, who, when told, had echoed her sentiments back to her, and then the late afternoon when she had biked alone to the bridge and stood, body pressed to the guardrail *exactly where it had happened*—trying to relive the event as it had originally taken place, as her parents had experienced it, to *understand*.

Aunt Sancy knew instantly which bridge she meant. One quick breath and her grin faltered, her gaze dropped. Silently she stood, running her fingertips over a color swatch. "You been talking to your Polk relatives?" she asked finally.

Meredith was vaguely aware of several Polk second cousins, who were living in Winnipeg. At least, that was where they had resided five years ago when her Polk grandparents had died. Since then, it was anyone's guess. Her eyes narrowed. "I haven't talked to any of them in years," she said shortly. "I looked it up in the *Post*."

Her aunt nodded.

"Because, of course, I *had* to look it up there," Meredith

added in a surge of bitterness. "No one in my life *who knew* would've told me. That my parents drove off a perfectly safe bridge, I mean—in the middle of the goddamn afternoon. *Because they were drunk.*"

Aunt Sancy winced noticeably. "That's not all they were," she said.

"What d'you mean?" demanded Meredith, her voice rising to a half-shout. Heart thudding, she leaned forward, her face centimeters from her aunt's.

"Whoa!" said Aunt Sancy, raising a protective hand. "I'm not hiding anything from you, hon. Give me a chance and I'll tell you about it. But before you take my head off, *think* for a minute. You were five years old when it happened. D'you think I should've told you all the ugly details then?"

Not ready to let go of her anger, Meredith stood silently, slammed by the deep thundering of her heart. Centimeters away, her aunt also stood without speaking, waiting her out. Gradually, in spite of herself, Meredith's anger began to retreat.

"You could've told me before now," she said grimly.

"Yes, I could've," agreed Aunt Sancy, glancing quickly at her, then away. "I've thought about it often, believe me— when you would be ready, what was the best time. When is anyone ready for something like that?"

"I'm ready now," said Meredith.

"Okay," said her aunt. "We'll go inside, have some iced tea. I've got a pizza baking for supper. Come on." Turning, she passed through the porch entranceway and into the kitchen, followed by a bewildered Meredith. "Sit down," said her aunt. "I'll pour us some tea."

Meredith sat down heavily at the table as her aunt opened a cupboard and took out two glasses. Through the open doorway came sounds of a late afternoon—aspen leaves shuffling, shouts of children at play. How could it be, thought Meredith, that the world went on—peaceful, rustling, and golden—while she sat, a dark, dull lump at its center, waiting ... well, waiting for what?

"Here you are," said Aunt Sancy, placing a tall glass of iced tea before her. Then, setting down her own, she sat opposite.

"Well?" said Meredith, her voice rasping in her throat, surprising her with its rawness.

"Drink some of your tea," her aunt said quietly; then, as Meredith hissed, she added, "*Please.* Drink some."

Meredith drank. To her surprise, the entire glass went down quickly—cool and soothing after her long bike ride home. "Okay," she said, setting it down, not willing to admit the accuracy of her aunt's instincts. "Now."

Aunt Sancy nodded again. "Cocaine," she said simply. "They were both flying on it. James was driving, neither were wearing seatbelts. There were no witnesses but there didn't need to be. What was left told the whole story."

"Cocaine?" Meredith repeated weakly. "You mean, like ..."

Her voice trailed off and she sat staring at her aunt.

"Like what?" prompted Aunt Sancy.

But Meredith didn't know like what. She wasn't stupid; she knew what cocaine was—had heard other kids talking, seen it on TV. The closest she had come to actual illegal drugs was a brief shared toke on some weed several neighborhood kids had been passing around last summer. It hadn't impressed her. Later, someone had told her dealers often passed off tobacco as weed to the naive, and she had figured she'd probably qualified. Probably still did.

"The *Post* just said alcohol," she stammered. "Not drugs."

"The *Post* was selective in its coverage," her aunt said dryly. "Elite bloodline, the high and holy Polk surname. Anyone else would've had their reputation dragged from here to Toronto and back."

"But why?" Meredith burst out. Agony, she was in agony; there was no other word for it—blood pounding everywhere through her, heart like a steel-toed boot, kicking and kicking.

Aunt Sancy's gaze softened. "What do you mean, why?" she asked.

"I mean ..." faltered Meredith. "Well, did they do that every day? Drugs? Is that the way they were?"

From across the table, Aunt Sancy's eyes caught and held hers. Dark, strong, and direct, they hung on, hung on. "Yes," she said.

Meredith hissed sharply. Heartbeats slammed through her; she sat, her hands clutching at nothing. "But he was in law school," she stammered. "He was articling."

"People go into law for various reasons," said her aunt. "Some of them are legal. Some aren't."

"What're you saying—my dad wanted to be a lawyer for ... *crime*?" whispered Meredith.

"I don't think I could ever begin to say what your father wanted out of life," Aunt Sancy said wearily. "The world can be an ugly place, Meredith. Ugly, *ugly* things go on. Entirely innocent people get caught up in them; life rarely goes the way you expect. When Ally first met James ..." Aunt Sancy stared off, thinking. "Well, I didn't like him much then, already. But he wasn't what he got to be later. It was law school that changed him—people he met up with there. Fast crowd, all of them with money of their own, just like him. So there were drugs, of course. High-flying designer capsules—you take one and you don't know who you are while you're on it; don't remember who you used to be when you come back down."

She shook her head. "It all looks good when you're in the middle of it. It looked good to Ally. And James made sure they were always right in the middle of things. So I guess she never asked questions. Or not the right questions. *Always* ask questions, Meredith," said Aunt Sancy, her eyes intense, piercing. "Especially when things look good ... real good."

Meredith's gaze flickered. "There was ..." she said hesitantly. "Well, in the *Post*, there was an article about a drug bust in Polkton the day before. Was he ... my dad ...?"

"Was he what?" her aunt prompted gently.

"Well, was he part of *that*?" Meredith exploded.

Aunt Sancy hesitated, shifted her glass along the tabletop, hesitated again.

"I want to *know*," Meredith said intensely.

"Your father was a gambler," Aunt Sancy said finally. "An extreme gambler and a stupid one. He built up debt, more than he could pay off, though God knows he came from enough money. Gambling debts mean you owe people something, sweetie. Scary people—people who like the meaning of the word 'bad.' Yeah, he was involved—exactly how and with whom, I can't say. Things were going on, building up ... and then the shit hit the fan, he and Ally were dead, and their involvement didn't matter anymore. At least, not to them."

Shock descended onto Meredith—dense, throbbing waves of it. "Are you saying ... he did it on purpose?" she asked. "Going off the bridge like that with my mom?"

Aunt Sancy blinked and breathed deeply. "I don't know," she replied. "No one does. Neither of them left a note, anything like that."

Meredith sat breathing, just breathing. "And it never got out?" she asked finally. "His gambling and drugs? The cops covered it up?"

Again Aunt Sancy blinked. "*Someone* did," she said.

Meredith swallowed. "But if it never came out," she faltered. "If the police never investigated my dad—how do you know all this?"

"I watched him," Aunt Sancy said tersely. "And I'm no angel myself, Meredith—you know that. I was never as bad as James but, back then, I knew my way around chemical euphoria." Pausing a moment, she stared off, then added,

"Chemical stupidity, more like. Now I'm older and wiser. If only we could be born that way. These days, no one could convince me to go anywhere near the stuff.

"But back then, like I said, I did my fair share, some of it with them. I also kept my eyes and ears open, watching James—first for your mother's sake, and then for yours. I mean, there you were, this tiny little girl, in the middle of ..." Aunt Sancy's voice trailed off, and she sat shaking her head.

Meredith stared at her. "I remember next to nothing about them," she said. "Just their faces, but all fuzzy and vague."

"Probably just as well," Aunt Sancy said darkly. "I want you to know, hon, that I stopped drugs completely two years before I adopted you. Someone had to be there for you. Believe me, I was trying."

Meredith sat, silence roaring in her head, trying to work out what her aunt was saying, what she wasn't saying. "I don't ..." she stammered, "... don't know what to think about this."

"You don't have to, sweetie," Aunt Sancy assured her. "It was an ugly part of your life, but now it's over—in the past. I'll take care of you."

"I know," said Meredith. "You do take care of me; you always have. I love you, Aunt Sancy. Really, I do."

Reaching across the table, Aunt Sancy gripped both Meredith's hands and they sat, blinking and sniffing as the wild wind of their thoughts gusted through them.

"I can just see you," Meredith said finally, withdrawing

one of her hands to wipe her eyes. "With your dark Goonhilly eyes and ears—snooping and spying."

Aunt Sancy grinned slightly, then nodded. "My beady, prying Goonhilly eyes?" she asked.

"I've got them, too," Meredith said fervently. "Goonhilly eyes and ears."

Another tiny smile came and went on Aunt Sancy's lips. "Hon," she said, "you're all Goonhilly."

chapter 11

F riday evening passed with Meredith stowed away in her room, reading a graphic novel and avoiding her aunt's concerned hovering. Her parents' wedding photograph, with its picture-perfect smiles, she did *not* glance at. Although relieved to have finally learned the basic facts concerning Ally and James Polk's deaths, Meredith felt battered by their harsh truth—as if a harvesting scythe had swept through her mind, obliterating the daydreams she had so carefully built up. Those daydreams now appeared foolish ... *Dumbness Incorporated*, she thought bitterly ... but they had been part of her, an important part—central to the way she had loved her world and herself. And so their loss left her feeling scraped raw; in some inner place, she hurt every time she breathed. That night, sleep was a long time coming and, several hours later, she woke to a dawn that lay listless and gray along the horizon. Staring out her bedroom window, Meredith felt an answering echo within—a dull, colorless numbness that seemed to have crept everywhere through her while she slept. As far as she could tell, this thick, dead feeling didn't change the way she looked or acted—at least her aunt showed few signs of noticing; as Meredith helped clean the apartment, then go grocery shopping, Aunt Sancy kept up her usual banter, sending out only the odd piercing glance, which quickly melted under her niece's reassuring smile.

After supper had been cleared away, Dean and Reb came over to make fudge, but even their company didn't dispel the dense, invisible heaviness that had moved in on Meredith. Her face smiled, her mouth talked, her hands stirred bubbling fudge and carried the resulting masterpiece to the living room, but inside her head she was light years away, floating somewhere between the apartment ceiling and the Milky Way.

Sunday, she woke to the same compressed gloom. Everywhere, it crowded in on her—an impenetrable cold that seemed to have taken over her bones. Sitting up in bed, she laid her forearms along the tops of her legs and stared at them, wondering where they had gained their recent weight, why it suddenly felt so impossible to move. Sluggishly, she swung her legs over the side of the bed and got to her feet. As she dressed, her gaze shifted around the room, landing everywhere but on her night table and its central framed photograph. For years, that picture had been the first thing she had looked at each morning—a message from the past, a promise of love that had renewed itself daily in her mind. Sure, there had been her aunt, love in the flesh and always there for her, day in and day out. But how could anyone—even a tattooed, Harley-riding angel like Aunt Sancy—compete with picture-perfect smiles and frilly wedding dress, framed and set behind glass? It was the ideal fairy tale, the exact image to capture a small girl's heart, and now, as Meredith finally gazed directly at her parents' photograph, she found herself blinking back tears.

Within seconds, the smiling picture morphed into a blur, leaving her with the mess inside her head. As Meredith stood forcing back tears, no words came to her—no recriminations such as "I hate you!" or "How could you do this to me?" Instead, what she experienced was a vast emptiness, like a lake in the rain—everything a gray gloom, half-formed thoughts hitting the watery surface, then losing themselves as if they had never been. Taking a quick breath, Meredith crossed her bedroom, took hold of the wedding photograph, and turned it face down on her night table. For several more breaths, she stood staring at it, half-expecting the photograph to resist, make some kind of protest. But nothing moved or cried out—not the photograph, not a single thought inside her head; all she knew was the deep, slow thrum of her heart.

Abruptly, several shudders erupted through her, as if

something was trying to evict itself from her body. Hugging herself, Meredith let whatever it was blow through her—ugliness there and gone. When the moment was over, she stood a while longer, still hugging herself to be certain, but nothing further surfaced; whatever had needed to leave her seemed to have done so. Cautiously, she let her arms sink to her sides and glanced around. Everything looked to be the usual—shapes and colors were as they had always been; shadows occupied their customary corners.

At the same time, she could feel that something fundamental had changed. The thick heaviness that had possessed her since Aunt Sancy's Friday evening revelations was gone, leaving her once again with an inner rawness—a sensation of being bruised and sore, but also of having come through a difficult experience and kicked free of it. Turning, she stared fixedly at the downed photograph on her night table.

Maybe my surname is Polk, she thought. *But from now on I* am *a Goonhilly. I don't care who you were—you're dead and gone, not part of me anymore. I won't let you be.*

Taking a deep breath, she strode from the room.

The following morning, Meredith walked into home form to find Morey and Gene deep in discussion. To her relief, Seymour's chair was empty, but no sooner had she sat down behind the drums than the Mol sauntered in and took his seat below her. Not once did he glance at her but, even so, Meredith found herself stiffening under an ugly wash of ... well, she thought grimly, whatever feelings were still hanging around since last Thursday's hallway mouth-clicking episode. Not that Seymour had given any sign of noticing her discomfort—upon his arrival, Morey and Gene had ditched their conversation and turned to him, anticipation animating their faces.

"Hey!" said Morey. "How was the biology field trip?"

Seymour smirked. "Interrupted," he drawled.

"So I heard," said Morey. "They take you away in cuffs like Pribram and Rogo?"

Seymour snorted. "You think I'm that stupid?" he asked.

"Not usually," said Gene, his tone dry.

"Nah," said Seymour, stretching out his arms and cracking his knuckles. "Take it from the Mol—an orange jumpsuit is not the way I intend to spend one nanosecond of my wonderful life."

Wide-eyed, her gaze fixed on him, Meredith was sucking in every word. Questions crowded her tongue but she held on, knowing her slightest comment could silence the Mol indefinitely.

"So what did you do?" probed Morey. "Dump your stash in the bush?"

"Sniffer dogs," Seymour said dismissively. "Basic rule of thumb: If you've gotta dump, head for the river."

"Ah!" Morey said knowingly, and the final bell rang, annihilating further conversation. As the national anthem kicked in, Meredith sat mulling over what she had just heard. Handcuffs, an orange jumpsuit, and sniffer dogs—they had to be talking about a drug bust, and apparently it was one that had taken place during a biology class field trip this past weekend.

Opening her binder, she pulled a Caramilk wrapper from the inside pocket, turned it over, and wrote across the back: *What are you guys talking about?* Then she passed the wrapper to Gene.

Eyebrows raised, he scanned her note and scrawled a response. Before returning the wrapper, he lifted it to his nose, took a hefty sniff, and rolled his eyes blissfully heavenward. With a giggle, Meredith accepted the wrapper and read what he had written in reply: *Pot fest on the biology field trip.*

And the cops were called in? Meredith wrote back.

Cops and dogs, Gene replied. *Couldn't see the forest for the weed.*

Curiously, Meredith studied the back of Seymour's oblivious head. Then she wrote: *Just weed?*

Mostly, Gene replied. *Some speed, maybe some acid. That's what I've heard.*

They had run out of space on the wrapper. Meredith started to tuck it back into her binder pocket, then was hit by a new question. Shooting Gene a glance, she once again extracted the wrapper, located a small, empty area at the top, and wrote: *What do you think about it?*

Gene took a moment to respond, frowning slightly and playing with his pen. Then, turning the candy wrapper over, he wrote *I deal with what's real* across the front, and handed the note back to her.

Puzzled, Meredith reread the note several times. It could, she decided, mean a number of things. So, as the last PA announcement was drawing to a conclusion, she scrawled, *What do you mean?* and passed him the wrapper again.

Gene looked taken aback. Quickly he scribbled something and passed her the wrapper.

Flattening it onto her binder, Meredith scanned his response: *Drugs lie.* Two words, that was the sum total of it, but their impact felt like a two-ton truck. *Tell me about it!* she wanted to scream as the image of a mangled guardrail flashed through her mind. Instead, she sat aimlessly folding one corner of the Caramilk wrapper back and forth and fighting off the sting of tears.

A hand touched her arm, and she looked up to see Gene observing her. "You all right?" he asked, but before she could reply, Mr. Woolger rose to his feet.

"Class," the teacher said briskly. "As you will recall, you still need to elect a representative to Student Council. You've had all weekend to consider the situation. Do we have a volunteer?"

Silence greeted his request. Face in neutral, Mr. Woolger had obviously been expecting this response. "Come, come," he said, making an attempt at congeniality. "It's only for the first semester. We'll get someone else to take over halfway through the year."

The silence continued unrelieved, and Mr. Woolger stood, conducting vaguely as he waited the class out. "Come, come," he repeated coaxingly. "Do you want to be the only home form in the school that doesn't have a representative?"

No ripple of shame disturbed the class; even their vital signs seemed to have deserted them. Finally, after an excruciating pause, Gene raised his hand. "I'll do it, sir," he said. "For the first semester."

Relief flooded Mr. Woolger's face and he said, "Thank you, Gene. Student Council's general meetings are Tuesday lunch hour, so they won't conflict with Jazz Band practices." Then, sitting down, he buried himself in desk work, the matter dismissed from his thoughts.

"Hey!" said Morey. Turning in his seat, he handed Gene a sheet of foolscap that had been torn from his binder.

"What's this?" asked Gene, scanning it.

Morey looked hurt. "It's a bouquet of flowers," he said pointedly. "Drawn by my own hand, as thanks for your sacrifice."

"Oh!" said Gene, turning the page this way and that. "Yeah, now I see it—a couple of dandelions and a thistle. And what's this?" Dramatically, he turned the page upside-down and exclaimed, "A daisy! How did you know that's my favorite flower? Thanks, Morey." Leaning forward, he gently patted Morey's shoulder.

Feigning further distress, Morey puffed out his lower lip. "I am wounded," he mumbled, turning to face the front of the room. "I draw you art from my heart, and what do I get in return? Mockery."

Seymour snorted. "Take it from me, Mor," he said sagely. "Class rep for half a year—that's a bouquet of roses, at least."

"Can't draw roses," pouted Morey.

"Can't draw dandelions, either," Gene said mercilessly.

The bell rang, and the class erupted into a cacophony of shifting chairs and footsteps. "Hey!" called a voice as Meredith started to step down off the third riser. Turning back, she saw it was Gene. "Now *those* are real flowers!" he proclaimed cheerfully. "Next time you get the urge to draw some, Mor—copy Meredith's daffodils."

At once Meredith felt it—multiple eyes focusing on her butt. Although this had been going on now for almost a week, today the eyes—at least these specific eyes—felt different, more personal. A flush shot through her but she fought it off determinedly, turning her back to Morey, then placing a hand on one hip and striking a jaunty pose.

"Sorry," she said, glancing back at him. "No roses." And she stepped off the riser.

"Wait a minute, Meredith!" called Gene, coming after her.

Surprised, she turned to face him. As the rest of the class headed for the door, he came to a halt beside her. *Tall*, thought Meredith, looking up at him. Maybe not as tall as Seymour, but he definitely had height where a Goonhilly did not.

"You okay?" he asked, his voice low.

"Oh, yeah," Meredith assured him. Unaccountably, she

was once again flushing. "It's the rain hat, y'know—I'm not used to it yet. Flowers on my butt ..." She shrugged.

Gene shook his head. "No," he said. "I meant the note. The last thing I wrote—you seemed ... upset, maybe, when you read it."

"Oh," said Meredith. Without warning, the stinging was back in her eyes. "It made me think of something, I guess. But I'm okay now, really."

"Okay," nodded Gene. "Well, I'd better get going, then. See you."

Turning, he headed for the door. Just as he reached it, memory erupted within Meredith. "Hey!" she called after him. "Your audition—did you ever have it?"

Gene grimaced. "Mr. Waltzing Spider Fingers," he called back. "Chang walked away with it. I've gotta grow more knuckles." Lifting a hand, he disappeared through the doorway.

Huh, thought Meredith, watching him go. Though Gene's tone had been calm, even cheerful, his initial grimace had been real enough—he had obviously wanted to make the youth orchestra. The guy knew how to lose.

Pensive, she started toward the door.

It was five to twelve, and Meredith had stepped into a washroom en route to her locker, her thoughts on the large wedge of fudge she had packed with her bag lunch. The last piece from Saturday night's batch, she and her aunt had bartered over it that morning at breakfast, Aunt Sancy finally wringing a commitment from Meredith to wash down the porch as compensation.

"You get the cavities," she had said complacently when Meredith had conceded. "And I get to put up my feet and watch you work. When you're finished, we'll start painting ... September gold."

Meredith smiled ruefully at the memory, realizing her aunt had probably planned out the discussion in advance. Still, she was always assigned one major chore to do on the weekend, and she knew Aunt Sancy was unlikely to give her a second in addition to cleaning the porch. So in the end, she thought, as she pushed open a stall door, her aunt had basically handed over a monster piece of fudge for free, without haggling for a thin slice, even a corner nibble.

Setting her binder on the floor, she straightened and reached for the rain hat chin-strings, intending to untie them. But instead of crinkly plastic, her fingers encountered only the denim of her jeans. Disbelievingly, she slid her hands around her waist but couldn't feel the rain hat anywhere, and when she peered over a shoulder, searching for some sign of it, nary a daffodil could be seen parading across her butt.

It can't be! Meredith thought incredulously. *I tied the strings with a double knot—I know I did.*

Wide-eyed, she leaned against the stall wall, riding out a minor wave of shock. Not that the loss of the rain hat was incurring major psychological damage or anything, she thought defensively. It was just a stocking stuffer, worth no more than a couple of dollars. All the same, it was hers—not public property. More to the point, what with last week's scrutiny and constant comments, she had found herself growing fond of the rain hat, *bonding* with it, even. There was no way around it—that rain hat had been her ally in time of need and now it was gone, its spritely yellow determination simply ... vanished.

How? she thought, still leaning against the stall wall. The rain hat couldn't have fallen off—she knew without a doubt that she had double-knotted the chin-strings. And it simply wasn't possible that someone could have unknotted it without her noticing. So what had the culprit used to get it off—a quick tug while she was navigating hallway crowds? The tip of a pen to tear the plastic? A pair of scissors?

Dull nausea swept Meredith, and she sat down on the toilet. The problem with a butt, she thought miserably, was that it was difficult to keep an eye on. Unless she wanted to scuttle crablike along a hall with her back constantly to a wall, her butt was always wide open. The only time she was safe was when she was seated, but she couldn't keep her butt continually planted. Head in hands, Meredith sat riding out her dismay. *The weirdest thing*, she thought listlessly, her eyes closed, *is how stupid this whole thing is. I mean, it's just a rain hat and a set of drums, but it's taking over my whole life. Why is Seymour putting so much effort into this? And why am I?*

Gradually, as she sat head in hands, her discouragement faded and her body returned to working mode. Getting to her feet, she cautiously fingered the rear seam of her jeans. *No gum*, she thought, swamped with relief. *At least, not yet.*

Well, so much for enjoying a massive fudge sugar-fix in the cafeteria. Her lunch hour mission was now obvious— to locate Dean and Reb, then head to the nearest drugstore in search of a replacement rain hat. *Preferably one with flowers*, she thought, her interest beginning to stir. *Bright, no,* brilliant *blossoms.* And under no condition was she buying a rain hat with ducks on it—with the way Neil Sabom's mind worked, she could just imagine the rhyme scheme he would come up with.

After using the toilet, she picked up her binder and headed out into the lunch-hour halls.

chapter 12

A lunch-hour trip to a nearby Shoppers Drug Mart proved to be a bust, but a visit later that afternoon to a downtown dollar store was successful, leading to a bin full of rain hats, each in its own pocket-sized plastic envelope. The rain hats' decorative designs included everything from Tweety Bird to the Simpsons, and narrowing down choices was a daunting task, but, in the end, Meredith selected four, of which her favorite featured thunderclouds with red zigzagging lightning bolts.

"The ultimate in pissed-off!" she declared triumphantly as she, Dean, and Reb left the store. "No one'll dare come near me in this."

"Maybe," countered Dean. "I still think you should've

bought the rain hat that had the target with an arrow stuck in it. It's better than the one you got with the seven dwarves."

"A target on my butt?" demanded Meredith. "No thanks!"

"Deanie," Reb said reprovingly. "Use your brain."

"Okay," replied Dean. "How's this for genius—duct tape! Use it to tape a rain hat to your butt, and the next time someone tries to cut off the rain hat, the tape will keep it in place."

Meredith frowned, considering, then asked, "But they'll be able to tell, won't they? They'll see the tape all around the rain hat."

"*Under* the rain hat, Mere," Dean said pointedly. "Wrap a piece of duct tape into a circle, stick one side of it to your butt and the other to the inside of the rain hat, and ... *voilà*!"

Understanding coursed through Meredith, and with it radiant relief. As simple as that, her problem had been solved. "Deanie, you are a genius!" she cried, throwing her arms around her friend and smacking her one on the cheek. "I am hereby announcing that I am calling Walt Disney and telling them to add an extra dwarf to the seven dwarves— one called Smarty that looks just like you. You'll be a major star—Smarty, the eighth dwarf!"

Dean beamed. "Major culture shock," she said. "Smarty, the Asian dwarf."

"Oh, yeah," Reb said musingly. "So, let's see—that'd make it Smarty, Sleepy, and Doc. And then there'd be Grumpy, Lumpy, and Dumpy. And, of course, Itchy ..."

"... and Bitchy," continued Meredith, catching Reb's drift.

"And don't forget Farty and Burpy, and—"

"Hey!" exclaimed Dean, cutting her off. "Thanks a lot—Smarty and Farty! Can't you come up with a better rhyme scheme than that?"

"And Itchy and Bitchy," Reb reminded her complacently.

"And no more gum on my bum!" sang out Meredith, raising two clenched fists. "My problem is solved. My agony is over. Life can now begin again. I feel it, I feel it—I'm about to take up *massive* space!"

In spite of her optimism, however, the thunder-and-lightning rain hat disappeared before she reached home form the following morning. Meredith felt it the second it went missing—a jerk, followed by a sharp tug—but by the time she had whirled around, the culprit was nowhere to be seen. Halfway along the hall leading to her locker, Meredith pivoted frantically under an overhead security camera, but there was no sign of the thunder-and-lightning rain hat anywhere—clutched in a hand, shoved into a back pocket, even trampled underfoot.

A heaviness descended onto her—remorseless, without end. Then a passing student clipped her shoulder, and the random carelessness seemed aggressive, personal. Ducking her head, Meredith shuffled to the wall and stood with her back to it as she slid a hand tentatively across her butt. Freshly warm from someone's mouth, she felt it immediately—a gum wad, sticky and *OOZING!* as Mr. Woolger would have put it.

Heat swarmed her face. *The bastards!* she thought. *It's*

so ... mean. I bet they don't even think about what they're doing. They're like a machine, or a horde of soldier ants. Seymour just has too many friends. They're everywhere and I can't avoid them—I have *to walk through the halls. If they keep this up, I'm going to be covered in gum wads—plastered in them.*

It was a grim, ugly truth, and there was no way around it. Shoulders slumped, Meredith stood blinking back tears. Stuck to her butt, the gum wad felt like a malignant tumor. *What do I do?* she wondered miserably. *Go to the nearest washroom, pull off the gum, then tie on the rain hat with the seven dwarves? Who am I kidding? It'll be five minutes* maybe *before Sleepy and Grumpy are pulled off. No, make that thirty seconds.*

And then it came to her—quiet, insistent, a kind of inner shift. This shift carried a bruised sensation, but also a flash of knowing similar to one she had experienced once in grade school, when several bullies had backed her into a wall and taken a few swings: This was going to hurt, yeah— but she would survive ... and they would not. As in, the bullies confronting her that day would never be anything but exactly what they were then; they didn't have the capacity to change, and would go through the rest of their lives stuck on repeat.

But she would not. And although the problem currently facing her wasn't one easily solved—still, she was now, as she had been in grade school, completely free to react to it in any manner she chose. She could be predictable, and wrap herself in another defensive rain hat—Grumpy, Burpy, or *whoever*, she thought dismissively. That, however, would dig her deeper into the rut she had been inhabiting for the past week, and she was tired of that rut. Tight, constrictive ... it was *boring*. She wanted space. She wanted to burst out of herself, shouting and singing. If there had to be a dwarf parading across her butt, she wanted it to be Happy, for God's sake!

Quietly, determinedly, Meredith hissed. Then, straightening her shoulders, she pushed out from the wall and strode, not to the nearest girls washroom, but to her locker, where she ditched her knapsack, along with the roll of duct tape, scissors, and extra rain hats that it contained.

"Hey," said the guy at the next locker. "You've got a wad of gum stuck to your butt."

"Oh, yeah?" Meredith said coolly. Unlike most of Polkton Collegiate's home forms, which had been assigned lockers in blocks, Home Form 75's lockers were scattered all over the school. That was what came with being the very last home form, Meredith supposed, and as a result, she didn't know the name of the guy right next door.

"And," he added, glancing bemusedly at her posterior, "something that looks like duct tape. Four pieces of it."

"Oh, yeah!" Meredith repeated, considerably less coolly. "Thanks." Pulling off the pieces of tape, she wadded them into a ball and stuck it to the inside of her locker door. The gum wad she left undisturbed. "What color is the gum?" she asked.

"Black," said the guy.

Meredith winced. Her jeans were blue; whether this was a Black Cat wad or not, there would be a stain, no two ways around it.

"What happened to the daffodils?" asked the guy.

"Someone picked them," said Meredith. "All of them."

"No shit," said the guy. "That's a bummer."

"You said it," replied Meredith. Closing her locker, she headed down the hall toward home form. Enclosed by the crowd, she braced herself and waited; the first comment came quickly.

"Hey dude," a male voice said into her ear. "You, like, sat on someone's Juicy Fruit."

Glancing to her right, Meredith saw a scraggly-haired guy sporting several lip studs. "I didn't sit on it," she corrected him. "Someone stuck it there."

The guy gaped back at her. "Huh?" he demanded. "You mean, like, on purpose?"

"Exactly," said Meredith.

"Strange hobby," shrugged the guy. "The Underwear Gummer." Cackling maniacally, he meandered on down the hall.

Wouldn't have to invent a new dwarf for you, Dopey, thought Meredith. Walking into home form, she stopped in surprise when she found the room milling with students. Then, recalling that it was Tuesday morning, one of the Concert Band's regular practice times, she stepped to one side to wait until the classroom had emptied out. On the third riser, she could see Gene setting the double bass into its case; beside him, a girl was putting away the tambourine and maracas. Directly below them, a trumpeter was also packing up; as Meredith watched, he pressed a valve on his trumpet, releasing a long line of saliva, which dripped to the floor.

Yuck! thought Meredith, recoiling. *Do they all do that? This place must be crawling!*

Gradually the room cleared of band members, and Home Form 75 students moved in to claim their seats. "Hey, Meredith," said Gene, glancing over at her as she started to step onto the third riser.

Before she could reply, however, a voice called out, "Stop this instant! Meredith Polk, this is an order: Do not move!"

Whirling around, Meredith spotted Mr. Woolger approaching, baton raised in alarm. "No closer!" he barked. "Back away from the instruments right now!"

Open-mouthed, Gene stared at the agitated teacher, but Meredith instantly got the man's drift. "It's gum," she told the teacher, feeling defensive in spite of herself. "Just a gum wad. Someone else stuck it there, not me."

"That may well be," snapped Mr. Woolger, distractedly waving his baton. "Nevertheless, you cannot bring gum into this room. I've told you many times—gum is not allowed in the music room. Take it out of here this instant. You may return when you've cleaned yourself off."

"But ..." stammered Meredith, staring at him. "It wasn't my fault. I didn't ..."

Forlornly, her voice trailed off. The teacher's words were entirely reasonable—she knew that. In fact, she had anticipated a negative reaction from him, albeit not one this extreme. The question now, she thought uncertainly, her gaze dropping, was whether every Polkton Collegiate teacher was going to respond similarly—kick her out until she had removed the gum wad, then let her back in as if this had solved the problem. When, in fact, it solved nothing. Because, sure, she could head to the nearest girls washroom and remove the offending wad, but by the time she returned to class, another wad could conceivably already have taken its place. And if not by that point, then within the hour, or by lunchtime, or mid-afternoon break. That was the reason she had decided to come to home form this morning without removing the gum wad first—she had finally realized how pointless this action would be.

"What happened to your rain hat?" asked Gene, breaking into her thoughts. Glancing up, Meredith saw that he had stepped down off the third riser and come over to stand beside her.

"Someone pulled it off," she told him, gulping around a sudden lump in her throat. "Yesterday. Then this morning, the new rain hat that I bought to replace the old one was pulled off, too."

Gene's eyebrows lifted. "So much for that, then," he said.

"Yeah," Meredith agreed heavily.

Quietly, Gene stepped behind her and assessed the situation. Shoulders hunched, Meredith tried not to wince too obviously. "Hey," said Gene, stepping back around to face her. "I've got a Kleenex. Want me to take it off?"

Heat stampeded across Meredith's face.

"Or we could ask one of the girls," added Gene, thinking better of it.

"No, that's okay," Meredith assured him. "Just get it off fast."

Several seconds of gentle prodding was all it took, and then Gene was holding out a wad of Kleenex, his face as flushed as her own. "We got the vermin," he grinned weakly. "But it left a stain. I don't know if it'll come out."

Meredith shrugged, her eyes flicking past his. "Whatever," she said. "Thanks."

"Excuse me, sir," said Gene, turning to Mr. Woolger, who was still standing nearby, conducting the procedure with his baton. "The gum-wad invasion has now ended."

Gingerly, the teacher plucked the Kleenex-wrapped gum from Gene's hand. "Are you certain you got it all?" he asked.

"Uh, I think so," drawled Gene. "D'you want to double-check?"

"No, no. That'll be quite all right," Mr. Woolger said fussily. Taking a step back, he bumped into Morey, who was peering over his shoulder.

"Sorry, sir!" gasped Morey, ducking an agitated swing of the teacher's baton. Pointedly ignoring him, Mr. Woolger strode to his desk, where he deposited the offending gum wad into a wastepaper basket and sat down.

"You okay, Mor?" asked Gene. "Mr. Woolger just about conducted you into the next galaxy."

"A bit woozy," admitted Morey, gently patting his flyaway hair. "Got spun around there in his armpit breeze. Now I know why you play bass instead of flute. But what's going on with you two?"

"Gum on my bum," Meredith told him, flushing slightly. "Again."

"*And* they got her rain hat," added Gene.

"Did you see who it was?" asked Morey.

Meredith shook her head.

"D'you think it's all been the same guy?" asked Morey.

At that moment, Seymour walked into the room, spotted the three of them grouped together and talking, and came to a dead halt. Swiftly, Meredith's eyes flicked across his, and away.

"Which guy?" she asked Morey.

"Y'know—the first time we talked about it," said Morey. "Last week. You said you thought you knew who it was, but you couldn't prove it."

"I still can't prove it," said Meredith.

Morey shook his head. "I don't get it," he said, puzzled. "*You*. Why would you be a target?"

A careful expression on his face, Seymour stepped up onto the second riser and sat down. Neither Gene nor Morey appeared to have noticed his entrance.

"I'll ask around," said Gene. "Someone's bound to know something. How about you, Mor?"

"Sure," agreed Morey. "I'll check it out."

A surge of relief burst through Meredith, so intense it left her momentarily shaky. "Really?" she demanded. "You will?"

"Sure," Morey said again as Gene nodded. "Why not?"

"Thanks!" exclaimed Meredith as the final bell went, cutting short her gratitude. Reflexively, all three turned to the risers to take their seats. About to follow Gene up onto the third riser, Meredith found her gaze drawn irresistibly to Seymour, who was maintaining a rigid forward gaze, apparently unaware of her presence.

In spite of herself, Meredith felt her heartbeat quicken and her palms grow moist. Then, before she could think twice about it, she walked over to the Mol and asked, "Are you a Boggs? I mean, are you related to the Boggs family?"

Surprise flickered across Seymour's face. "My grandmother is a Boggs," he said, not quite looking at her.

Gotcha! thought Meredith. Stepping up onto the third riser, she sat down on her throne.

chapter 13

S he got hit with another gum wad during the lunch-hour break. When, exactly, it happened, she wasn't able to pinpoint, but sometime during a cafeteria conversation with Dean, Meredith stepped out from the wall she had been leaning against and was followed by a wet, stringy, tightly-clinging yellow mass.

"Uh-oh," Dean said mournfully. "Don't look now, but ..."

"Butt?" clarified Meredith, and her friend nodded. "Okay," sighed Meredith, her heart beginning a slow, deep pound. Turning to peer over her shoulder, she spotted her long yellow tail. Whatever brand of gum this was, its ooze factor was high—she could feel its warm, wet presence seeping through the seat of her jeans. Which, she realized, her interest beginning to quicken, should add exponentially to its stretchability factor.

"Watch this," she told Dean, taking a careful step forward, then another, and another. Resolutely, the gum tendril held.

"Whoa!" said Dean, grinning slightly.

"Too bad Reb's at the dentist," said Meredith, now seven steps out from the wall and continuing her forward momentum. "She should catch this—it's as good as the monster wad from math class." Behind her, she could see the gum wad holding firm to its position on the wall, the impossibly long thread connecting it to her butt taut as a tightrope. From a nearby table, an admiring whistle cut the air, and conversations faltered as students turned to look. Cautiously, Meredith took another step, and another.

"Twelve," Dean called after her. "Thirteen."

Someone began to applaud; others called out encouragement. Fifteen steps, sixteen, seventeen—still, the gum tendril held steady. Abruptly, a figure stepped out of the gathered onlookers and swung a hand through the yellow strand, causing it to sag to the floor.

"Hey!" cried Dean, starting forward. "What did you do that for?"

The guy who turned to face her was Neil Sabom, the expression on his face so stern that, for a second, Meredith wondered if he had been telepathically possessed by his father. Without a word, the principal's son fixed Dean with a contemptuous glare; then, turning it on Meredith, he let loose with several rapid-fire mouth clicks before pivoting and stalking off into the crowd. Open-mouthed, Dean stared after him.

"Whoa!" she said again. "Does that guy have problems, or what?"

At that moment, a vaguely familiar voice called out from the watching crowd. "Hey, Meredith!" it singsonged. "Your name's Meredith, right?"

Turning, Meredith saw Ronnie Olesin seated atop a nearby table, her feet straddling the bench that ran alongside. Pudgy face piqued with interest, her pale blue gaze was fixed on the wad still glommed to Meredith's butt.

"You're a walking target!" she crowed. "Might as well hang out a sign: Open for business!"

Ronnie's tone was gleeful, the implications of her comments breathtakingly nasty; both slammed into Meredith like a speeding semi. At the same time, she was becoming aware of the apprehension that had reared through her at the mere sight of the other girl. All over herself, Meredith could feel it—the weird vibes Ronnie Olesin gave off. No question about it—this girl creeped her out big time.

Beside her, Dean let loose with a loud hiss and started toward Ronnie. Quickly, Meredith blocked her with an arm. "Don't," she said quietly. "She's trouble. Just leave it."

"She's a bitch, whatever else she is," muttered Dean.

Without warning, the girl seated next to Ronnie threw back her head and hooted with laughter. "Yeah!" she half-shouted, bumping Ronnie's shoulder with her own. "You got it, Big R! Open for business! Open for business!"

Dean's eyebrows skyrocketed. "Slow circuit," she mumbled under her breath. "That one's on a definite time delay."

Lana Sloat, thought Meredith, eyeing the second girl. Like Ronnie, Lana was in Grade 11—give or take a few credits. Thin and lanky, with an uncertain hangdog look, she generally skulked at the fringes of school activities—usually in Ronnie's wake and functioning as her sidekick. Nothing about her presence did anything to dispel Meredith's unease.

"Yeah, it's a drag," she said, trying to sound noncommittal. "Someone in this school has a real thing for plastering me with gum wads."

Ronnie's eyes gleamed. "Maybe he's got the hots for you," she sneered. "A secret admirer. Or not so secret—have you figured out who it is?"

"No," Meredith said shortly. She was beginning to actually taste her dislike of this girl. The problem was how to cut and run, with Ronnie sitting next to the only available exit route.

Apparently struck by inspiration, Lana leaned forward and blurted, "A rearview mirror—tape one to your forehead, dozo! *Then* you'll see the bugger coming up behind you!"

Face in an expectant grin, she glanced at Ronnie, as if seeking her approval. For a long moment, Ronnie sat motionless, seemingly considering her sidekick's suggestion. Finally she nodded, and Lana's grin widened.

"You got it now!" she announced loudly to Meredith. "Get

yourself a rearview mirror and your problems are solved, dozo."

Uncertainly, Meredith glanced at Dean, who was wearing a carefully pained expression. That it would be unwise to offend Ronnie went without saying. Extending the conversation, however, wasn't high on the agenda, either.

"What d'*you* think?" Dean asked abruptly, crossing her arms and fixing Ronnie with her gaze. "What would *you* do if this was happening to *you*?"

"Me?" demanded Ronnie, startled by Dean's directness. "Nothing like *that* would ever happen to *me*."

"Pre - tend," drawled Dean. Beside her, Meredith winced. Mount Matsumoto was clearly running out of patience; the condescension in her voice was impossible to miss.

Ronnie got Dean's drift. Stiffening, she leaned forward as if about to speak but, before she could get out the words, a voice called authoritatively from the cafeteria's central aisle. "Hey—you there!" it barked. "You two, sitting on the tables!"

Glancing toward the speaker, Meredith spotted Ms. Runcie—a business teacher on lunch-hour patrol. "You there!" the woman repeated, pointing at Ronnie and Lana. "Get off the tables! There is no sitting on cafeteria tables!"

"Shit!" hissed Ronnie as she caught sight of Ms. Runcie. "It's the fuckin' Nazis. We're outta here." Surging to her feet, she ducked into the crowd, followed by Lana, and the two girls began bulldozing their way toward the nearest exit.

"Come on," said Meredith. Grabbing Dean's arm, she

took off in their wake, using the space the girls had opened up to weave a quick route through the crowd. "No, not that way," she said to Dean as they emerged from the cafeteria— halfway down the hall, Ronnie and Lana could be seen veering into a stairwell. "Over here." Crossing the corridor, she pushed open the door to a girls washroom.

"Whew!" said Dean, following her in. "For a second there, I thought you actually wanted more social interaction with those two. What *is* the inside of their skulls made of—papier mâché?"

"Forty-watt bulbs," replied Meredith. "The lights are on, but nobody's home." Now the encounter was over, it was the last thing she wanted to talk about. Ronnie and Lana were, simply put, out of sight, out of mind. "Look," she continued, turning to face the mirror. "Can you help me clean off this gum before gym? Check to see if there's a stain, okay?"

Placing both hands on the washroom counter, she tried to avoid her resigned reflection as Dean checked out her butt. "Yeah," her friend reported dismally as she removed the remaining gum. "It's pretty yellow, Mere. Well, the stain's actually a light green because your jeans are blue. And you can still see the black stain you got this morning."

"My best jeans!" exploded Meredith. "I won't be able to wear them ever again. If this keeps up the way it's going, I'll have to toss all my clothes. Maybe I *should* start wearing Pampers."

Face distressed, Dean leaned against the counter beside her. "I wish I knew what to do," she sighed. "If only I could walk along behind you all the time and fend them off."

Turning her back to the mirror, Meredith tried unsuccessfully to get a sight line on the two stains. "8:35 AM," she said gloomily. "And 12:40 PM. Two moments of doom, documented on my butt. What a pain in the—"

"Hey!" said Dean, her expression coming out of its dejected slump. "That's it! I mean, why not? Your jeans are already stained."

"What're you talking about?" Meredith asked half-heartedly, her attention still focused on her reflection.

"Document it!" exclaimed Dean. "As in, *right on your jeans*, beside each stain. The black stain happened at 8:35, right?"

Eagerly she dug through her pencil case, pulled out a marker-pen, and held it up. "Beside each gum-wad stain, we write the time and date," she explained rapidly. "So the buggers know we're tracking them, and not giving in just because you've stopped wearing a rain hat. You keep wearing the same jeans every day, so the stains only happen to one pair, and the list of dates gets longer and longer—*if* they don't give up when they see *you're* not giving up, that is."

Face alight, she waited as Meredith worked it through. "Okay?" she asked encouragingly.

"Yeah," said Meredith, nodding slowly. "Yeah—it could work. If I wear the same jeans every day, the stains won't matter so much."

"Great!" said Dean, uncapping her pen. "Bend over, sweetheart."

"God—I hope no one walks in right about now," muttered Meredith, trying not to cringe as Dean's pen tip dug industriously into the seat of her jeans. "And write neatly, Deanie. I don't want anyone mixing up what you're writing with a bull's eye and an arrow."

"Now *there*'s an idea," Dean said musingly, then placed a firm hand on Meredith's shoulder and pushed her back into position. "Just kidding. Come on!"

"Smarty Pants, the eighth dwarf," muttered Meredith.

"There," said Dean in a satisfied tone. "8:35 AM, September 17, and 12:40 PM, September 17. Right?"

"Right," said Meredith, straightening, then turning to observe her newly documented butt in the mirror. There, in backwards capital letters, she saw the two dates clearly parading across her posterior. "I feel like Watergate," she said, feeling slightly awed. "Or WikiLeaks. A crime in progress. Something *profound*."

"The profoundest butt in the universe," affirmed Dean.

"Thanks, Smarty," said Meredith.

"You're welcome, WikiButt," grinned Dean.

The willow tree swayed languorously, its long tendrils a late September amber. Stretched out beneath it and drinking in the rich scents of autumn, the Feet were putting in their obligatory five minutes of silence before beginning to speak. *Funny*, Meredith thought idly, *how different I feel during this time from any other*. Body splayed, her mind easing out of its usual busy pace, she could feel her breathing slow and deepen until it seemed almost to be rising out of the ground beneath her back. To either side, she sensed Reb and Dean going through the same process. *It's a gift*, she thought suddenly. *This time—it's a gift they give me, and I give them.*

"Is five minutes up?" asked Reb, her voice plaintive.

"Close enough," said Dean.

"Okay," sighed Reb. "There's something I want to tell you guys about. Except I don't really know how to talk about it."

"What's it about?" asked Meredith.

Reb hesitated. "Barry," she said finally. "At least, I *think* it's about him."

"Mr. x's and o's?" Meredith said teasingly. "Your new fave game, which you play only with Barry before class—"

"Not anymore," said Reb, cutting her off.

"How come?" asked Dean. "I thought you really liked him. He didn't ...?" Her voice faltered and she fell silent, leaving her sentence incomplete.

"Insult my boobs?" Reb finished for her. "No, he didn't do anything like that—not even once. He's actually quite a decent guy, at least *that* way."

"What was it, then?" asked Meredith. Turning her head, she angled it to bring Reb's profile into view. Gaze fixed on the willow's golden canopy, Reb's expression was troubled.

"You," she said softly, unaware of Meredith's scrutiny.

"Me?" asked Meredith, startled.

"Yeah," said Reb. "It's happened a couple of times,

actually. He just up and said things about you, out of the blue."

Something heated shifted in Meredith's throat. "Like what?" she asked.

"Things that weren't true," said Reb. "Not even *remotely*. Believe me, I told him he was wrong the first time he said anything. I thought that'd be the end of it—I mean, he knows I've known you for years. But then, there he was the next day—saying something different."

"Like ... what?" Meredith asked again. "Specifics, Rebbie."

"Well ..." Reb's reluctance was obvious. "He said you weren't a good friend for me. You're arrogant and shallow. You use people and don't care about your friends. You're a social climber."

Warmth flared in Meredith's cheeks. "Where'm I climbing to?" she asked gruffly.

"That is *bull*!" exploded Dean to her left. "You told him that, didn't you, Reb?"

"You bet I did!" asserted Reb. "I know Meredith Polk. Next to my parents, Mere—you love me more than anyone."

"Hey!" interjected Dean.

"You too, Deanie," added Reb. "Of *course*. I just meant—"

"I know what you meant," said Dean, mollified, and the three lay a moment, contemplating Reb's revelation.

"Maybe he's right," Meredith said finally, her voice tentative.

"What're you talking about?" exclaimed Dean, pushing

herself up onto an elbow and staring at her. "Of course he's not right!"

"Well, not *everything* that he said," said Meredith. "I'm not shallow—at least, I don't think I am. And I don't think I use my friends."

"Not these two friends," affirmed Reb.

"But ..." said Meredith, hesitating. "When I think about how I've been this year ... First, I went after the throne in home form. That was kind of arrogant."

"*How* was it arrogant?" demanded Dean. Still braced on one elbow, she sent her dark gaze boring into Meredith.

"I just wanted it," said Meredith, "so I went after it. I didn't think about anyone else—that I might be taking it from someone else who wanted it, too. Well, actually, I *did* think about someone else wanting it—I made damn sure I was there really early the first day so I could snag it first.

"And ..." Again she hesitated. "Well, once I got the throne, I basically dumped the kids I hung around with in home form last year—Kirstin and Sina. Not that I don't say hi to them in the halls, but I hardly ever talk to them in home form anymore. I never even think about them, really—except when I look down on the backs of their heads in the front row. That's kind of arrogant, isn't it?"

Dean and Reb were silent, mulling over her words. Then, with a dramatic sigh, Dean slumped back onto the ground. "I don't think it's *arrogant*," she said determinedly. "Maybe it's not *thinking* about things enough ... kind of careless. But arrogant is believing that you're better than other people—a superior race. Like, Asians rule—that kind of thing."

"We *know* you, Mere," added Reb. "If you were arrogant, we'd know. And if we knew, we'd be honest enough to tell you. That's what friends are for—right?"

Meredith blinked back unexpected tears. "Okay," she hedged. "But there's one thing you've forgotten about—my genes."

"Jeans?" asked Dean, confused. "Your WikiButt ones?"

"No—my Polk genes," said Meredith. "It's in my blood. Remember Ancestor Great Hand? And then there were my Polk grandparents, who were out-and-out snobs—BMW addicts. And ..."

Briefly, she hesitated. Though it had taken place four days previous, she hadn't told her friends about her aunt's recent disclosure, or the framed wedding picture still lying face down on her night table. "Well, there's my dad," she said slowly, and told them the entire story. "He grew up rich, spoiled, and arrogant," she finished off. "He paid for it in the end, but y'see what I mean—that's the way the Polks *are*. And *I'm* a Polk. I've got their genes. So, chances are I got the arrogance gene. And maybe ..." Pausing, Meredith breathed deeply. "Well, maybe *that's* why I went after the throne."

Silence followed her last statement, Dean's and Reb's brains in overdrive, working their way through this latest data. Then another emphatic sigh sounded to her left, and Dean let loose.

"First off," she announced, "if I was in your home form,

I would've done the same thing, and I'm not a Polk. If I'm not a Polk, I can't have the Polk-arrogance gene. Maybe I have a Matsumoto-arrogance gene, and Rebbie has a Looby one—"

"I have the Looby-booby gene," broke in Reb.

"Right," said Dean. "Obviously, I missed out on that one. Anyway, I don't think this has anything at all to do with genes. I think it has to do with *wanting* something. You wanted to have fun, Mere. Is that arrogant? Is it arrogant to want to have fun?"

"No," Meredith said uncertainly.

"Of course not!" asserted Reb. "Fun is good, not bad. Unless, of course, you want someone else's fun, or someone else wants yours."

"And Seymour can't have your fun, Mere—no matter how much he wants it!" snapped Dean. "He lost the throne and he's just going to have to sit in a corner, sucking his thumb, until he gets over it."

"End of story," Reb said softly, "*if* we were the only ones telling it. I wish we were. The thing that bugs me the most about this whole thing is *why* Barry kept on making comments about you, Mere. Even after I basically told him to shut up."

"Seymour?" demanded Dean.

"I think so," sighed Reb. "When Mere pointed out how Barry was chewing gum that first time he talked to me in class—well, I didn't want to think there was a connection. But now I think there probably is. Lord of the Underworld and all that."

"Lord of Bull Shit," sniffed Dean. "I bet he doesn't think it's arrogant when *he* wants something."

For a moment, the three lay silently, watching the drift and sway of willow leaves. Then, gently, a hand touched Meredith's right arm.

"I didn't want to hurt you, Mere," said Reb, her voice concerned. "But I thought I should tell you. What're you thinking?"

Meredith lay, her eyes following a breeze through the tree above her. Confusion burned in her, and sadness—as brilliantly as September leaves against a perfectly blue sky.

"I'm thinking it's so beautiful," she said finally. "This tree, Grade 10, the whole world. Why does it all have to get so fucked up?"

chapter 14

The next morning, Meredith arrived at her locker by 8:20, intending to hit the library before classes and get in some research on a history assignment. This early in the day, the halls were relatively empty and, as she closed her locker and headed along the corridor, few students could be seen. Around the corner and a ways down the next hall, even the music classroom stood silent. *No Concert Band practices Wednesday mornings*, Meredith recalled as she approached. *What does Woolger do with all that peace and quiet?*

Quickening her pace, she strode toward the classroom, noting that the door, now several meters ahead, stood ajar. Casually, thinking nothing of it, she glanced in as she passed, then came to an abrupt halt. Quietly, she stepped backward and pressed herself to the wall. Hyper-alert, she waited, but hearing no sound from the room, slid forward and peered around the doorframe. Inside the classroom, nothing had changed since her previous glance, the room's sole occupant giving no sign of having noticed her presence. Seated behind the drums on the third riser, Seymour Molyneux was regarding the rows of empty chairs before him, his eyes hooded and body motionless, except for the steady chewing of his jaw.

Heart thudding, Meredith considered her options; then, with a deep breath, she walked into the room. Three steps in was all she took, and those three felt monumental—far more so than her original action two weeks earlier when she had first taken a seat behind the drums. As soon as she entered the room, Seymour fixed on her—his gaze intent, but not particularly surprised. Without speaking, they sized each other up, Seymour continuing his placid chewing while Meredith's heart went into overdrive, body-slamming her with repeated thuds.

"You're here early," she said finally, fighting to keep her voice steady.

One eyebrow raised, Seymour observed her without speaking.

"Just visiting?" she asked, to break the silence. "Or are you planning some kind of coup?"

At once she realized that she had put herself at a dis-advantage by speaking again without first having received a reply, but to her relief, this time Seymour answered.

"It's your throne," he said, his voice languorous, unruffled.

"It's not a *throne*!" snapped Meredith.

"It is," he said calmly. "And you're a queen."

"I am *not* a queen!" burst out Meredith.

In response, Seymour sat simply eyeing her.

"Why is this such a big deal to you?" demanded Meredith, taking a step forward. "I mean—sticking gum on my bum, getting your friends involved. It's just a place to *sit*, you know."

A silent shrug was Seymour's only comeback. Stunned, Meredith gaped at him. *That's it?* she thought, anger rearing through her. *You sic half the school on me, and cover me with gum wads and who knows what kinds of germs—and all you have to say about it is a shrug?*

"How long d'you plan to keep this up?" she demanded, crossing her arms to contain their shaking. "The entire fucking year?"

Her obvious anger had some effect. Unhurriedly, almost philosophically, Seymour straightened in his seat, as if pulling himself together for an important communication. "Meredith," he said quietly, gazing somewhere past her left ear. "Meredith *Polk*."

For the briefest of seconds, Meredith got the sense this wasn't the first time Seymour had mused the syllables of her name aloud; as much time as she had spent pondering his behavior, he had probably invested twice as much into trying to predict hers. Any pride she might have taken from this realization was, however, fleeting—her entire awareness having focused in on what the Mol was about to say next.

"I have a suggestion to make," he said, watching his fingers slowly steeple themselves. "You and I will switch places. It'll only be for one year, and next year—after I've graduated— you can go back to sitting here behind the drums. That way you can keep your thumb in the pie, and you'll still be sitting close to Gene, for whom you're developing such an *obvious* attraction."

Instant heat flooded Meredith and Seymour smiled, acknowledging his direct hit. *Well!* thought Meredith, furious at having betrayed herself so easily. Maybe she couldn't help flushing, but she wasn't going to give him more than that. "What *pie*?" she asked, throwing all the contempt she could muster into her tone.

Again Seymour shrugged. "The power pie," he said simply. "Those who want to rule get their thumbs in."

"I don't want to *rule*!" exclaimed Meredith.

"You went straight for the power seat," commented Seymour.

"So what?" expostulated Meredith. "No one was in the room except me; I got here first; the seat was empty. Why shouldn't I sit behind the drums if I want to?"

Seymour gave another tiny smile and Meredith felt it— the way her blustering self-defense, her need to explain, had caused some invisible balance in the room to shift toward him. "Power is all appetite," he informed her coolly. "It sees, it wants, it takes. It's a universal law, and it works the same for you as the rest of us. And here's another universal law, Meredith *Polk*—the most basic law of chemistry, physics, and human dynamics: the law of action and reaction. Any time you act, someone else reacts. Only so many thumbs can fit into the same pie."

"And this particular pie takes only one thumb?" Meredith shot back.

Seymour raised an eyebrow, but didn't deign to speak. Eyes narrowed, Meredith raked her gaze over him. The longer the two of them spoke, the more she felt her awe of the Mol diminish, and the less off-balance she felt. "What about the rest?" she asked, glancing at the front row where she had sat last year. "The ones who don't get their thumbs in?"

"They go hungry," said Seymour. "But they don't concern us. What concerns us, Meredith, is your hunger and my hunger. As far as that goes," he added, patting the back of the chair where he usually sat, "sitting in this seat here, you won't go hungry. You'll get your share of the pie—less than what you're getting now, granted, but enough. Because when you sit here, it'll be a sign to everyone that the situation has changed and you're now with me. They'll know we've talked, we've come to an agreement, and I've taken you on as one of my friends. I have a lot of friends, Meredith. Any one of my friends is friends with all my other friends. I think, in the end, you'll find it pleasanter to be one of my friends' friends ..." He hesitated, then said simply, "Than not."

Dumbfounded, Meredith gaped at him. "You're psychotic!" she exploded. "Deranged! You talk like you think you run the entire school."

"Not the entire school," Seymour said impassively. "That's not necessary."

"Oh!" snapped Meredith. "And what is?"

For a moment, Seymour remained silent. Then he said, "You'll find out. Either way. Think about it. Do you really want to spend the rest of the year covering your ass? You'll have other chances, you know. It's really just a matter of timing—success usually is. All you have to do is lower your sights for nine more months—the rest of your Grade 10 year—and then the power will be yours. *All* yours, Meredith Polk—for whatever you want to do with it."

Leisurely, as if he had all the time in the world, Seymour got to his feet, stepped down off the third riser, and sauntered toward Meredith. Instinctively, her heart racing, she stepped backward, but the only sign Seymour gave of noticing was several rapid-fire clicks with his mouth. Then he was passing her and ambling through the open doorway, leaving her alone in the empty room.

She sat, eyes staring but seeing nothing, in one of the library's back study carrels until five to nine, then got to her feet and headed for the exit. Coming through the doors, she hit it—the swollen mass of students streaming both ways along the hall. *How many of them does Seymour control?* she wondered as she watched the throng pass. What percentage of the Polkton Collegiate student body was friends with Seymour Molyneux ... or more importantly, *wanted* to be—five? Ten? Twenty-five? Even two percent could make her life miserable—*was* making it miserable, she corrected herself.

But the fact was, Meredith told herself grimly, whatever Seymour's buddy percentage, their main weapon—drooling *OOZING!* gum wads—had been neutralized. Now that she had stopped worrying about stains, Seymour's weapons of butt destruction had lost their shock and awe factor. Sure, gum wads were an inconvenience, but she could wash her WikiButt jeans daily if she had to. Sooner or later, Seymour would have to see the light and give up ... because she wasn't going to. That was all there was to it. End of story.

End of story perhaps, but regardless, Meredith realized with a start—the first warning bell was now two minutes gone and she had to make tracks. Stepping into the crowd, she joined the flow headed for the school's tech wing. Pressed in on all sides, she didn't expect immediate commentary on her new WikiButt decor, and didn't get any. Resolutely, she descended the short staircase that led out of the school's main building, turned into the corridor leading to the tech wing, and walked toward the music room's open doorway.

The moment she entered the classroom, she saw him. Off

to one side, Seymour was leaning against the cupboards that contained the numbered instrument cases, apparently reading a textbook. On the second riser, his seat sat empty, and on the third stood the drum set—steel ribs gleaming, proud, and uninhabited. For three long seconds, Meredith hesitated, her gaze darting between Seymour, propped against the cupboards, and his vacant chair. Next to that vacant chair sat Morey, turned around and engrossed in discussion with Gene; every other student in the class was also seated and similarly engaged.

Again, Meredith's gaze flicked between Seymour and their two empty seats. The Mol's message was abundantly clear—he was giving her the chance, here and now, to renounce her claim to the throne, abdicate, and settle for a lower rung on the ladder, an *obedient* rung where she belonged. Briefly, Meredith tried out the scenario in her mind, imagining, just *imagining* the process of walking to the second riser, stepping up onto it, and sitting down with her back—her *entire* back—exposed, unprotected, and facing King Mol.

At that moment, perhaps sensing her presence, Seymour glanced toward the door. As he caught sight of Meredith, his gaze sharpened and his features tightened—a fist closing around its prey. The shift in his expression was fleeting; a second later, the muscles had relaxed and returned to their habitual cool, but in that instant she had seen it— his intention, raw and unmasked, on his face. The guy wasn't playing around, she realized, staring at him. For the

Mol, this was no idle fancy; he wasn't engaging in some diplomatic contest of wills. As far as he was concerned, the drum set was his by rights and, sooner or later, he would be parking his butt there. It was only a matter of time ... the amount of time that she, Meredith *Polk*, wanted to waste deceiving herself.

For what seemed a stretched-out eternity, Meredith stood riveted, unable to move. Blood thundered in her veins; dueling voices shouted in her head. *Action*, she thought weakly. *Reaction*. Then, on legs that felt thick as old-growth tree trunks, she got herself going, and lumbered past a slit-eyed Seymour and up onto the third riser, where she plopped down heavily behind the drums.

"Hey, Ms. Big," grinned Gene.

"Hey," she replied vaguely.

The final bell rang. Over by the cupboards, Seymour snapped shut his book, strode to the second riser, and sat down.

The day's commentary on her butt turned out to be surprisingly disinterested—by lunch, only a few students had noticed Dean's recorded dates, and both gum-wad stains were so faint, Meredith had to explain the connection. After the almost continual hilarity that she had received in response to the daffodil rain hat, this was deflating, but she kept up her radar, constantly scanning her surroundings for Seymour's next move. And so she was ready, even anticipating the gum-wad assault when it was launched, midway through the lunch hour. Coming down a stairwell with Reb and Dean, Meredith heard the sudden thud of footsteps behind her, and was partway into a swift turn when a hand slapped itself hard against her jeans' rear seam. Which placed her, finally, in a position to catch a quick, blurred glimpse of her attacker; one hand covered in beige mush and an expression of glee on her narrow face, it turned out to be Lana Sloat. Before Meredith could react, however, Lana shoved her with her clean hand, knocking Meredith off balance and into Reb, who fell against the wall.

"Watch it!" cried the startled Reb, raising a defensive arm and unintentionally elbowing Meredith in the chin. Stunned by the whack to her jaw, Meredith nevertheless forced herself to focus on Lana, who was now backing away and grimacing at the gooey evidence that connected her right hand to Meredith's butt.

"Hey!" yelped Dean, darting back up the stairs toward Lana, but, pivoting, the other girl took off, leaving a telltale trail of gummy strands.

"Yuck, what is this!" cried a nearby girl, taking a swing at a sticky tendril that had attached itself to her tights.

"Gum!" exclaimed a guy, trying to shake a persistent strand off his sleeve. "What—are they going after everyone now? I thought it was just that Polk kid."

"It *is* just the Polk kid," called out Meredith. "The Polk kid is over here."

Homing in on her, students crowded around to survey the

mess caked onto the seat of her jeans. "That was more than one gumball," observed a guy who sported some promising chin fuzz. "There was a lot of it left on her hand, too—she couldn't get it all off."

"It was Lana Sloat," volunteered yet another speaker—Cathy Kotelly, a girl Meredith knew from her English class. "You know—Flunk-Out Sloatie."

The stunned sensation in Meredith's jaw was beginning to subside. "Yeah," she said uneasily. "I saw her. I don't think she expected the gum to be that sticky."

"Why is she after you?" asked the first girl, as she detached the gum tendril from her tights. With a disgusted look, she flicked it off her fingers. "Did you piss her off?"

"Not that I know of," said Meredith.

"Watch out for her, Meredith," advised Cathy. "She's not as stupid as she looks—at least, not when she wants something."

Swallowing hard, Meredith said dismissively, "Ah, it's just her idea of a joke. She saw someone get me yesterday, and probably thought it'd be fun to try it herself."

At that moment, several students standing on the stairs above Cathy parted to let Dean through. "Hey!" announced Dean, breathing quickly from her failed attempt to run down Lana. "We've got to go to the office to report this. And we need witnesses. You guys all saw it. Will you come with us—y'know, to corroborate?"

"No thanks," grimaced the girl in the tights, taking a pointed step back. "Not if it's Lana Sloat."

"Just tell them to check the cameras," advised Mr. Chin Fuzz, pointing to a nearby security camera. "They should have it all on film."

"Yeah, but you can still come with us," protested Dean. "I mean, you should! You saw it happen."

"Not me," said Mr. Chin Fuzz, raising both hands. "Didn't see a thing." Without another word, he edged away. Glancing around the now almost deserted stairwell, Meredith saw that of the original group of witnesses, only she, Reb, and Dean remained—even Cathy had vanished.

"Don't worry, Mere," said Reb from beside her, breaking her extended silence. "Dean and I will vouch for you. And I'm awfully sorry about hitting your chin. Does it hurt?"

"Some," admitted Meredith, fingering the sore spot. "But not too bad."

"C'mon then," urged Dean, starting down the stairs. "It's 12:40, and I've got Art at 1:00. We've got to talk to someone in the front office before you clean that gunk off, so they can see it for themselves."

"Yeah," agreed Meredith. "But first we go to the nearest can, Deanie—so you can record the time and date next to the scene of the crime."

Cheered by the prospect, the three headed to the nearest girls washroom.

Several hours later, Meredith was standing inside the tech wing's north exit, the seven-dwarves rain hat tied firmly over the mess on her butt as she waited for Dean and Reb to show. All things considered, she thought musingly, the afternoon hadn't gone too badly. After viewing the evidence, one of the school's vice-principals, Ms. Bishaha, had watched smilingly as Meredith tied on the rain hat, then heard out the rest of her story. Next, she had used the PA to summon Lana to the front office. Lana had, of course, denied the entire episode, but a cursory examination of her right hand had revealed a thin but suspiciously sticky film. Ms. Bishaha hadn't even bothered to check the security cameras.

"You can go now," she had told Meredith, Reb, and Dean, who were already late for their 1:00 classes. "Lana and I will deal with the rest of this without you, won't we, Lana?"

Head slumped, Lana had merely grunted; still, as Meredith reviewed the scene in her mind, she felt nothing but relief. *If only everything was that easy to solve*, she thought, squinting into the bright sunlight that streamed through the glass doors. *Seymour and the drums, the Boggs and the Polks. My dead* criminal *parents, creepy Ancestor Great Hand. I'm sure it was his left hand on that map—it had to be. Everything the Polks do comes from the dark side. It's a sort of curse, but not something outside of them that comes after them. It's* inside *them—in their genes. No matter what Deanie thinks, the Polks do have an arrogance gene; they're just a left-hand kind of people. Even Grandma and Granddad Polk, with their perfect house and* BMW. *Maybe ...* Here, Meredith's thoughts faltered and she frowned. *Well, maybe Seymour's right and that* is *why I went after the throne. I'm a Polk, so I'm arrogant and want power ...*

"Hey, Meredith," said a familiar voice, and she turned to see Gene coming toward her, toting the double bass in its case. "You're wearing another rain hat."

"Whoa!" she said, eyebrows rising as she took in the size of the case close-up. "That's massive. How far d'you have to carry it?"

"To my car," said Gene. "I parked on Quebec Street so I wouldn't have to drag it far. Got a minute?"

"Sure," said Meredith.

"C'mon outside," said Gene. Pushing open the door, he stepped out into the breezy afternoon, Meredith on his heels. Without comment, he crossed the school lawn and stopped beside a dusty, weathered-looking Chrysler parked close to the north exit. Unlocking the rear-passenger door, he slid in the double bass. Then he glanced cautiously around.

"I asked some guys like I said I would," he said, his voice dropping even though no one else was close enough to overhear. "About the gum wads, right?"

Dense, electric, a pulse started up in Meredith's throat. "Okay," she said carefully.

"Well," said Gene, his face troubled, "what I've heard is it's Seymour. Not that he's doing the actual attacks, but he's pulling the strings. It's because of the drums. You're sitting where he wants to sit, so ..." He shrugged.

Meredith nodded. "Yeah," she said. "I ran into him before home form today, and he admitted it. He says it's a tradition—the oldest guy always sits there, and this year it's his turn. If I—"

"A tradition!" exclaimed Gene, interrupting her. "Since when?"

Startled at the sharpness in his tone, Meredith hesitated. "Since ... the beginning of Polkton Collegiate, I guess," she said.

"Meredith," Gene said emphatically, "they've only been using the music room as a home form for five years— because of the new Riverdale suburb and all the students it brought into the school. It's because of overcrowding— they ran out of regular classrooms and had to use ones they wouldn't normally use. Otherwise, they'd never let non-music students *near* the music room. Every seat in the room is taken—haven't you noticed?"

Stunned, Meredith stared at him. "I never thought about it," she faltered. "So ... Seymour's lying?"

"Does that surprise you?" asked Gene.

For a moment, Meredith just looked at him. "No," she said finally. "Not if I think about it. But just off the top of my head ..." Her voice trailed off.

Gene nodded. "You're not a natural liar," he said. "So you wouldn't be as likely to see it coming from someone else."

"Are *you* a natural liar?" countered Meredith.

"Not a *natural* one," said Gene. "But I'm probably naturally more suspicious."

His comment brought a new question to Meredith's mind, but she wavered on it. Nice as Gene was being, he was a year older and she didn't know him that well. Sitting where she did in home form, it wouldn't be smart to risk burning her bridges with both him and Seymour. On the other hand, she reasoned, destroying bridges ran in her family. "Well," she said, her eyes flicking across his. "If you know he's a liar, why are you friends with him?"

Gene's eyebrows rose. "I talk to him in home form," he said mildly. "But, believe me, I'd never let myself get stuck one-on-one with him in a situation where I'd have to depend on him."

Unconvinced, recalling the many endless, amicable home form debates, Meredith just looked at him.

"Hey," said Gene, raising both hands defensively. "Remember—up until today, I didn't know it was *him* doing this to you. How come you're wearing a rain hat again? With ..." Ducking around behind her, he took a quick glance. "Doc and Sleepy?" he grinned questioningly.

Meredith hesitated, then decided to go with the change in subject and described Lana's assault. "I don't know if Seymour was behind it," she concluded uncertainly. "I mean—Lana *is* friends with Ronnie Olesin, and Ronnie's *always* in trouble. Neither of them would need any encouragement from Seymour."

"I dunno," said Gene. "Seymour's got a long reach."

A sick feeling nudged Meredith's gut; decisively, she shoved it away. "Seymour to Lana Sloat is, like, light years," she scoffed. "He wouldn't even *look* at her if he passed her in the hall. But the other kids who've come after me ..."

Pausing, she considered, then blurted, "What I don't get about this whole thing is—*why*? Why do kids who barely know Seymour do what he tells them?"

"Probably for different reasons," said Gene, leaning against his car. "Not *every* kid does, y'know." Gazing off toward the school, he frowned thoughtfully. "But the kids who do? Yeah, there are enough of them. I've been watching Seymour in action for a couple of years now—him *and* his rapt audience. And what I think is, in the end, there are two kinds of people—the kids who are willing to suck up the lie Seymour puts out, and the kids who aren't."

"*The* lie?" Meredith repeated, confused.

"Yeah," said Gene, more firmly. "Seymour's like a drug— he lies *constantly*. Tries to make you think he's got the answer to everything; he's the force at the center of the universe and if you stick with him, you've got it made. He puts on a good show—I'll give him that much—and there are always kids who want to be entertained. But in the end, that's all he is—a performance. *Not* real life, and *not* a friend. Not even *close* to a friend."

"Huh," said Meredith, watching him closely. Sensing the intensity of her gaze, Gene grinned sheepishly. "Mom calls me 'Mr. Preacher,'" he said. "That's on a good day. On a bad one, I'm 'Mr. Disgusted.' If I was one of the seven dwarves, I'd be Grumpy."

Meredith frowned, too tied up with the thoughts inside her head to smile. "Hey," she said awkwardly. "If you were me, and you had this whole mess to deal with, would you keep on with it? Or would you give up on the drums and sit on the second riser like Seymour told me to?"

Gene looked incredulous. "Meredith," he said, "on the first day of your Grade 10 year, you walked into home form and snagged one of Seymour Molyneux's personal dreams. Do you *really* want me to tell you what you should do with your life?"

Meredith stood silently working this one through, but Gene wasn't finished. "Do you know how many kids have tuned into this?" he asked. "They *know*, Meredith. Out there—sitting in the cafeteria, walking the halls—they know you took something from right under Seymour's nose, and they're talking. You've managed to give the finger, big time, to the Mol. There are guys who are *insanely* jealous."

"Oh," said Meredith, taken aback. "Well, what about you? D'you want to give him the finger, too?"

"There are days when I'd like to get hold of his ego and play Keep Away with it," admitted Gene. "Bounce it around, pass it back and forth, not let him have it for a while. But other than that?" He shrugged. "I've got better things to do than get a hate on for someone. Which reminds me—I've got to be home by four to take my brother to his swimming lesson. So, see you tomorrow, eh?"

"Yeah, see you," said Meredith, watching him go around to the driver's side of his car and get in. "And—thanks!"

"Hey!" called Gene, planting both hands onto the car roof and pulling himself up through the window. "I can tell you one thing, Meredith Polk," he grinned at her over the roof. "In a million years, I'd rather be sitting next to you in home form than Seymour."

With a wave, he drove away from Meredith's ear-to-ear grin. *Damn arrogance and power!* she thought exuberantly. *I don't care why the heck I went for the drums—I've got them, they're mine, and I am going to ride them all year!*

chapter 15

With an emphatic grunt, Aunt Sancy set down the two cans of paint she had carried up the back staircase. "Okay," she said breathlessly. "That should do it. I'll just lever off these lids, and in an hour we'll be living inside dandelion yellow."

Getting down onto her knees, she worked off the lids with a screwdriver, stirred up the paint's warm brilliance with a stir stick, then passed Meredith a paintbrush. "You get first honors," she smiled.

An answering grin on her face, Meredith reached for the brush. About her, the porch stood empty of its usual clutter. Over the last few evenings, she had been clearing it out, and scraping and washing it down in anticipation of this moment. As reward for her efforts, Aunt Sancy had said they could paint it midweek, even though it was a school night. *I can't believe it*, marveled Meredith as she carried an opened can to the inner wall. *Dandelion yellow, September gold—it'll be the first thing we step out into it every morning and come home to every night.*

Awed, she dipped her brush into the glowing paint and ran it across the grayish wall in front of her. "Whoo-hoo!" cheered her aunt from across the porch. "All winter long, we'll be living inside the sun."

Again, Meredith dipped her brush and ran it across the wall. The change in color was intense—the deep pulse of tawny gold engulfing the cracked, faded white. Reveling in its richness, Meredith decided to focus on the inner wall where she could work more quickly, and leave the external ones, with their complicated window frames, to her aunt. To her left, she could see her reflection in a darkening window, hair tied in a bandana and dressed in some old clothes, but she was soon lost to anything except the glow spreading across the wall in front of her, then up through her arms and into her chest.

"I now know what I'm going to do with my life!" she announced, holding her dripping paintbrush aloft. "I'll be a house painter, and paint every house dandelion yellow—top to bottom. No matter what the house owners ask for."

"Could do worse than a painter," agreed her aunt. "Grandpa Goonhilly was a carpenter, and he supported his family just fine on that."

A frown creased Meredith's forehead as she noted the underlying defensiveness in her aunt's voice. Even in the middle of something as celebratory as this, Sancy Goonhilly's resentment of the Polks remained right at the surface, entirely undiminished. "Maybe I'll be a painter *and* a carpenter," said Meredith, trying to steer her aunt clear of a potential funk. "D'you think Grandpa Goonhilly would've liked this color for a porch?"

"Oh, *he'd* love it," Aunt Sancy said immediately. "So would Grannie Goonie."

Meredith hesitated. In her bedroom, her parents' wedding picture was still lying face-down on her night table. For three days now, she had been looking everywhere else when she had been in there, determinedly banishing their faces from her mind—but still, the pretty smile of her mother tugged at her thoughts, willing her to pick up the photograph and return it to its central, upright position in her life.

"And my mom?" Meredith asked carefully. "Would she have liked it?"

Across the porch, the smooth strokes of Aunt Sancy's brush paused. "Ally liked yellow," she said after a moment. "She wore it a lot. I think her wedding bouquet was yellow."

"Yellow and white," affirmed Meredith. "But a lighter yellow. No dandelions."

Aunt Sancy laughed shortly, then said, "Y'know, I believe that'd actually be quite pretty—a wedding bouquet of dandelions. Not that the Polks would've allowed it—every detail of that wedding had to be approved by Johanna, and dandelions would've been considered gauche. Lower class. Something a *Goonhilly* would do."

"Well, *I'm* a Goonhilly," Meredith said stoutly. "And so are you."

"*All* Goonhilly," asserted her aunt. "And proud of it."

Again a frown crossed Meredith's face. "Grannie Goonie was a Pegler," she reminded her aunt. "You're part Pegler, too."

"Another family from the lower class," said Aunt Sancy, without missing a beat. "Where I come from, we're all plebs—through and through."

Slowly, Meredith lowered her paintbrush. Without warning, short heated breaths were rising through her; inside her head, thoughts whirled, intermixing the image of her parents' wedding portrait with the *Polkton Post*'s snapshot of the broken bridge guardrail and the partially submerged car. Pain—maybe it was a decade old, but there was still so much of it, a huge inner bruise. But no words— nowhere inside herself could Meredith get a fix on the words that went with this ache.

"Sometimes," she said finally, her voice hoarse, "you're *too* Goonhilly, Aunt Sancy."

The silence that dropped onto the porch then was immense. The very air stiffened; on the other side of the porch, the quiet rhythm of brush strokes ceased.

"Exactly *what*," asked Aunt Sancy, her tone dangerous, "do you mean by that?"

I don't know! Meredith wanted to shout at her. *I don't like the Polks any more than you do!* But something dense and heavy had hold of her—something that weighed down her brain and muffled her thoughts.

"You make it sound like a disease," she said shakily. "Being a Polk. Like there's nothing good in it—they're the enemy, the Taliban."

"That's pretty close," snapped her aunt. "Yeah, I'd say that's pretty much the category they belong in."

"The Taliban?" demanded Meredith, turning to face her aunt, who remained crouched opposite and staring grimly out a window.

"The enemy," replied Aunt Sancy. "Dave and Johanna Polk—citizens emeritus, donators to charity—ha! Gamblers, gangsters, drug syndicate *shit*, more like! All those flights he made to Colombia and Mexico—you think those were for his frozen food business?"

Face contorted, she pivoted and pinned Meredith directly with her gaze. "Cocaine *crook*!" she declared. "Dave Polk was flying it in by the plane-load, then distributing it up and down the east coast. Family of goddam *thugs*—the Polks go back generations in that muck."

A sheer whiteout of shock hit Meredith. Open-mouthed, she stared at her aunt. "What ... are you saying?" she faltered. "Granddad Polk was a ...?"

"You heard me!" snapped her aunt, no warmth anywhere in her expression. "Your respected, super-citizen grandfather was tied in with the drug trade big time. That's where your father first picked up his habit, though Dave and Johanna had theirs under better control—I'll grant them that much. In fact, they had everything pretty much under control ... or so they thought. Then, somewhere along the line, something went wrong; Dave miscalculated, stepped on the wrong toes. All of a sudden, his yacht blew up— taking him, your grandmother, and their multiple facelifts into oblivion. All that wasted Botox—what a pity."

"They were ... *murdered*?" whispered Meredith.

Her aunt didn't even bother to nod. "When the lawyers went over their estate, they found out that the great and mighty Polks were bankrupt," she said heavily, staring at the wall above Meredith's head. "I suppose, living high-off-the-hog the way they did, it came as no surprise. Maybe it was all those people your grandfather was paying to keep quiet. Probably, in the end, it was for the best—if you'd inherited much money, the scum kissing your grandparents' asses would've come smooching after yours. Since you were penniless, they weren't interested, which was fine with me."

Stunned, Meredith gaped at her aunt. Inside her brain, nothing moved. When she finally spoke, the voice that left her mouth was unfamiliar—rough-edged and guttural.

"Was it?" she heard herself growl. "Was it, Aunt Sancy?"

Throwing down her paintbrush, she tore out of the porch, through the kitchen, and down the hall to her bedroom. Without hesitating, she headed for her night table, where she slammed down the photograph of her Polk grandparents. Grabbing the support stand, she yanked at the cardboard backing and lifted out the photograph. Next, she repeated the process with her parents' wedding portrait. For a moment then, she stood staring at the two pictures—their smiling faces smudged by glowing yellow fingerprints.

With a moan, she sank to her knees and began ripping them up. The pictures shredded easily—too easily ... or too quickly; when the two photographs lay scattered in fragments, anger was still ramming itself through her, and Meredith found herself reaching for the last standing photograph. Mercilessly, she tore at the snapshot of her Goonhilly grandparents, and then, finally, when there was nothing left to reach for—no dreams and no illusions—she covered her face with both hands and began to sob.

She didn't know when her aunt arrived in the doorway but, at some point Sancy Goonhilly was there, surveying the destruction, then cautiously crossing the room and kneeling beside her. "Meredith," she murmured. "Meredith, oh Meredith." Without asking, she slid an arm around her niece and, when Meredith stiffened, silently took it back. Around them, the room breathed heated and raw—its heartbeat racing, throbbing, throwing itself at them both.

"There!" Meredith burst out finally, hands still covering her face. "They're gone. I've done what you wanted. I got rid of them, and now I'm not a Polk anymore."

For a moment, her aunt was silent. Then, breath ragged, she muttered, "That's not what I wanted. I—"

"You do *too* want it," accused Meredith, lowering her hands and gazing directly at her aunt. "Every time we've talked about this, it's always ended up being about how good the Goonhillys are and how bad the Polks are. And I know they were bad—what they did was wrong ... *evil*—but it's not my fault. And you make me feel, somehow, that it *is*—that somehow I'm *them*, that I'm responsible for everything they said and did. And that no matter what I want or do, I'll always be them—what they were. I can't be just me because I'm *polluted* by their genes, and the only way to be safe is to somehow get rid of my poky-Polkness and be a Goonhilly—*just* a Goonhilly. A goodie *goodie* Goonhilly."

Briefly, Aunt Sancy's expression hardened, and then she breathed long and deep, releasing something. "Meredith ... I've been stupid," she said. "Really, *really* stupid. I should've seen how this was affecting you. I don't know why I've hung onto it so long. It was an ugly mess ... everything about the Polks was ugly—"

Abruptly, she stopped speaking. Surprise crossed her face and she shook her head, as if telling herself internally to shut up. "No!" she said forcefully. "*Not* everything. The Polks—well, they've always had ambition. The ability to go after what they wanted. Of course, *what* they wanted was a problem, but I see that ability in you too, Meredith—you see what you want and you reach for it. You're a go-getter. I've always told you that part of you was Goonhilly, but it's Polk. The Goonhillys ..." Here, Aunt Sancy smiled fondly. "Well, we're a contented bunch for the most part. But you, Meredith—you'll *do* things in life, see what needs to be changed and try to change it.

"And as for the rest of the way the Polks were—well ..." She shrugged, then added, "In the end, I got you out of the deal, and you're the light of my life, sweetie. Painting our porch gold was the best way I could think of to tell you that. I was hoping you'd figure that out."

A shuddery sigh ran through Meredith. "So you didn't adopt me to get the Polks' money?" she asked.

Head bowed, Aunt Sancy studied her own hands. "That's something you're going to have to work out for yourself," she said after a pause. "I don't think anyone else can tell you something like that."

Air breathed in and out of Meredith's lungs, in and out. *Tired*—she felt so tired. "I'm not sure," she said tentatively, looking at the scattered photograph fragments, "I'm glad I did this."

"I've got the negatives," Aunt Sancy assured her. "If you ever want them again, I can get more prints made—for your photo album, maybe?"

"Yeah," said Meredith. "I think I need to be by myself in this room for a while. Too many ghosts."

"Too many ghosts," agreed her aunt. This time, when she placed an arm around her niece's shoulder, Meredith didn't pull away.

When she walked into home form Thursday morning, Meredith made a point of stopping and chatting with Sina and Kirstin before heading to her third-riser seat. As they conversed, she thought she could feel Seymour's gaze riding her—speculative, calculating the signs she might be sending him. But when she turned and continued toward the drums, he appeared oblivious to her presence, deep in discussion with Morey. Behind them sat Gene, observing their conversation with a quizzical expression. As Meredith slipped in behind the drums, he raised an eyebrow at her and lifted a finger to his lips. Then he returned to watching Seymour and Morey. Puzzled, Meredith joined in on the surveillance, quickly tuning in to the intensely calculated quality of Seymour's and Morey's apparent casualness. The biggest giveaway was the manner in which they had physically positioned themselves—facing one another, but carefully angled so they weren't likely to catch even a peripheral glimpse of Gene. They were shutting him out, obviously; the question was why?

Opening her binder, Meredith pulled out another Caramilk wrapper from the front flap and wrote across the inside: *Don't they like you anymore?* Then she passed it to Gene. A smile crossed his lips as he read her note; scrawling a response, he passed the wrapper back.

Morey found out what I found out, Meredith read. *We had a disagreement.*

As usual, Gene's response was making her work to figure out what he was getting at. *About me?* she wrote back, and Gene nodded, then scribbled, *He's declaring his loyalties.*

Eyes widening, Meredith homed in on Morey. Blonde hair frizzed out wild as ever, he was keeping his gaze fixed on Seymour as if his life depended on it. At the same time, he looked weighed down by guilt—hunched and rigid—and Meredith was momentarily seized by the urge to poke him, just to see how he would react.

So she did. Leaning around the drums, she jabbed Morey in the shoulder—firmly, so he couldn't ignore it. His response was electric—jerking away with a yelp, his eyes darting around to meet hers.

"What did you do that for?" he demanded in aggrieved tones, flexing his injured shoulder.

"I dunno," said Meredith, settling back into her seat. "Just felt like it, I guess."

For a moment, Morey stared at her. "Well … *don't*," he said huffily. Then, carefully re-positioning himself, he resumed his conversation with Seymour, who, along with Gene, had been silently observing the proceedings.

Returning to the Caramilk wrapper on her binder, Meredith wrote, *Contact with the alien race has been established. Soon, entire new civilizations will result.*

Don't hold your breath, Gene replied.

The bell rang; the national anthem lumbered past; PA announcements regarding field hockey and drama tryouts followed. Slouched behind the xylophone, Gene appeared to be absorbed in a chemistry textbook. One riser down, Meredith noticed what appeared to be the same textbook lying atop Morey's binder. Eyebrows raised, she glanced from one textbook cover to the other. Then, leaning over, she tapped the front of Gene's opened book and asked, "Are you and Morey in the same chemistry class?"

"Desk mates," said Gene.

"No kidding," said Meredith. Leaning back in her seat, she returned to studying Seymour and Morey. PA announcements complete, they had once again taken up their discussion, Seymour intensely cool as ever, and Morey intensely ... *well, intense*, thought Meredith. More than intense, actually—the guy looked miserable, even frightened. Whatever it was that he had heard while asking around about the gum-wad assaults, it had really scared him. As she registered this, a trembling passed over Meredith, but she fought it off. There were two ways of responding to this thing, she told herself—Morey's and Gene's. Afraid or ...

Well, is Gene scared? she wondered, giving him a sideways glance. Still scanning his textbook, he looked unperturbed, but she couldn't say the situation didn't frighten him—she didn't know him well enough. Suddenly, glancing between Gene and Morey and their matching textbooks, Meredith felt guilty. These guys were friends—probably had been for years. Expecting Reb and Dean to stick up for her was one thing; Gene was from a different social stratum entirely.

Flipping over the Caramilk wrapper, she wrote across the front: *You can talk to them if you want. Don't worry about me.* Then she slid the wrapper onto the page Gene was reading.

Deliberately, he pinned the wrapper with one finger and read her latest missive. Eyes narrowing, his gaze shifted to Morey, still angled in his seat and talking earnestly to Seymour, then to the Mol himself. Slowly, a tiny smile on his face, Gene scrawled something across the wrapper and returned it to Meredith.

He started it, she read. *I'm pouting.*

Meredith spurted laughter. One row ahead, Seymour and Morey stopped talking, and she could see it in them—the instinct to turn toward the mirth, discover the joke, and join in. Instead, their faces still rigidly casual, they again took up conversation. To Meredith's right, Gene made no comment, but simply read on, a grin on his face. Leaning back in her chair, Meredith tucked the Caramilk wrapper into her binder flap and sighed. Complicated as things were in her life right now, she reflected, Morey's situation was ten times worse. No question about it—chem class with a pouting desk mate ... especially *this* pouting desk mate ... was going to be a drag. While she hadn't yet had the pleasure of encountering Mr. Disgusted directly, Meredith had the feeling he wasn't the kind of guy you wanted to be mixing acids and bases with. But like Gene had said in his note, Morey was the one who had started it. So it was up to the accordion player extraordinaire to end it.

The bell rang; she got to her feet, stepped down off the third riser, and headed to Math.

chapter 16

It was the end of the lunch hour and the halls were swarming with students en route to their first afternoon class. Books under one arm, Meredith was moseying along the corridor one floor down from her history class, when she glanced up and saw Morey trudging toward her. Head down, he didn't appear to have noticed her; slowing her pace, Meredith came to a near halt and watched his approach.

She knew the instant he saw her. His head came up; every frizzed flyaway hair lifted a centimeter higher; then, turning his face ninety degrees in the opposite direction, he proceeded past her without speaking. Open-mouthed, Meredith turned and watched him traverse the rest of the corridor. Once he was safely out of visual range, Morey rotated his head to a forward-facing position and picked up the pace until he disappeared into the cafeteria entrance at the hall's north end.

Seconds passed before Meredith got going again. It wasn't that she had expected Morey to greet her like a bosom buddy; the few times they had encountered each other previously in the halls, they had nodded but hadn't stopped to chat. Still, when she had initially caught sight of him, Meredith's response had been upbeat—the thought that here, coming toward her, was a chance to say, "Fuck you," to Seymour's invisible omnipotence, possibly enact a minor revolution. And so to see Morey react in this manner, refusing even to look her in the eye when the Mol was nowhere to be seen ... *well, it's unbelievable!* she thought, staring after Morey's disappearing backside. More than unbelievable—it was pathetic.

At that moment, a brief, familiar, come-and-go pressure yanked Meredith out of her thoughts and back to the crowded school corridor. Realizing what had probably taken place, she went into a slight sag, then sighed and started for the nearest girls washroom.

"Hey!" said a voice beside her. "They got you again."

Glancing over, Meredith spotted Cathy Kotelly. "Yeah," she said resignedly. "How big is it? And can you tell me how glommed on it is?"

"Come over here for a sec," said Cathy, taking her by the arm and pulling her toward the wall. Stepping behind

Meredith, she took a discreet look. "It's not too bad," she said reassuringly. "Got a Kleenex?"

"I've got one," said another voice, and a hand appeared, dangling a loose tissue. Cathy took it and, after a second's furtive fumbling, presented the gum wad for Meredith's inspection. Cherry red, it appeared to be about average in the size and oozability categories.

"Thanks, you guys!" exclaimed Meredith, gratitude spurting through her.

"No prob," shrugged the girl who had offered the tissue. "There's a stain, though—red like the gum. And there's some other stuff on your butt, too. What is this—writing?" Leaning in close, she scrutinized Meredith's posterior.

God! thought Meredith. As a small audience began to gather, she explained the situation yet again. "So, y'see—I started to date the wads," she told the girl who was still hunched down, busily reading, "because I couldn't catch the kids who were sticking them on me, and it was a way of tracking it, I guess. Dumb, maybe, but ..."

"Butt?" quipped the girl, straightening. Older than Meredith, with several lip studs, she looked to be in Grade 11. "I do calligraphy," she said, breaking into a smile. "I'm on the Poster Committee. I can document this latest stain in gothic if you'd like." Opening her pencil case, she took out a fancy-looking marker-pen.

"What—right here?" stammered Meredith.

"Sure," said the girl. "We'll get it done before your next class."

Meredith swallowed, then decided to go for it. "Okay," she said. Depositing her books on the floor, she turned to face the wall and placed both hands against it, as if about to go through a body pat-down. "Do your thing," she said over her shoulder.

"By the way," said the girl as she uncapped her pen, "my name is Naslini. Just so you know who to go after in case you decide to sue."

"Thanks," mumbled Meredith, as visions of some of the nastier graffiti she had seen danced through her head. Behind her, scattered giggles could be heard from the growing audience as Naslini's pen poked and prodded.

"Sweet!" said someone.

"All right!" agreed another.

Finally a smattering of applause erupted, and Naslini gave a triumphant "Ta-da!"

"What does it say?" demanded Meredith, twisting to catch a glimpse of her handiwork.

"September 19, 12:55 PM," grinned Naslini, returning her pen to her pencil case. "I'm not stupid. There were way too many witnesses."

With an airy wave, she headed down the corridor, and the watching students began to drift away. Retrieving her books from the floor, Meredith was about to head off to her class when she caught sight of someone observing her from across the hall. A senior, he was familiar—in fact, she was certain he had been part of the group that had been gathered around Seymour by her locker last week. One eyebrow raised, the guy was watching her now with the same expression he had been wearing the moment he had turned to let Seymour know she was approaching.

Instinctively, Meredith glanced around, but Seymour was nowhere in sight. When she returned her gaze to the senior across the hall, he had moved on and was ambling casually toward the cafeteria, but Meredith wasn't fooled— the guy's brain was in overdrive and, before the afternoon was out, she knew Seymour would have heard every detail of what had just taken place.

Well, so what? she told herself, fighting a wind-flare of nerves. *I don't need the Mol's permission to talk to other kids. I'm going to do whatever I want, and you can just suck it up, Seymour.*

Turning into a stairwell, she headed up to the third floor. But as she neared the top of the steps, Ronnie Olesin unexpectedly appeared in the doorway, apparently headed downward. Hastily, Meredith deked left, trying to avoid the other girl but, catching sight of her, Ronnie grabbed Meredith's arm.

"Wait a sec, bitch!" she ordered, her grip tightening. "You're not going anywhere."

"Let go of my arm!" cried Meredith, pulling back in alarm.

"I'll let go when I'm good and ready!" snapped Ronnie, her eyes narrowing.

"Let go or I'll scream!" insisted Meredith, pulling harder.

"Hey!" said a guy, coming up the stairs behind Meredith. "What's going on?"

Ronnie let go. "I'm warning you, bitch!" she said, her face contorting as she jabbed a finger at Meredith. "You got my friend into trouble yesterday over *nothing*. I'm telling you now—you're going to the office today after school to tell Bishaha you lied about Lana putting gum on you, or you're looking at your own grave."

Bright fear swept Meredith, and she almost choked on the clutch in her throat. Then, without warning, something tore open inside her and she was fiercely, *savagely* angry. "Who the hell d'you think you are?" she shot back, knocking away Ronnie's jabbing finger. "You don't run me or anyone else at this school. Just fuck off—you *and* your bubblegum-brain buddy."

Veering around Ronnie's enraged face, Meredith forced her wobbly-edged joints to carry her up the last two steps and out of the stairwell. "You wait!" Ronnie shouted after her. "You just wait and see!"

Her words were a grenade going off in Meredith's head. Heart sinking, she knew she had done it then, but there was no going back, and all she could do was suck in the rampaging, *demented* things she wanted to yell in reply. Grimly, she continued onward, the corridor slipping past in a blur—nothing she could distinguish or later remember. But as she reached the open doorway to her history class, one particular sound penetrated the roar in her brain—a nearby rapid-fire clicking that could only be coming from someone's mouth. Whirling around, Meredith scanned the crowd, but no one looked suspicious; she didn't see anyone she would peg as being a cohort of the Mol.

Did I really hear that? she asked herself confusedly. *Or is my brain in overdrive?*

Shoving the matter out of mind, she entered her history class.

That evening, Meredith knelt beside her aunt in the kitchen doorway, staring out at the freshly painted porch. Ceiling, floor, walls—all of it gleamed with dandelion-yellow gorgeousness, the glow of it so intense, Meredith could feel it lighting her up from the inside. *Home*, she thought. *The color of home.* Sighing, she laid her head on her aunt's shoulder.

Aunt Sancy's arm came around her and squeezed. "It's the exact perfect shade," she said warmly. "You sure know how to pick a color swatch. I ... Oh—*damn*!"

"What?" asked Meredith, lifting her head.

"The light switch," said Aunt Sancy, annoyed. "How are we going to turn it off? It's five steps from here to that wall, and the floor's wet. We'll have to leave it on all night. And if this paint isn't dry by morning, we'll be climbing out of the living room window. Won't the Altgelds love that?"

But the paint was dry by morning, and after her aunt had left for work, Meredith stood a moment, alone in the porch, letting its dandelion glow sink into her. She couldn't believe how happy the color made her—how simply seeing its rich gleam from inside the kitchen brought an instant smile to her face. *The color of home*, she thought again, turning to take in every angle. *Of Aunt Sancy and me.*

An intense shiver of delight ran through her. "I love you, Aunt Sancy," she whispered. Then, pulling on her windbreaker, she headed down the stairs and toward whatever the day was holding for her. As for an exact definition of whatever, she figured that was pretty much wide open. She hadn't told her aunt last night about Ronnie's hallway threat—next to the excitement of finishing off the porch, everything else in her life had simply faded away. Besides, telling Aunt Sancy about Ronnie would have meant having to tell her about the ongoing gum-wad saga, which would have led inevitably to Seymour's involvement. In spite of her aunt's contrition earlier in the week, Meredith wanted to avoid anything that might trigger further discussion about the Boggs, the Polks, and their various genetically inspired evils. Neither she nor her aunt needed any more of that. Besides, thought Meredith as she strode along the street, today was the last day before the weekend; she could easily avoid Ronnie and Lana for seven hours, and Saturday and Sunday would give them time to calm down.

But when she arrived at her locker, she discovered the situation was hardly in calm-down mode. Taped onto the front was a piece of foolscap. Across it, someone had scrawled a lopsided sketch of a bomb, with angry vibration marks scribbled on both sides and *tick!* written several times in the margins.

"D'you know who put this here?" she asked some nearby

students, but no one had noticed anything of significance. Jerkily, Meredith tore the sketch from her locker, wadded it up, and tossed it onto the floor. If this was Seymour's latest move, she thought as she set off down the hall, he was getting derelict for ideas. The bomb sketch was grade-school, something to be expected from a ten-year-old. Why someone with his brains would have bothered with something like that—

Without warning, the memory of Ronnie's contorted face flashed across Meredith's mind. *You wait!* she heard the girl shout again. *You just wait and see!* Halfway along the corridor, Meredith faltered, her stomach corkscrewing as she considered the possibility. Yeah, she concluded reluctantly—a scrawled picture of a ticking bomb was Ronnie's style. In fact, it had her Neanderthal modus operandi written all over it. The only question was: How had she discovered the location of Meredith's locker? Not that this information was top secret but, to date, Meredith had never seen Ronnie in the tech wing, and it hadn't even been twenty-four hours since yesterday afternoon's confrontation.

For a second, Meredith contemplated backtracking down the hall to retrieve the wadded-up threat and take it to Ms. Bishaha in the front office. But then she ditched the thought. When all was said and done, she had no proof Ronnie had drawn the picture, and even if she had—so what? A picture was just a picture; anyone should be able to handle something like that. Sure, Ronnie had a rep for fighting, but only with her fists—she wasn't known to carry a knife. And anyway, here on school property, Meredith figured she was safe enough. After all, in spite of endless scheming, even Seymour and his Underworld buddies hadn't managed more than a few gum wads and some bizarre mouth sonics. No, she resolved, the best thing to do was simply walk away from the whole thing. Given space, Ronnie would cool down. Anger was like ping pong—if you refused to pick up the paddle, your opponent couldn't play the game.

Satisfied with her reasoning, she turned into the music room and headed toward the third riser. Most of the class was already in their seats and, in the far corner, she could see Mr. Woolger fussing with something in an open cupboard. Stepping up onto the third riser, she slipped into place behind the drums. Directly in front of her, Seymour and Morey were engaged in what appeared to be yet another lively, scintillating conversation, while to her right slouched a silent, brooding Gene.

"Hey," said Meredith, glancing at him. "Party pooper."

Gene stuck out a morose lower lip. "Don't like the party," he said. "Hey—what're you doing at lunch?"

Heat blew fleetingly across Meredith's face. "Nothing," she shrugged.

"I have Jazz Band practice," said Gene. "But there's something I want to show you. Can you meet me at the north tech exit right after morning classes?"

"Sure," said Meredith, intrigued. "Where are we going?"

Gene's eyes darted toward Seymour and he shook his head. "Wait until lunch," he said, and impatient as Meredith was, she had to settle for that.

She was en route to math class when she first heard it that morning—rapid-fire clicking, there and gone in the press of the hallway crowd. Whirling around, Meredith scanned the area, but no one looked particularly suspicious—of the fifty or so nearby students, the clicker could have been anyone or no one. When the sound came a second time, however, just after she had taken her math-class seat, Meredith immediately narrowed down the possibilities to a several-desk radius, then even further to the smirk on one student's face—Barry Otash. But just to make sure, she leaned forward and poked Reb, who was hunched over her own desk, getting in some last-minute work on a mystery equation.

"Have you heard any weird sounds around here lately?" Meredith asked, trying to make the question as open-ended as possible.

"Yeah," groaned Reb. "It's Barry. He's been madly clicking away since I sat down. I heard him tell someone he has a cavity ticking like a bomb in his mouth."

"A *bomb*?" repeated Meredith, startled.

Reb's gaze intensified, homing in. "Seymour?" she asked significantly.

"I ... dunno," faltered Meredith, glancing again at Barry. But before they could discuss the matter further,

Mr. Jiminez stood up to begin the day's lesson. Anything he had to say, however, was lost on Meredith as she sat pondering her own equations: *clicking + Seymour = bomb*. Or was it: *Ronnie + threat = bomb*? Whatever—the clicking in Meredith's brain was about to blow sky-high. When Math ended, she took an alternate route to her next class, where it was less likely mouth clickers would be lying in wait. Unfortunately, her English classroom was situated halfway along a corridor, and as soon as she stepped into this hall, the clicking started up again. Glancing around, Meredith spotted the likely culprits ... two male seniors, their backs to her as they headed down the corridor. Neither had been with the Mol last week during the initial mouth-clicking episode.

How many kids has Seymour pulled into this? wondered Meredith, as she watched the two seniors recede down the hall. *And what are those guys thinking about as they click away like that—a cricket? Gunfire? Or a bomb ticking inside their mouths? Was it Ronnie who drew that bomb, or Seymour?*

Though she pondered these questions throughout English, no answers were forthcoming, and by the time she reached the tech wing's north exit, she was disgruntled and ravenous. "Okay, Mr. Disgusted," she called, catching sight of Gene by the doors. "I've been wondering all morning what this is about. It better be good!"

Gene raised a mysterious eyebrow and intoned, "Follow me and all will be revealed." Then, pushing open one of the doors, he headed out onto Quebec Street. "This way," he said, setting off along the sidewalk. "It's half a block down Melrose Avenue. Not too far."

"*What* is?" probed Meredith, quickening her pace to keep up.

"You'll have to see it to believe it," said Gene. "I'm not sure I do yet." Reaching the corner, he turned onto Melrose. "It's on this side," he said. "About five cars down."

"Five cars?" repeated Meredith. "So it's a car?"

"Sort of," said Gene. Coming to a halt beside a black four-door, he added, "It's *in* a car. *This* car. Check out the rearview mirror."

The make of the car before Meredith was unfamiliar to her; its only identifying logo, written in chrome, said *Soul*. Shifting her gaze to the car's interior, she spotted Gene's reason for bringing her here—her daffodil rain hat, dangling from the rearview mirror. Indignation exploded across her so intensely she felt slapped. "That's ... psychotic!" she spluttered. "Deranged!" Taking hold of the nearest door handle, she attempted to open it, then progressed around the car, trying the others without success. "Fuck!" she howled, glaring at the oblivious vehicle. "It's hanging *right* there ... and I can't get at it."

"Hardly likely Seymour would leave his car unlocked," Gene said dryly.

"Seymour?" demanded Meredith.

"It's his car," affirmed Gene.

"He owns a car called a Soul?" squeaked Meredith. "And

it's *black*!" Astounded, she stared at the kidnapped rain hat. "It feels like it's my *butt* he's got in there," she admitted. "I want it back."

"D'you know how to pick a car lock?" asked Gene. "It's not one of my finely hewn skills."

"Hardly," snorted Meredith. "If only I had a camera on me. My cell's too cheap to take pictures."

"I'd take one for you if I could," said Gene. "But I don't carry a cell."

Turning, he started back toward the school, and Meredith fell in at his side. "How come?" she asked.

"How come no cell?" he replied. "Ah—I like living on my own time. If you've got a cell, people think they own you."

"Oh," said Meredith, startled. "I guess. I never thought of it like that."

"Mr. Disgusted again," Gene said sheepishly. "As my mom would say."

"Does she have a cell?" asked Meredith.

"Oh, yeah," Gene said decisively. "Doesn't yours?"

Meredith hesitated, then said, "I don't have a mom. Or a dad."

"No?" said Gene. Momentarily his face blanked, as people's usually did when she presented them with this information. "I didn't know that," he murmured almost to himself, and, to her relief, he didn't follow this up with an apology.

"It happened a long time ago," she said hastily, smoothing

over the moment. "I live with my Aunt Sancy. And *she* has a cell."

"Ah," Gene said knowingly.

"She's not a Polk," Meredith added, watching her feet scuff through the leaves scattered along the curb. "Being a Polk is ..." Her voice trailed off, and she considered ditching the thoughts coming at her. But beside her Gene remained silent, as if waiting her out, and so, tentatively, she continued. "Well," she said, "I'm not proud of being a Polk. People think I should be because of ole Gus, my ancestor, but from what I've heard, the Polks were actually pretty pathetic—at least my dad and granddad were. My aunt pretty much hated them when they were alive. She still does, really."

"How come?" asked Gene.

"Because she's decent," said Meredith, the answer coming to her firm and concise. "She's got a clear head, and she can see straight, and she's tough to fool. She knows scum when she sees it, and that's pretty much what my dad was—scum."

"Huh," Gene said cautiously.

"But, y'see," Meredith added, just as cautiously, "he was also my dad. And ..." A frown crossed her forehead; without warning, she was blinking back tears. "Well," she said hoarsely, "I *want* a dad, y'know?"

"Yeah," nodded Gene. "Good dads are worth anything. Mine's pretty decent. I don't know where I'd be without him."

"What's he like?" asked Meredith.

Gene hesitated, then said, "Someday I'll tell you. When we have more time. Right now, I'm late for band practice and I've got to run. Sorry."

"That's okay," Meredith assured him. "Thanks for showing me the rain hat."

"No prob," said Gene, and headed toward the tech wing's north entrance. Meredith stood, watching the door close behind him, then turned left and headed down the short slope that ran along the northwest corner of the school's practice field. Crossing the field, she continued around the school to its south face, where she found Reb and Dean sprawled on the front lawn, halfway through their lunches and soaking up the sun.

"Hey," she said, settling down beside them. "Listen to this." And, pulling out her own lunch, she told them about the bomb sketch and the kidnapped rain hat.

"It's Seymour!" declared Dean when she had finished. "*All* of it—the drawing *and* the clicking. It's got to be."

"The sketch sounds more like Ronnie to me," demurred Reb. "Wha—"

"Hey, Meredith!" interrupted a voice. Turning, Meredith spotted a guy named Hamza from her history class jogging toward her. "Hiding out from Ronnie Olesin?" he asked as he passed.

"Ronnie?" asked Meredith, straightening in alarm. "What d'you mean?"

"She's looking for you," Hamza tossed over his shoulder

as he continued toward the curbside smoking crowd. "On the warpath—her *and* Lana Sloat."

"Where did you see her?" Meredith shouted at his receding back.

"Cafeteria," Hamza replied carelessly, intent on his date with nicotine heaven.

Aghast, the three girls sat staring after him. "Well," Reb said weakly. "So much for it being Seymour. Ronnie must've drawn that bomb."

Distractedly, Meredith lifted a sandwich to her mouth and set it down again. "I guess," she muttered.

"What're you going to do, Mere—tell Ms. Bishaha?" asked Reb.

"What's there to tell?" asked Meredith. "Ronnie hasn't done anything yet."

"Yeah, but she's threatened to," said Reb. "And, y'know ... with her track record ..." Her voice trailed off and the girls sat silently, tasting fear. "I feel sick," mumbled Reb. "Like I'm gonna throw up."

"But you're not," said Dean, taking a quick breath. "You're not going to throw up because you *can't*. None of us can. Meredith is in trouble and we've got to stick by her. More than that—we're gonna take up space, exactly the way *we* want to ... just like we said. Right?"

Startled by the fierceness in Dean's tone, Meredith and Reb just looked at her. Wide-eyed, Dean stared back. "Beware," she reminded them hoarsely. "Beware, Polkton Collegiate. We are going to take up massive space."

"Yeah," muttered Reb. "That was okay under the willow. But in real life, you hardly ever get things exactly the way you want them."

"Well, *I'm* with you, Mere," said Dean, ignoring her. "After school, I'll meet you at your locker. Don't take a step off school property without me. We'll go to my place, and if Ronnie follows us, we'll call the cops on our cells."

"Sure," said Meredith, her heart slow-thundering in her chest. Then from her other side came a deep, gulping sigh.

"Okay," said Reb. "I'll admit it—I'm scared. And I'd probably be useless if ... well, if anything happened. But I'm your friend for *sure*, Mere. I'll be at your locker after school, too."

Intense chills swamped Meredith; she felt exhausted and dazed. "Thanks," she heard herself say as if from a long way off. "Thanks a million, and a million times more after that. It's just today, I think, that there's anything to worry about. It's Friday, and over the weekend, Ronnie'll cool down. When she does, things'll be okay again."

"Over the weekend," Reb echoed softly, as if reciting a prayer.

"The weekend," agreed Dean. "All we have to do is make damn sure about today."

chapter 17

The afternoon passed in a nauseous blur. Everywhere Meredith went, she heard clicking, and though she would have been the first to admit this was mostly in her head, still her stomach went into a queasy lurch every time she had to round a blind corner. It didn't help that the real clicking she encountered in the halls was all anonymous, there and gone before she could identify the perpetrators. And while the clickers in her gym class were easily identifiable—Penny Gugomos and Sandra Clulee, the Chiclets girl—their schoolgirlish smirks did little to calm Meredith's nerves.

Then, a half hour later, as she was coming down a corridor en route to her history class, she caught sight of

Seymour at the opposite end, and though he gave no sign of noticing her, the moment was far from inspirational. While she hadn't spotted Ronnie anywhere, several students had passed on versions of the bloodthirsty threats she was apparently spewing, and Meredith felt the other girl's presence continually, like a storm flickering along the horizon. By her late afternoon class, she was leaving sweaty palm smears on her desk top, and by the time she reached her locker at 3:30, a headache was brooding deep inside her skull. When she spotted Dean, determinedly waiting for her, Meredith had to fight off the urge to cry.

"Hey, Mount Matsumoto," she said weakly.

"Ready to blow," replied Dean.

Minutes later, Reb arrived, flushed and apprehensive. Hastily, Meredith stuffed her weekend homework into her knapsack, and checked to ensure her cell phone was in her jacket pocket. Before starting down the hall to the north exit, she glanced uncertainly at her two friends. There was so much that could potentially take place in the next ten minutes, and they had no plan other than to stick together. Steadfast, Dean met her gaze; Reb's flickered once, then hung on.

"Come on," said Dean, turning toward the exit. "We're outta here."

As they came through the doors, there were easily one hundred students within calling distance—playing hacky sack, unlocking their bikes from a nearby bike rack, or simply hanging around. Giving the crowd a quick scan,

Meredith felt relief lift through her on electric wings. "She's not here!" she gushed, turning to her friends. "She must be waiting at a different exit."

Without hesitation, they started down the walkway that led to Quebec Street. To their right, students sat chatting on a waist-high wall that extended halfway to the public sidewalk; as the three girls reached its end point, a guy from Meredith's English class called out to her, asking about the day's quota of gum wads. Reflexively, she turned to reply, then froze in alarm as two shouting figures burst out from behind the wall and grabbed her arms. Faces leering, Ronnie and Lana shoved her roughly off the walkway so Meredith was suddenly bent double, tripping over her own feet. Dimly, she was aware of Dean launching herself, followed by the abrupt disappearance of the hands gripping her right arm. But then another shove sent Meredith staggering forward until she fell heavily onto her side. Landing on the grassy slope that buttressed the practice field's northwest corner, she began rolling downward, with someone clinging to her shoulders and cursing.

Bleached blonde hair whipped Meredith's eyes and mouth, but it was the voice she tuned into—Ronnie's, without a doubt. Dizzy, the breath knocked out of her, Meredith tried to pull free, but each time she rolled over, the textbooks in her knapsack jammed themselves painfully against her back, and Ronnie had both her arms pinned. Finally, the world stopped rotating and the two girls came to a halt, Meredith flat on her back and Ronnie glommed onto her and panting into her face.

"Think you're so great," sneered Ronnie as she levered an elbow across Meredith's throat. "Little Miss *Polk*. Think your name gives you the right to run this school—even the vice-principal jumps for you. Well, you don't run me and my friends. You got Lana in trouble, and now you're gonna pay for it."

Before Meredith could respond, Ronnie lifted her free hand. There, above her head, gripped by that hand and outlined by the late afternoon sun, Meredith saw a large rock.

"Oh, my God!" she gasped, watching the rock rise. "No, Ronnie! Polk is just my name. I don't run this school; I don't run anything. Please stop. Just *stop*."

Everything shifted to slow-mo. Off to one side, Meredith could hear sounds of a struggle and voices calling out to her. But wherever Dean and Reb were, it was too far away—much too far to reach her before Ronnie's hand arrived at the peak of its arc and started down.

"Please," pleaded Meredith, squirming and twisting, trying to work her way free, but Ronnie was heavier, much heavier—a malevolent weight. "Please *don't*."

Without warning, the world snapped back into regular time, and the hand holding the rock dropped directly toward Meredith's face. Lunging desperately, she managed to jerk herself sideways so the rock struck a glancing blow off the side of her forehead. Pain slammed through her—gigantic, a tidal wave reeling through her head.

"Awesome!" grunted Ronnie. "I'm getting a hundred bucks for this, and I'm going to lay you out good and flat."

Again she lifted the rock. Pain swung nauseatingly inside Meredith's skull; it was all she could do to force open her eyelids and watch, horrified, as the hand ascended a second time.

Abruptly, Ronnie was rammed from behind. Grunting loudly, she pitched forward, the rock flying from her hand as someone landed on top of her. At once, Ronnie began to squirm, but then yet another body landed on the heap, grabbed her arms, and started dragging her free of the pile. Still pinned, Meredith could only turn her head, and what she saw was Gene, kneeling over Ronnie, one knee pressed to her chest.

"You move," she heard him snarl, "and I'll fucking tear out your throat with my teeth. Vampire Cree."

A hand passed over Meredith's face, tracing the edges of the wound the rock had left. "Mere," said Reb, her voice breathless. "Mere, it's me. Are you all right?"

Groggily, Meredith tried to focus on the face hovering above hers. Reb was breathing rapidly; in the intensity of the moment, Meredith could smell the sausage-and-onion sandwich her friend had eaten for lunch. "Reb," she whimpered, her thoughts slurring drunkenly. "Watch out for the ones who want to be important. Watch out especially for yourself when you want to be important. Because, Reb, you're my friend. I love you and I don't want to lose you. And I love Dean and Aunt Sancy. I love my whole life. Hang onto me. Don't let me go. Don't let me go off the bridge."

"The bridge?" asked Reb, sounding confused. "What bridge? We're at school, beside the practice field. You're not going off any bridge."

"It's the hand," mumbled Meredith, struggling to keep her eyes open. "I saw it—the evil hand, coming to get me like I always knew it would. The Polk curse—I've got it, too. Because I was proud. I was proud and wanted power."

"Mere," said Reb, starting to cry. "Shhh, Mere. There's no bridge and there's no curse. You're going to be all right. Gene's got Ronnie, and Dean and another guy took down Lana. About fifty kids called 911 on their cells. The cops are coming, and an ambulance just got here. Can you hear the sirens?"

"Excuse me, miss—can you let me in?" asked a voice. Hastily, Reb ducked aside, and a man in a paramedic's uniform leaned over Meredith and began probing the wound on her forehead. "How did this happen?" he asked.

"It was this rock," said Reb, kneeling beside him and holding out the rock for his inspection. "Ronnie Olesin hit her with it. You can see the blood on it."

"Okay," said the man. "Keep it for the police." Turning to one side, he opened a medical bag and extracted a small flashlight. "Look straight ahead," he told Meredith, lifting up her right eyelid and flicking a beam of light in and out of her gaze. "Can you see my finger?"

"Yes," Meredith said obediently, squinting at the finger he was holding up. "Fuzzy. It's a fuzzy finger."

"Good," said the man. Glancing over his shoulder, he called out and, a moment later, two uniformed women appeared with a stretcher. "Easy now," said the man as they lifted Meredith onto it. Seconds later, she was strapped in and being wheeled up the slope.

Lights flashed at the curb; off to her right, Meredith thought she saw a blurry Ronnie being guided into a police cruiser. All around the ambulance, gawking students crowded close; as Meredith was lifted into the back of the ambulance, she heard Gene ask which hospital she was being taken to.

And then the doors shut, enclosing her in a small, quiet place. To one side sat the male paramedic, and beside him, one of Polkton Collegiate's Tech teachers—Mr. Neebe.

"Hello, Meredith," Mr. Neebe said gently. "I'll be with you at the hospital until one of your parents gets there. Just to make sure everything's okay."

Meredith's eyes closed, taking her into darkness.

She was kept overnight for observation, and released Saturday morning with the recommendation she stay home from school for several days and skip gym for at least a week. The emergency ward doctor overseeing her case didn't seem overly concerned. Meredith had been lucky, he assured Aunt Sancy. Her shaved left temple and the bandage covering her ten stitches looked dramatic, but the rock had merely torn open the skin; she would have a headache for a few days, but was expected to recover quickly and completely. Indeed, on Sunday afternoon when the police came to the apartment to interview her, Meredith was able to answer their questions coherently—while she sometimes had to stop and wait out the throbbing in her head, the officers departed looking satisfied with her performance.

Aunt Sancy wasn't so easily convinced. "Why didn't you tell me about this?" she kept asking, her expression simultaneously reproachful and guilt-stricken.

"Ronnie only threatened me on Thursday," Meredith pointed out, wincing at the ache that started up in her head whenever she thought about the assault. "Then that night, we painted the porch and we were so happy—talking about Ronnie would've been a real downer. Besides, I didn't know *this* was going to happen."

By *this*, she meant Friday's assault—she still hadn't told her aunt (or the police) about the ongoing gum-wad saga and her suspicions regarding Seymour, and there was no way she was going to bring it up now. The pain in her head was simply too volatile—a dark, formless presence that lurked, waiting for the slightest opportunity to launch itself. Loud sounds, bright lights, sudden movement ... even unexpected thoughts inside her own head could cause a flare-up, and all Meredith wanted was to keep that pain quiet and at bay. So she spent the weekend answering questions put to her as simply as possible, then crawling back into bed, closing her eyes, and letting herself sink past the hurt in her head into uninterrupted sleep.

Monday morning, Aunt Sancy announced that she had taken the day off work in order to accompany Meredith on a visit to their family doctor. They returned home with another recommendation for several days' rest and a prognosis of complete recovery. "I checked out the x-rays taken at the hospital," Dr. Boisot told them. "Bruising of brain tissue is minimal—your headache should ease off shortly. But no school until it has ... and no homework!" he winked. "Homework is much too stressful for a healing brain."

And so, homework-free, Meredith curled up on the couch and watched DVD's while her aunt fussed around the apartment, baking muffins and catching up on housework. Late in the afternoon, the land-line phone rang. Immediately, Aunt Sancy buzzed into the room and picked it up; for the past several days, she had been intercepting all of Meredith's calls and taking messages. Up to this point, Meredith had been too dozed-out to care, but now she straightened and looked beseechingly at her aunt.

"Hello, Gene," said Aunt Sancy, smiling at the phone. From what Meredith had gathered, her aunt and Gene had met in the hospital waiting room while she was being examined. Gene had had to leave before the doctor had finished stitching her up, but Meredith had emerged to find one highly impressed aunt. "Yes, she's much better today," Aunt Sancy told Gene warmly. "I'm sure she'd be happy to talk to you."

Carrying the phone across the room, she handed it to Meredith. "Find out when he can come for dinner," she mouthed before leaving the room. "I promised him whatever he wanted, and he said steak and cheesecake."

Gene—here for dinner? thought Meredith. Slowly she lifted the receiver to her ear, relieved neither Gene nor her aunt could see the flush taking over her face. "Hi, Mr. Disgusted," she said.

"Try Mr. Heart Attack!" burst out Gene at the other end. "Are you all right?"

"Headache," said Meredith, wincing at the loudness of his voice. "I've got ten stitches. But the doctor said the wound is just surface."

"So no concussion?" asked Gene.

"A small one," said Meredith. "I've got this headache that never goes away. But Dr. Boisot said it should clear up in a couple of days. So it's nothing like Sidney Crosby."

"When will you be back at school?" asked Gene.

"Thursday, maybe," said Meredith. "Has Seymour taken over the drums yet?"

"Over my dead body," growled Gene.

Meredith's lips wobbled into a smile. "I'm supposed to ask when you can come for dinner," she said, her heart quickening. "You ordered steak and cheesecake, I hear."

"I didn't *order* it," protested Gene. "Your aunt asked what I liked best, and that was all I could think of at the time. She was pretty much swamping me in hugs."

"Well, she should've," Meredith said stoutly. "You're a hero, y'know." A warning throb stabbed her skull and she paused, waiting it out. "You maybe saved my life. I know you saved my brain."

Without warning, she was engulfed by a memory of the assault—lying on her back, Ronnie lifting the rock for the second time, then grunting as she was rammed from behind—and all of a sudden, Meredith was sobbing, tears burning her eyes and her throat choking up as pain swarmed her head.

"Meredith?" asked Gene, his voice sounding a long way off. "Meredith, are you okay?"

The receiver slid from Meredith's grasp as her aunt lifted it from her hand. "That's it for now, Gene," Aunt Sancy said quietly into the phone. "She's too tuckered out, but thank you for calling. You're welcome to call again tomorrow, if you'd like."

Then, hanging up the phone, she sat on the edge of the couch and stroked Meredith's face, making gentle, soothing sounds until, exhausted, her niece fell asleep.

chapter 18

Two days passed before Meredith's headache subsided enough to allow visitors. Since Aunt Sancy had returned to work Tuesday morning, this left Meredith alone in the apartment—alone with the nonstop thoughts parading through her mind. As the hours progressed, she began to grow uneasy; solitude had never bothered her before, but now it was definitely creeping her out. Every time she moved, she thought she saw something shift nearby—shadowy and indistinct, there and gone in the corner of her eye. Gradually, this shifting clarified into the image of a hand, fingers outstretched and rising from the floorboards, or clutching a rock and arcing above her head. Then, early Tuesday afternoon, she felt something slap against her butt—the sensation so tangible, it sent her own hands darting across the rear seam of her sweats to discover ...

Nothing! she scolded herself fiercely the fourth time it happened. *There's no one here but me! It's nothing—nothing!*

Nothing or not, however, the disembodied hands continued to come at her—silent, predatory, without explanation. When Aunt Sancy returned Tuesday evening, bringing her steady cheerfulness and chitchat, the shadowy hands retreated, only to reappear Wednesday morning as the roar of her aunt's Harley faded down the alley. Although Meredith knew these phantasms weren't real, every time another hand came at her, she found herself jerking back, vivid with alarm. *Stupid!* she told herself angrily. *You're making this up! It's the concussion—it's driving you crazy. Cut it out!*

But she couldn't seem to cut it out. And rather than fading upon command, the hands grew more frequent—even with the TV turned up so loud, Meredith worried one of the Altgelds might desert the downstairs bakery counter and come pounding on the porch door. Finally, curling into a ball, she lay motionless, with her face pressed into the absolute darkness of the couch back. Shadowy hands that didn't exist, she told herself, couldn't get at her if she couldn't see them. And she sure as hell didn't want to see another of their grasping, reaching forms; if she did, she was certain fear would crash in on her like a second doomsday rock, tearing her open right to the—

Knocking started up at the porch entrance, one hand pounding to be heard over the blare of the TV. *The Altgelds!* thought Meredith. Shoving herself up off the couch, she turned off the TV and scurried along the hall to the kitchen, where she spotted Dean and Reb pressed to the outer porch door and waving at her through the window glass. With a gasp, Meredith rushed to let them in, the shadowy hands banished in a burst of excited chatter. Ten minutes passed with Dean and Reb admiring the porch paint job, then shedding their coats and sitting down at the table as Meredith plugged in the kettle and got out a box of Girl Guide cookies.

"Have you heard anything from the police yet?" asked Dean, opening a cookie and licking out the frosting. "Have they charged Ronnie and Lana?"

"Yeah," said Meredith. "Ronnie has a court appearance next Monday. I'm not sure about Lana."

"Well," sighed Reb, dunking a cookie into her mug of tea. "At least now you know it wasn't Seymour. What I can't figure out is why Ronnie went after you on school property. There must've been a hundred witnesses."

"She's not very bright," said Dean. "Her or Lana. And Ronnie's been suspended for fighting at school before."

Reb's face twisted. "I keep thinking about it," she muttered. "How it could've been so much worse. If Gene hadn't been there—"

"What d'you mean, *Gene*?" broke in Dean, pointing a

half-eaten cookie at her. "You got to Meredith before he did! And I never got to her at all!"

Startled, Meredith homed in on Reb. "*You* got to me first?" she asked. "I thought Gene ..."

"Gene got there a second after me," Reb assured her. Hunkered down in her chair, she stared at her tea. "When Ronnie and Lana grabbed you," she continued almost reluctantly, "Dean went right after them. I was ... slower. But it was Dean and I together who pulled Lana off you, and that left just Ronnie. I was trying to get away from Lana so I could help you, but she was hanging on like the dickens. Then this other guy—I don't even know his name—ran over and tackled Lana, and I got free. I turned and saw you at the bottom of the hill, just as Ronnie was lifting that rock."

Here Reb paused, moaning softly. "You were so far away," she murmured. "And ... well, I was so *scared*. My brain stopped working and my whole body turned into, like, a junkyard of clunky stuff so I could barely run toward you. I couldn't even think enough to lift my hands so I could shove Ronnie off, and I just ran straight into her." Blinking rapidly, Reb glanced at the bandage on Meredith's forehead, then away. "It was my boobs that took her out, y'know."

For a long moment, Meredith stared open-mouthed at her friend, and then a shout of laughter broke out of her. Instantly she winced, both hands going to her temples.

"Mere!" gasped Reb. "Are you all right?"

"Yeah," groaned Meredith, lowering her hands. "Remind

me not to laugh again. But d'you remember—under the willow? Beware the Looby boobs!"

In another long moment of astonishment, the three sat gaping at each other.

"Well, holy tamoly," grinned Dean, her eyes flicking across Reb's chest. "Talk about taking up space, Superwoman."

"Hardly," said Reb, flushing.

"Oh, yeah," said Dean. "You qualify, babe."

"Do you ever!" burst out Meredith. "Super Boobs—you are my brave, brave friend! And you, too," she added, looking at Dean. "You helped just as much. You two and Gene—together, you probably saved my life. You're just ..." She pressed her lips together, fighting off another surge of tears. "... the *best* friends."

With a gulping sigh, she made it past the urge to cry. Obvious relief on their faces, Reb and Dean refocused once again on dunking cookies into their tea. "Who would've thought?" murmured Dean. "A couple of weeks ago, it was just gum wads on your butt. And then, suddenly, there was Ronnie with that rock. In a way, y'know, it *is* Seymour's fault. He started the whole thing."

"You can't blame Seymour for Ronnie," objected Reb. "*He* wasn't holding the rock." Silent a moment, she watched the steam rise off the surface of her tea. "Mere," she said hesitantly. "You said something just before the paramedics got there. About going off a bridge, and a hand—an evil hand."

A frown creased Meredith's forehead. "I did?" she asked.

"Yeah," said Reb. "The evil hand was coming after you because ... oh, something about being proud and wanting power."

A vague flicker crossed Meredith's brain. "Are you sure?" she asked, confused. "I don't remember saying anything like that."

"Reb," said Dean, touching her arm. "Maybe we shouldn't. I—"

Again, something flickered across Meredith's brain, and then the phantasmal hands were back, or just one of them—holding a rock and outlined in brilliant sunlight as it rose above her head. Without warning, intense pain flashed through the left side of her head and both her hands went up, as if fending something off.

"Oh, my God!" gasped Reb. "Forget I said anything, Mere. Just forget it."

"No," said Meredith, staring at her upraised hands. "It's okay. I think ... I remember now." Slowly lowering her hands, she shifted her gaze to the empty space between her friends' faces. Stunned, she felt stunned ... and somehow *opened*, as if a heaviness that had been inhabiting her brain for days had just dissolved, revealing what lay hidden beneath it. "I guess, y'know," she said, fumbling through her thoughts, "I've been thinking about Ronnie and that rock—well, it was sort of like fate. I mean, I've always had a feeling about a hand—a creepy feeling, and it's always been about just *one* hand. Because of Gus Polk, of course, and the way he used *his* hand to draw that map of Polkton. Here we all are, two centuries later, living on top of his arrogant hand. It's always creeped me out."

She paused, thinking, then added, "And, well, to be honest, arrogance runs in my family—the whole Polk family, not just Gussie. And not just arrogance, either—like I told you about my dad, sometimes it's actual evil. Except the evil was more than my dad. Way more. Listen." Quickly, she explained her familial connections to the drug trade. "So, you see," Meredith continued, still keeping her gaze between her friends' concerned faces. "It's in my Polk genes, really—power and evil. The Polks want power and it makes them do evil things. And I'm sort of like that, too—like Seymour said, I went for the drums because I wanted power."

"You wanted to have fun!" protested Reb. "That doesn't make you *evil*!"

"No," said Meredith. "But it did have something to do with wanting power. I wanted ... to be at the center of things, and I didn't wait until Grade 12 to go for it. Even Seymour waited until he was a senior. And like he said, every action causes a reaction. I wanted power, just like a Polk, and Seymour wanted it too, probably just like a Boggs. And we both went for the throne and our paths crossed like Polk Avenue and Boggs Street, right over Gus Polk's creepy *evil* hand.

"And *then*," she added with a quick breath, "hands started coming after me, but always just one hand at a time—like the hands sticking gum onto my butt, and then

Ronnie with that rock. It was like I reached for power with my arrogant Polk hand, and the hand of ..." Meredith hesitated, then blurted, "*doom* came after me—fate, like I said."

Obviously taken aback, Dean shifted in her chair. "But Seymour didn't hit you with the rock," she objected. "He wasn't anywhere around when Ronnie came after you."

For a third time, something flickered across Meredith's brain. "Ronnie said something," she faltered, "about getting a hundred bucks for taking me down. As if someone was paying her to go after me."

The shock that hit her friends' faces then was enormous, dropping their mouths and bugging their eyes. "She didn't say who," Meredith added hastily. "With everything that happened after, I forgot about it until now—when Reb made me think of it."

"Well, you'd better tell the police!" exploded Reb. "Right away!"

"I will," promised Meredith. "But what do I tell them? I can't say it was Seymour, because Ronnie didn't say that. And if he was involved, I doubt he would've talked to her directly. You know how he operates—he would've sent a cousin of a friend of a friend ... someone he's never seen with. And then, too—if he did send her a message through someone, I doubt it had anything to do with bashing in my head with a rock. Probably she was told to rough me up a little." Pausing, Meredith thought for a moment, then added hesitantly, "And then fate stepped in and turned Ronnie's hand into the evil hand that I always knew was coming to get me, and she hit me with that rock."

Wide-eyed, Reb gaped at Meredith. Then, lifting a hand and pointing at Meredith's forehead, she exclaimed, "But, Mere—Ronnie hit you on the *left* side! So it was her *right* hand that she hit you with, not the left. *Not* the evil left hand of darkness."

Instantly, Meredith's hands were at her forehead and fingering the bandage. *Left, left*, she thought, bewildered. It just wasn't possible that the bandage was on the left side of her forehead, but there it was. Cautiously, she fingered it again. Why hadn't she noticed it was the left side?

"Okay," she mumbled, trying to work her way through an absolute barrage of thought. "Let's not say left or right. Let's just say *a* hand—a hand that reaches for power. A hand that *wants*. What I mean is—is it evil to reach like that? Is it wrong to want? Because that's when the trouble starts—when you want something and reach for it. Especially in *my* family—the Polk side, at least. Look at how they reached, what they wanted. Where it got them ... *and* me."

Reb's gaze flicked across Meredith's bandage. "Mere," she murmured, her face troubled. "No Mere, no ..." Then, as if her mind had suddenly opened onto something entirely new, her expression cleared. "The reason Seymour called it wanting power is because that's the way he thinks," she declared. "Like Neil Sabom and his daffydildos, right? But really, your sitting behind the drums is about wanting to be *alive*, isn't it? Like when you wake up in the morning and everything is gorgeous and glorious, and you want to get up singing and shouting. It's just wanting to be *alive*. What's wrong with that?"

"But it was more than that," insisted Meredith. "If I'm really honest, I know I wanted to be at the center of things, to be popular and important. I wanted *some* kind of power—I felt it."

"Okay," Reb said reluctantly. "So you wanted to be popular. But you didn't want to go around selling cocaine or anything like that, did you? I mean, isn't that just the way life is—a little bit of the bad mixed in with the good? Nobody's perfect. You've just got to try, do your best. Because if you sit around waiting until you're perfect before you do anything, what does that leave—people like Seymour running everything. And who wants that?"

The room silently waited for Meredith's reply. Motionless, she sat staring straight ahead; then, from some inner place, a vast breath lifted through her, clearing something out. "Seymour," she admitted.

Across the table, Dean hunched rigid, face scrunched in confusion as she struggled to absorb everything she was hearing. Finally, with a sigh, she reached across the table and took hold of both Meredith's hands. "Mere," she said, her voice wobbling. "This is ... weird. I don't know what to say here. I—"

She paused for a moment, then forged onward. "I don't know about the Polk family and creepy ancestral hands," she said. "How can a ghost's *hand* reach out of the past and get at you hundreds of years later?"

"Not a *ghost's* hand," protested Meredith. "I don't mean Gus Polk was coming after me last Friday after all those years. I mean something bigger, more ... universal. The hand of fate, no ..." She hesitated, thinking about the shadowy hands that had been haunting her over the past two days, and then, finally getting it, blurted, "... *reaction!* It was the hand of reaction that got me in Ronnie's hand. You both saw it happen. You can't deny it."

"Yeah, okay," Dean agreed reluctantly. "It did. But even if that's true, Ronnie's hand wasn't the only hand there last Friday. There were *tons* more hands there than just hers. And the *other* hands were doing their damnedest to help you. You should've seen Gene. He saw Ronnie on you and he just *ditched* that big violin he was carrying—"

"Double bass," corrected Meredith.

"Double whatever," said Dean. "He ditched it and took off down the hill toward you. I swear he took a flying leap straight at Ronnie." Pausing, she blinked back tears. "And then, too, there were the paramedics and the cops, and ... Well, that's a *lot* of hands. So maybe you're right. Maybe some kind of evil Polk destiny-hand did come after you last Friday, trying to take you out just because you *wanted* something. But if that's true, *it lost out* to the twenty or thirty hands—left *and* right—that were trying to save you."

"And my boobs!" interrupted Reb.

"Yeah," said Dean, flashing her a grin. "There's just no

kind of fate anywhere that could win out against Reb's super boobs."

Once again open-mouthed, Meredith sat, her gaze shifting between her friends' earnest faces. Inside her head, it felt as if parts of her brain were rearranging themselves— as if some dark gothic grip that had hold of her for years was finally letting go. Because Reb was right—a person couldn't sit on her butt forever, waiting for perfection to drop down onto her before she acted. And Deanie was right too—the hands of reaction that had been trying to save her had been at least as numerous as the ones out to get her. In the end, it had probably come in around fifty-fifty. All things considered, those were decent odds. Action, reaction—it was simply part of life. And that was a positive, not a negative.

"Y'know," she said, breathing deeply. "I'm going to call the cops *now*."

chapter 19

That evening, Meredith's aunt drove her to police headquarters, where she gave a second interview in which she described everything that had happened with Seymour to date.

The officer taking her report nodded when Meredith told her about Ronnie's one-hundred-dollar comment. "I'm familiar with Ms. Olesin's statement," she said. "As you may know, she has admitted to the assault. She has also made frequent references to a male student, who was supposed to be paying her one hundred dollars for the attack on you. She couldn't name him though. Blond hair, tall, Grade 11 or 12—that's all she can say about him."

"What if she had a school yearbook?" asked Meredith.

"Maybe she could identify him from that."

"I'll drop off your copy sometime in the next couple of days," interjected Aunt Sancy. Then she drove Meredith home and informed her that she would be spending the rest of the week resting in the apartment. "I'm not open to discussion on this," she said flatly. "The last thing you need right now is to be sitting behind that Boggs *criminal* in home form while the police are investigating him. Friday, I'll drive you to Dr. Boisot's for another checkup. If he says you've recovered enough, I'll consider Monday. Maybe. *If* you don't pester me about it."

And so, cell phone glued to one ear, Meredith endured another four days of enforced rest. From the frequent calls that she received from Dean and Reb, she learned that neither Ronnie nor Lana had been spotted on school property since the previous Friday; rumor had it they were currently residing at the youth detention center. Seymour, on the other hand, was everywhere to be seen, quietly surfing Polkton Collegiate's undercurrents as he always had. Or perhaps not. Friday lunch hour, Meredith answered her cell to discover Reb on the other end, handing off to someone who turned out to be Gene.

"Meredith!" he said so enthusiastically her phone gave off static. "How are you?"

"Okay," she replied, embarrassed to find herself flushing in the middle of an empty apartment. "I saw my doctor this morning, and he said I can come back on Monday."

"Great!" said Gene. "There's something you should

probably know first, though. Seymour was on pins and needles this morning. *Definitely* on edge. We're still not talking so I don't know what's bugging him, but there's *something* going on."

Meredith's heart started up a slow, solid kick. "I did another interview with the cops Wednesday night," she said hesitantly. "About the drums, the gum wads, and Seymour. Aunt Sancy took me in to talk to them again because I remembered something Wednesday afternoon." Then she told him about Ronnie's one-hundred-dollar comment.

Gene whistled. "That explains it," he said. "They've obviously contacted him. Now *there's* a situation where I'd like to be a fly on the wall."

"All I told the cops was what happened," said Meredith, feeling suddenly defensive. "I didn't say Seymour offered to pay Ronnie. I just told them what *she* said."

"Of course," Gene said immediately. "Like I said, you're not a natural liar."

Relieved, Meredith let out a whoosh of air.

"Mind you," added Gene, "Seymour *is*. And he has a *lot* to lie about here. So you're going to have to get yourself ready for that."

"I guess," said Meredith, swallowing.

"I'll back you, though," Gene assured her. "I saw one of the gum wads on your butt and the rain hats—including the one Seymour had in his car. And I've been here every day, watching him like a hawk. So if you need me, I can testify about every breath he's taken in home form this year."

Meredith rode out a wave of emotion. "*Thanks!*" she said, blinking back tears. Off in the distance, she could feel a headache prowling.

"Okay," said Gene. "I've got band practice—what else is new? See you Monday, eh?"

The weekend plodded by. When Aunt Sancy tried to engage Meredith in discussion about her return to school and her pending home form encounter with Seymour, Meredith gave noncommittal replies. She didn't have a clue what she was going to do when she first saw the Mol—speak to him or spit at him. Truth be told, she was going into paroxysms at the mere thought of it. But what would be the point of talking about it? No one could predict Seymour's behavior, and anyway—like Gene had said—he was on pins and needles. Sure, relatively speaking, she was on ice picks, but at least she wasn't the only one suffering.

Monday morning, she resolutely pulled on her WikiButt jeans. Before falling asleep the previous night, she had prepared several rationales for her aunt in case the first one wasn't enough: Number One: *It'll give me confidence.* Number Two: *It's my symbol for not giving up.* And the clincher, Number Three: *It's what a Goonhilly would do.* In fact, as Aunt Sancy herself had admitted, it was more likely what a Polk would do. But, upon spotting the jeans, her aunt didn't raise a fuss—merely raised her eyebrows, then went into a long, slow smile.

"Never a dull moment," she murmured, and left it at that until they had climbed onto the Harley twenty minutes later. Then she swung into high gear. "Now you remember, Meredith," she said as they started off down the alley, "I talked to Mr. Sabom last Friday, and he said he was on top of the whole thing. If you experience any trouble—*any at all*—you're to go straight to him. I don't like the fact that you'll be sitting anywhere near that Seymour character in home form, but you should be safe enough with an entire class around you." Face taut with uncertainty, she maneuvered through morning traffic, then pulled up to the curb outside the north tech-wing entrance. "Off with you, now," she added brusquely. "Skedaddle. And call me at lunch to let me know how things are."

"Twelve-fifteen on the nose," affirmed Meredith.

"Fine. I'm off to deliver this yearbook to the police now. Outta my sight," said her aunt, and Meredith was released from her concern. Within seconds of climbing off the Harley, she was swarmed by curious students who crowded in, gaping at the bandage and her shaved temple. What with the barrage of questions directed at her, Meredith didn't even think to glance in the direction of the practice field, where she had been assaulted. By the time she reached her locker ten minutes later, she had learned that it was common knowledge Ronnie and Lana were now residing at the youth detention center, but no one seemed remotely aware of Seymour's possible role in the affair. Ditching her knapsack and windbreaker, she collected the necessary books and headed toward home form. Greetings continued to swamp her as she progressed along the hall, and then, finally, she was turning the corner into the corridor that led to the music classroom, her attention homing in on the looming doorway of Home Form 75.

Deep in her gut, a thud started up. *Here we go*, she thought, swallowing. *Poky-Polk-Goonhilly meets Godzilla.* With a long, slow breath, she stepped into Home Form 75. At once Seymour's gaze was on her—narrowed, intent, his mouth tightening. But instead of locking into his stare, Meredith found her gaze shifting to Gene, who was straightening in his seat, a welcoming grin on his face. An answering grin lit Meredith's, and she started toward the third riser and the uninhabited drums.

"Meredith," called a voice to her left. Turning, she saw Mr. Woolger beckoning her toward his desk. "How are you?" he asked, his eyes riveted to her bandaged forehead.

"Fine, sir," Meredith assured him. "It looks worse than it is."

Mr. Woolger nodded. "I'm glad to hear that," he said. "I have a message for you—from Mr. Sabom. He wants to see you in his office."

"Oh," said Meredith, startled. "I'll go see him after home form."

"No," said Mr. Woolger. "He said expressly that he wanted to see you as soon as you arrived. In fact, my understanding is that he's in his office right now, waiting for you."

"Oh," repeated Meredith. "Okay. Thanks." Doing an about-face, she headed out the door and along the corridor that led toward the front office. At one minute to nine, the halls were mostly empty—only the odd student scurrying to beat the last bell. And so, undeterred by further questions, she reached the front office just as the final bell went off; accompanied by its shrill wail, she pulled open the door and walked toward the receptionist's desk.

Multiple pairs of secretarial eyes zeroed in on her bandage, and she was swiftly escorted into Mr. Sabom's office. "Meredith," he said, standing up behind his desk and reaching out to shake her hand. "I was relieved to hear from your aunt that you're going to be okay. How are you feeling today?"

"Fine, sir," said Meredith, retrieving her hand from his firm grip. Then, unsure how to conduct herself in an actual face-to-face encounter with the Phoenix, she glanced awkwardly around the small room.

"Please, sit down," said Mr. Sabom, pointing to one of several chairs, and Meredith slid gratefully into the nearest one. "Thank you for coming in straightaway, like I asked. You're probably wondering why I wanted to see you." Sitting down behind his desk, Mr. Sabom steepled his hands. "It has to do with something you told the police ... in your second statement to them, I believe it was."

Deep in Meredith's gut, a thud started up again. Unease— she was definitely crawling with it. Not because of the topic of conversation; obviously, it was to be expected. But something undefined lurked in the Phoenix's expression— guarded, almost predatory. Meredith didn't know how to read it. "Yes, sir?" she said tentatively.

"There seems to be some kind of problem in home form with a fellow student," said Mr. Sabom. "Over seating arrangements, I believe?"

"Not with me," Meredith said hastily. "I don't have a problem with the seating arrangements."

Mr. Sabom frowned slightly. "But that's not what you told the police," he said.

Confused, Meredith frowned back. "I didn't tell the cops I had a problem with seating arrangements," she protested.

"But, in fact, you did," said Mr. Sabom. "In fact, you indicated that tension over the current seating arrangements in Home Form 75 may have led to Ronnie's attack last Friday."

"Well, yes," hedged Meredith. "Sort of. But not the way you're saying it. There *is* tension, yes—but *I* don't have a problem with the seating arrangements."

"But you were concerned enough over that tension," said Mr. Sabom, leaning forward, "to mention it to the police. *And*, in the process, to make a serious allegation against one of our senior students, Seymour Molyneux."

The thud in Meredith's gut deepened until she was vibrating to it. "Seymour has been trying to get me to trade seats with him since the start of the year," she said in a heated rush. "He's gotten other kids involved by getting them to stick gum wads onto my desk seats in my classes, or my butt when I'm walking through the halls. I know *for sure* that he did this because he admitted it to me himself last week. And after Ronnie hit me with the rock, she told me someone was paying her a hundred dollars to attack me. So *that's* what I told the cops—nothing more, nothing less. I didn't say Seymour put her up to it."

"But you implied it," said Mr. Sabom.

"The cops *asked* me if anyone other than Ronnie had anything against me," protested Meredith. "Last Wednesday, Seymour said that unless I gave up my home form seat to him, I'd have to keep my ass covered for the rest of the year. Then, Friday, I got attacked. I thought I should tell the cops about it."

"Why didn't you tell a teacher—say, Mr. Woolger—about what Seymour said to you?" countered Mr. Sabom.

Flushing, Meredith sank back into her chair. *Guilty*—for some reason, the Phoenix's tone had her swarming with soldier ants of guilt. "Because it was just *words*," she blurted finally. "I never saw him actually *do* anything."

"Exactly!" exclaimed Mr. Sabom, an expression of satisfaction taking over his face. "Words. Conjecture. *Speculation*. What we have here is a complete lack of evidence of any wrongdoing on Seymour's part." Taking an emphatic breath, the principal leaned back in his chair. "Meredith," he said, his voice ringing with confidence. "My guess is that you have entirely misunderstood some off-the-cuff remark Seymour made to you. Wherever you go in life, I can assure you there is going to be tension. It's part of the human condition. The trick is to be able to put it into the proper perspective.

"Now, I'm sure you didn't make your allegation against

Seymour out of malicious intent," Mr. Sabom continued reassuringly. "With regards to his character, I can tell you that I have known the boy personally since he was in grade school. He's a friend of my son's. So I know without a doubt that under no circumstances would he be involved in something the likes of which you've been describing."

"But, sir—" protested Meredith.

Shaking his head, Mr. Sabom cut her off. "We'll leave it to the police to investigate," he said. "I have no doubt Seymour will be entirely vindicated. In the meantime, however, I think it would be in everyone's best interests to transfer you to Home Form 34. It's just around the corner from the front office, in the east corridor—Room 103, a math classroom. The teacher, Ms. DuClot, knows you're coming. I've had an extra desk brought in for you."

"But—" stammered Meredith, stunned.

Again, Mr. Sabom shook his head. "You said there was tension, Meredith," he said firmly. "And you seem to be under the impression this tension is threatening your physical safety. Under the circumstances, I should think you would be glad to transfer to a different home form."

"No!" cried Meredith, rising to her feet. "I like where I'm sitting in Home Form 75. I want to keep sitting there. This isn't fair. *I'm* not the prob—"

Mr. Sabom raised a warning hand. "It's not up for discussion," he snapped. "The decision has been made. Ms. DuClot is waiting for you."

Getting to his feet, he crossed to the door and opened it.

Her head pounding, Meredith stood gaping at him; then, clutching her books, she shot past him and out into the office. But her encounter with Polkton Collegiate's principal was not quite complete.

"Meredith!" he called as she headed toward the exit. "Those jeans you're wearing. They're the ones you've been using to … *document* the situation?"

Turning to face him, Meredith said warily, "Yes, sir. It's to document the gum wads—when each one was stuck on me. It's just times and dates—no swear words, anything like that."

Mr. Sabom's face took on a stern expression. For a second, Meredith half-expected the infamous lock of hair to ascend directly from the top of his head. "You will go home at lunch and change into something else," he ordered. "Those dates are an *invitation* for more of the same. Wearing them is *asking* for trouble, and it's my job to keep this school trouble-free."

Meredith didn't bother to reply. Whirling toward the exit, she strode past the staring secretaries and out into the empty hall, where she stood leaning against a wall and breathing heavily. Somewhere in the vast, pounding space that was her brain, thoughts floated—images of herself storming into Home Form 75 and accusing Seymour in front of the entire class, Gene rising to his feet to support her, even Morey joining in on her behalf.

Behind her, the office door opened. "Meredith," said a voice, and Meredith turned to see one of the secretaries observing her. "D'you need help finding your new home form?" she asked.

"No," choked Meredith. Wordlessly, she headed down the corridor toward Home Form 34, the secretary's gaze on her back until she turned into Room 103.

The school library was the usual sonic conglomeration of shuffling papers, clicking computer keyboards, and the odd muffled cackle. Getting up from the work table where she had been conferring with several classmates, Meredith headed to the back of the room to check out the stacks for information on the Canadian Senate. *Somewhere in the 900s*, she mused, perusing the shelves, then paused as she heard a stifled burst of laughter. Curious, she edged to the end of the aisle and peered out at a row of study carrels that lined the library's south wall. Most were empty, but clustered around one in the far corner, she spotted a clutch of senior male students. Hunched over a laptop at their center sat Seymour Molyneux.

Later, Meredith could not have said where her rage came from. That she was angry at the Mol went without saying, and the situation had been dramatically compounded earlier that day by the Phoenix's actions. But upon seeing Seymour sitting there with a casual grin on his face, probably clicking his way through a video game, something came over her—immense, catastrophic. Suddenly, she was breathing electric air and shaking as if plugged into high voltage. Without thinking, she stepped into the rear aisle, raised a furious, apocalyptic arm, and accused, "You!"

Harsh-edged and guttural, her voice carried just far enough to be heard by Seymour and his friends. Glancing up from the laptop, the group focused, en masse, on her bandaged forehead; even in her heightened state, Meredith noted how every one of their eyes widened in the same startled dismay. *They know*, the thought came to her. *They all know what Seymour knows.*

"You did it!" she hissed, her hand still raised and pointing. "Everything that's happened—it was all because of you."

Seymour blinked once. In the silence that followed, she saw the pulse beating in his throat. "Did what?" he asked, a slight quiver in his voice. Quickly, he cleared his throat.

"You *know* what!" growled Meredith, not quite able to name it even now. "*And* you got me transferred to Home Form 34."

Seymour's eyebrows lifted. Even through her rage, Meredith could see his surprise. "That's why you didn't come back this morning?" he asked.

Meredith's eyes narrowed and she continued to stare him down. Returning her gaze, Seymour waited a full ten seconds, then gave in and spoke again.

"Who kicked you out?" he asked cautiously. "Woolger?"

"Sabom," she snapped, watching the way Seymour took this information into himself—like a slow wave, an appealing scent, a congratulatory handshake. His shoulders relaxed, he settled back into his chair, and a carefully relieved expression spread across his face. Finally, he smiled. Around him, his buddies took on more obvious delight—tapping exuberant fingertips across the top of the carrel and expelling triumphant grunts of air.

"You got it, Mol," muttered someone, but at an understated shake of the head from Seymour, the group laid off—their bodies quieting, their gaze drifting away from Meredith's face.

"Looks like your problem is with Sabom," drawled Seymour. "I'd suggest you go talk to him."

Then, as if she were a backyard scene across which he had drawn a curtain, Seymour redirected his attention to the laptop. On cue, his friends crowded in, cutting off Meredith's view of his face. She had been dismissed—and as if to emphasize the fact, some inner switch clicked off, draining the rage from her body. Abruptly, she was confronted with the full reality of her situation—that of a Grade 10, head-banged twerp who had just snarled an utterly false accusation at one of the school's most popular senior students. Exactly what did she think she was doing here? There was no way to prove Seymour had hired Ronnie to attack her, and, on its own, gut instinct wasn't enough to go around making enraged, grandiose statements—at least, not in public.

You got it, Mol. The memory of the muttered phrase shifted like a pickaxe in Meredith's gut. So, she thought grimly—her battle with the Lord of the Underworld was well and truly over. By hook or by crook, his own admitted actions or ones she could only speculate about, Seymour had gotten what he wanted. The throne was now his to claim whenever he chose, and she had been relegated to a back corner desk, floor level with everyone else in Home Form 34.

Silently, Meredith retreated down the aisle.

fternoon classes had let out for the day. Still numbed with disbelief, her mind on lockdown, Meredith was trudging through the halls en route to her locker when a hand touched her arm.

"Meredith," said a familiar voice. Glancing right, she saw Gene keeping pace, a puzzled expression on his face. "What happened this morning?" he asked. "Why didn't you come back?"

Frustration erupted in Meredith, shattering her numbness. "Sabom!" she exploded. "He kicked me out of Home Form 75. I've been transferred to 34."

Astonishment took over Gene's face. "What for?" he demanded.

"Because I told the cops about Seymour," said Meredith. "Sabom read my report or heard about it, and now he's saying there's so much tension over seating arrangements that he's got to transfer me for my safety."

"Why not transfer Seymour?' asked Gene.

"Because Sabom thinks I'm imagining the tension," spat Meredith. "He said I just misunderstood something Seymour said, but he was still transferring me so I'd feel better."

"Whoa!" said Gene. "That explains it."

"Explains what?" asked Meredith.

"Come over here," said Gene, guiding her out of the corridor and into a quiet stairwell nook. "Today at lunch, I walked into the music room and overheard Woolger on his cell. He was telling someone about an argument he overheard in the music room last week—said he was in one of the practice rooms and the arguers didn't know he was there."

"That must've been me and Seymour!" Meredith interjected excitedly. "When Seymour admitted to masterminding the whole gum-wad thing, and said I'd better keep my ass covered. If Woolger heard him say—"

Reluctantly, Gene shook his head. "Woolger said he didn't hear most of what went on," he said. "The practice room door was probably closed—those rooms are soundproofed. But he kept insisting that something was going on. 'You've punished the wrong kid, Neil,' he said."

"Neil?" asked Meredith, thinking of daffydildos.

"That's the Phoenix's first name," said Gene.

Meredith rolled her eyes. "He named his son after himself," she muttered. "Figures."

"Huh," said Gene, his gaze on passing students as he worked things out in his head. "What comes next, I wonder?"

"Seymour takes over the drums," Meredith said morosely. "Just like he planned from the start."

"If he does, I'll sit in his lap!" declared Gene. "And I'll suck my thumb! Or I'll make him suck it!"

Meredith spurted laughter. After six hours, locked into bitter resignation, it was a welcome release. "Bounce!" she hooted. "Really hard!"

Gene grinned. "Hey," he said. "What're you doing now?"

A flush blew through Meredith and she took a quick breath. "Nothing," she said, not quite meeting his eyes.

"A couple guys and I are heading down to Taylor's Music Store in my car," said Gene. "I need new strings for my electric bass, and Joe Akinloye has to get some pads for his sax keys. Navasky's just along for the ride. Want to come with?"

"Yeah!" exclaimed Meredith, a grin taking over her face. "Sure!"

"My locker's one floor down," said Gene. "I have to stash some books and then we're outta here."

Together they headed down the stairwell.

Ensconced in sleeping bags and toques, the Philosophical Feet were lying under the Matsumotos' willow, watching its stripped branches ride a brooding sky. Heavy winds had dominated the past few days, and only the odd leaf still proclaimed itself brilliantly against the sullen clouds. Fixing her gaze on one lone leaf-soul, Meredith sighed. Cold, wet weather was in the forecast; this looked to be the last day available for willow-communing until spring.

"Hey," she said, breaking their initial five-minute period of silence. "I talked to Gene today at lunch."

"What—*again*?" demanded Dean, her tone teasing.

On cue, Meredith flushed. "As a matter of fact," she said primly, "I ran into him outside the music room."

"Oh, yeah," Reb said knowingly.

"Come on, you guys!" protested Meredith, half-laughing. "You know my locker's down the hall. *Anyway*, he told me about something that happened this morning in Home Form 75. He said it was like watching the inside of Seymour's mind put into action. I guess Seymour has been biding his time, hoping everyone would forget about me, and this morning he sauntered in like it was any old day. Gene said Woolger was on him like a hawk, though—just sat at his desk, eyes glued as Seymour moseyed over to the third riser and stepped up casually behind the drums. Then, just as Seymour was about to park his butt, Woolger jumped up from his desk. Gene said he damn near exploded—his baton was *possessed*. 'No one is allowed to sit behind the drums anymore!' he shouted. 'They're too easily damaged. Now that this classroom has an extra seat, no one will sit there at all.'"

"Sweeeeet," Reb drawled appreciatively. "So what did King Mol do then?"

"Froze," said Meredith, relishing the image. "With his royal butt midair—centimeters from the throne that's never going to be his. Gene said, for a second he thought Seymour was going to cry. Then he hauled his sorry ass down to his old seat."

"Where he belongs!" pronounced Dean in an immensely satisfied tone.

"Yeah," said Meredith, the enthusiasm fading from her voice. "But he's still getting away with everything he did to me. Today makes it two weeks since Ronnie attacked me, and it looks like the cops aren't going to charge Seymour—even though Ronnie used my yearbook to identify Frank Yockey as the guy who hired her to attack me. Of course, Frank denied it, and Ronnie's say-so on its own isn't worth much. Besides, Frank isn't buds with Seymour; there's nothing to connect them. And ..."

She paused, poking around the tumble of thoughts in her head, then burst out, "I know Seymour hasn't gotten what he wanted in the end, but Ronnie and Lana are left carrying all the shit and he walks. What kind of crappy world is that? Then there's what they did to me—just picked me up and moved me to another home form as if I was some sort of *thing*. And even though lots of people stuck up for me, it didn't change anything. Woolger tried; Aunt Sancy went in and talked to Sabom; even Gene went to the office, but Sabom wouldn't listen to him, either. It's just so *wrong*.

Don't any of us matter unless we're at the top of the heap, running things? On the *throne*?"

To either side, she could feel Reb and Dean silently working their way through everything she had said. "D'you think," Dean asked tentatively, "Sabom really believes what he told you—that Seymour is completely innocent?"

"Nah!" declared Reb. "If the Phoenix thought Seymour was innocent, there wouldn't be a need to cover up anything. And he's sure working overtime to protect the Mol's butt. At least, that's the way it looks. But that's the problem, isn't it? We don't *know*. And there's no way to find out for sure."

"Well, there is one thing we know for sure," said Dean. "Seymour Molyneux is a complete shit."

"You got that right," muttered Meredith.

"No argument there," agreed Reb. "But that's *him*—not us. Not the Feet—we're still best friends, and we will be through thick and thin. And tomorrow night, Meredith's aunt is cooking a heroes' dinner for us, and Gene and Carl ..."

Carl Rueda, thought Meredith. A short, skinny minor-niner with glasses, he didn't look the type to fling himself into harm's way for a complete stranger.

"And after that," Reb continued determinedly, "there's still most of Grade 10 to go, and it's going to be *great*. Beware, Polkton Collegiate—the Feet are here, and we're going to take up space! This morning, Mr. Canilang talked to me in my French class, and asked me to join the yearbook committee. He said they needed help on layout. It's going to be so much fun! And you're going to be super busy working on the new auditorium mural, Dean ..."

"Yeah!" chimed in Dean. "I'm psyched. Mr. Mattar just asked me yesterday, and I'm still flying. I hope I get to do some of the actual painting—more than just tracing the design onto the wall."

Temporarily forgotten, Meredith lay listening to the eager chatter of her friends. *The yearbook committee, the new auditorium mural,* she mused. Direct personal requests by teachers for extracurricular student participation seemed to be going around; earlier in the day, she had also been approached by an instructor—Ms. Vorona, the drama teacher—and asked to help out with set construction for the school's December production of *A Midsummer Night's Dream.* Excited, she had immediately agreed. And when Gene had told her at lunch that Mr. Woolger had just appointed him assistant conductor for the Concert Band, she had been elated for him, too.

Now she wasn't so sure. All four of them approached and offered plum extracurricular positions within two days—could it be a coincidence? Or was it, rather, the basic, ultimate law coming into play: action and reaction. Together, the four of them had become aware of something that normally remained hidden from view. What that something was exactly, Meredith wasn't certain, but she knew it was connected to power and its under-the-surface machinations—who held the reins, who was allowed to reach for them, and who was not.

And so, it seemed, they were being targeted. Previous to the assault, the Feet and Gene Bussidor had gone largely unnoticed by the powers-that-be; their spare time and how they chose to spend it hadn't been viewed as significant by anyone at Polkton Collegiate but themselves. But now, suddenly, their leisure time—or more exactly, the leisure time they spent together—appeared to have become a matter of importance to ... someone.

Not that she believed for one second that Mr. Woolger, Ms. Vorona, Mr. Canilang, and Mr. Mattar, Dean's art teacher, were in some kind of conspiracy. No, this "conspiracy"—if that was what it was—was Mr. Sabom's and Mr. Sabom's alone. Probably the Phoenix had approached each of the teachers individually, and suggested they invite a particular student to participate in an extracurricular activity in order to help get that student's mind off what had, no doubt, been a traumatic event. It was even possible Mr. Woolger had been intending all along to ask Gene to take on assistant conductor status. Like Reb had said, there was no way to know for sure. Meredith's head had been bashed with a rock and the throne stolen out from under her butt, and she would never know with absolute certainty if Seymour had, indeed, been the one behind the scenes, holding the reins.

Was that the way things worked? she wondered. Kids in families with connections screwed up, and then someone in a position of authority covered up for them? That was the way things appeared to have gone for her father and her Polk grandparents. What about the Phoenix—had he, too, sometime earlier in his life, needed something smoothed over, and now he was passing on the favor?

Well, she thought determinedly, the Mols and Saboms of the world weren't the only ones making things happen. They weren't the only ones capable of causing actions and reactions. And the name Polk belonged to her, too. Her father, grandparents, and Ancestor Great Hand were now dead; she was currently the only Polk left in poky-ole-poke Polkton, and she was going to make that surname mean *Meredith*. Yeah—Meredith Polk was going to take up space, and she was going to make that space mean *her*.

"You're quiet, Mere," said Reb, breaking into her thoughts. "What're you thinking about?"

Meredith hesitated. "This morning," she said slowly, "Ms. Vorona asked me to help out with set production for *A Midsummer Night's Dream*."

Breath held in, she waited for her friends to clue into the significance of what she had just revealed, but all Reb said was, "Sweet!"

"What d'you want to do?" added Dean. "Paint or build?"

Briefly, Meredith teetered on the edge of voicing her suspicions, and then she let the moment go. Reb and Dean were true friends; unquestionably they had put themselves on the line for her, but now they wanted to move on and believe in what the world was offering them. She didn't have the right to interfere with that. *Odd*, she thought. She had always assumed that when she came flat up against the truth, it would be a friend, someone to share a smile with.

Now, for the first time, she felt the bleak aloneness of it—the way it moved in and changed things ... important *core* things.

Everything changes, she reassured herself half-heartedly. *Doesn't it?*

"I don't think I will, though," she replied in answer to Dean's question. "Probably I'll wait a while, and rest my head. It could use the break."

Above her clung several last dandelion-yellow leaves, trembling in the breeze. *Hang on*, she thought at them fiercely. *Hang on.*

Aunt Sancy leaned the Harley onto its stand and they slid their helmets over the handlebars. Then, Meredith leading, her aunt following, they walked up the incline that led to the bridge. A sidewalk ran along the west side; together they proceeded to the bridge's center and stood looking out over the water.

They didn't speak. Without glancing at her aunt, Meredith laid her forearms along the top of the guardrail and rested her chin on them. Below her, water streamed past, quiet and unperturbed. Eyes narrowed, she watched its flow, trying to imagine her parents' fatal crash, but the event didn't come to her, erupting into her mind the way it had three weeks previous. No matter how she tried, she couldn't call it into her thoughts; the episode was somehow now over for her in a way it hadn't been the last time she had come here.

I'm not living in the land of the dead, anymore, she

realized. *This is goodbye. Whoever you were, Mom and Dad, and whatever the reason you chose to do what you did—it doesn't really matter anymore. At least, not so much that I'm desperate to find out. I've got a home, and someone I know really loves me, and I'm okay. It's enough. I guess I thought I had to live inside what you did—that your lives would somehow always be my life, too. Now I know I don't; I'm a completely separate person and I like that. I like me.*

A sigh meandered through Meredith; she felt her entire body lift with it, then slowly, gently, release. Turning her head, she glanced up to find her aunt smiling at her.

"Okay?" asked Aunt Sancy.

"Okay," said Meredith. Tired—she felt hugely, sweetly, softly tired. At peace. "Let's go home," she said, and led the way back off the bridge to the Harley.

Epilogue

It was mid-afternoon, ten minutes into the last class of the day, and Meredith was barreling along a corridor, sent by her History teacher to the library to pick up an instructional DVD. In both directions, the hall stretched empty—classroom doors closed, the linoleum and pale yellow walls reflecting back the overhead fluorescent lighting. Then, ten meters ahead, the door to a guys' washroom opened and a student stepped out, turned, and started toward her.

It was Seymour. Split-second recognition shot through Meredith and her stride faltered. Suddenly, her heart was thundering; the shock of seeing him—close-up, personal, and alone like this—ricocheted through her like a bowling ball. For the first time since she had started at Polkton Collegiate, she felt a rush of gratitude for the school's hallway security-camera system. Swallowing, she forced herself to maintain her gaze as Seymour's passed casually across hers, then returned with what looked to be a gasp of incredulity.

No, realized Meredith, *contempt.* The expression taking over Seymour's face as he strode toward her was undeniably one of scorn. And along with it, as clearly as if he had spoken aloud, she could hear his thoughts.

Nothing! he hissed at her in his mind as he passed by, one meter to her right. *You are nothing!*

And then he was gone, his steady footfalls receding down the hall. Grimly, Meredith forced herself not to turn around and watch him go. By the time she reached the library entrance, her heart had eased up on its pounding and her sweaty armpits cooled to damp patches. Leaning against the corridor wall, she let her whirling thoughts calm. Though this wasn't the first time she had seen Seymour since her transfer out of Home Form 75, it was the only one, other than their library encounter, in which they had been close enough for conversation.

Conversation hadn't happened and probably never would, she realized. Seymour just wasn't the kind of guy who got off on reconciliation. All things considered, he was probably a lot like her father—made allowances for, pampered, unchecked. Someday, perhaps, he would face his own bridge—but, unlike her mother, Meredith knew she wouldn't be along for the ride.

With a deep breath, taking in space—filling herself with it—she continued on into the library.

What is intriguing about this story is that you have shown that a small detail of the high school world, such as where someone sits during home form, can lead to destructive results. How did you decide to use such a trigger to this story?

I didn't consciously decide to use the drums as any kind of trigger. The story started for me with the image of a fifteen-year-old girl headed along a busy school hallway, intending to snag the most sought-after seat in her home form. And with this image came the understanding that this would bring her into conflict with a popular senior student who also wanted that particular seat. The rest of the story evolved from this point as I wrote—I don't sketch out plots in advance; rather, I follow a story as it reveals itself to me. So I didn't plan a trigger in advance—the story developed out of that initial image of one girl reaching for something she wanted—something that would be considered unexpected for someone of her social standing.

Meredith is not alone as the story begins, but in the end she really *is*, as she discerns that she and her friends are being "bought off," in a sense. So there's no happy ending. Why do you think it's important that the story concludes in this way?

I see the ending as positive. And I don't see Meredith as standing alone—her relationships with the Feet, Gene, and her aunt remain strong and caring. Yes, she's the only one who sees a pattern in that they've all suddenly been offered plum extracurricular-activity positions; she's also smart enough to understand that this is the kind of realization a person needs to be ready for internally in order to absorb, so she doesn't point it out to Dean or Reb. That's not a failure on anyone's part—the Feet have really stood by Meredith, but they simply aren't ready to see this aspect of the situation yet.

Meredith, however, is and I think it's a plus for her that after everything that's happened to her, she's still determined to look reality in the eye and see it for what it is. The information she gains from this—that someone wants to distract her from really thinking through what has been perpetrated against her—leads to her decision to temporarily withdraw from the action-reaction flow of events and mull things over on her own, so she can understand her situation more fully. A wise choice—sometimes the power of inertia is the best way to handle an overwhelming episode of action-reaction.

So again, I don't see the ending as negative. It may not be euphoric, but at the end of the book Meredith is strong, determined, self-aware, and surrounded by people who care about her. And she has learned to see herself as someone who acts on the flow of life events, rather than merely reacts—as an initiator rather than a receiver—a skill she will continue to fine-tune throughout her life.

The acquisition of power—asserting power and holding onto it—is one of the themes you explore in this story. Because of her family background, Meredith worries that she has somehow sought power that isn't rightly hers. Do you think teenagers tend to seek power as they learn about how to get along in the world?

The term "power" is very loaded. It can mean anything from terrorism and armed insurrection to writing a meaningful novel. And seeking after power, both in personal relationships (the ability to express and stand up for yourself) and performance at school and in society in general is part of every teenager's *natural* development. Coming into adolescence means growing into an understanding of yourself as an individual—separate from parents and family. Power is essential to that ability to stand on your own—not the power of a raised fist, but the strength to stand apart, clearly assess what is going on around you, and *then* act as you see fit (rather than as you're told to act). Often the most powerful person in a room is the quietest— the individual sitting off to one side and observing what is going on, thinking her/his way through an event. It's important to try to be conscious in everything you do—to act rather than merely react. This approach takes longer. It's generally less dramatic and glamorous to take time to think your way through a situation to a thoughtful, balanced response—but in the end it's more powerful, more rooted in who you are, who you want to be.

Seymour seems to be able to manipulate things to achieve his own ends, and even appears to enlist the principal in that manipulation. Do you think a teenager, no matter how accomplished, could do this?

Seymour is manipulative, certainly, but I don't see him as controlling anyone but himself. Everyone who cooperates with his agenda does so of their own free will, generally because they hope to get something out of it—most often popularity, peer approval. But Seymour can't manipulate everyone. Besides Gene, quite a few other students randomly assist Meredith in the halls, and Mr. Woolger certainly doesn't fall for Seymour's act—in the end, he blocks Seymour's attempted rise to the throne.

I also don't see Seymour as enlisting Mr. Sabom's cooperation. My guess is they haven't discussed Meredith's allegation the morning the principal summons her to his office. Mr. Sabom is acting on information he's received from the police, not Seymour. So I don't think Seymour's power to manipulate comes from himself—it's given to him by everyone who cooperates with him. In effect, the illusion of Seymour's "power" is created by others, in the same way that we regularly create celebrities and superstars. When you "worship" someone else, you give them part of your own power—the respect you need to give yourself.

When you are in your teenaged years, there's a tendency to feel you can develop independence, strike out on your own, free yourself from the past, carve out a fresh identity. What do you think the chances are of totally freeing yourself from your family background, as Meredith struggles to do?

One hundred percent, but it takes decades of committed effort. Meredith has made a strong start—she's reached for power and the hand of reaction has clunked her on the head for it, but she's managed to come through it more or less intact. The reason she has survived the Polk "curse" when her parents and grandparents did not is because she spent so much time previous to the assault nurturing positive relationships with the Feet, Gene, and Aunt Sancy—Meredith has invested in positive, inclusive power, where her parents and grandparents actively sought out corruption. So when Meredith arrives at her moment of need, her friends come to her aid, whereas her parents and grandparents died alone.

In my own experience, freeing yourself of negative family influences—whether you see these as psychological or karmic or both—is a gradual process. Essential to this process is continual self-respect and the willingness to see your family for what it truly is—both in its failings and positive aspects. This can be a very difficult process, and a lengthy one. If you're involved in it, be gentle with yourself. Self-tenderness is a gift you need to give yourself over and over.

You have written many books for teenagers. What is there about this audience that you find so compelling?

I've written twenty-two books in twenty-two years, of which seventeen are for young adults. There's a teenager inside me that still has things to say, ideas to work out on the page. I like her; I like listening to her; we get along. So we keep on writing together.

Thank you, Beth.